REIGN OF THE WITCH QUEEN
BOOK 2

A Crown of Wind and Water

ANDREA ROSE

A CROWN OF WIND AND WATER by Andrea Rose

All rights reserved.

Copyright © 2026 by Andrea Rose

Second Edition. Previously published as WIND AND WATER by A.S. Fenichel

No part of this book may be reproduced in any form or by any electronic or mechanical means, including information storage and retrieval systems, without written permission from the author, except for the use of brief quotations in a book review.

This book is a work of fiction and any resemblance to persons, living or dead, is purely coincidental. The characters are productions of the author's imagination. Locales are fictitious, and/or, are used fictitiously.

AI RESTRICTION: The author expressly prohibits any entity from using any part of this publication, including text and graphics, for purposes of training artificial intelligence (AI) technologies to generate text or graphics, including without limitation, technologies that are capable of generating works in the same style or genre as this publication. The author reserves all rights to license uses of this work for generative AI training and development of machine learning language models.

Edited by Penny Barber

Copy Edit (First Edition) by Oopsie Daisy Edits

Cover design by Artscandare

Interior illustrated character art by Vivien Ginter

Table of Contents

Reign of the Witch Queen	7
Prologue	9
Chapter 1	19
Chapter 2	35
Chapter 3	51
Chapter 4	67
Chapter 5	83
Chapter 6	99
Chapter 7	117
Chapter 8	131
Chapter 9	145
Chapter 10	161
Chapter 11	179
Chapter 12	195
Chapter 13	211
Chapter 14	227
Chapter 15	241
Chapter 16	255
Chapter 17	271
Chapter 18	287
Chapter 19	303
Chapter 20	323
Chapter 21	343
Chapter 22	363
Epilogue	377
Also by Andrea Rose	385
About the Author	391

For Mom.
This book was the most difficult to write in my career. The passing of my mother, Eleanor Fenichel, brought me to a place of deep sorrow that made writing about two people falling in love and fighting for all the right things nearly impossible. I tried to push through. I attempted to tell myself that I was strong enough to grieve and write simultaneously. I suppose I was. The book took longer than planned, but I wrote it, and I'm incredibly proud of this story.

As always, thank you to my husband, Dave, for supporting me and putting up with a writer in the house.

REIGN OF THE WITCH QUEEN

In the beginning, there were two worlds.
The human world is bound by earth, fire, water, and air.
The elven world glows with the fifth element, magic.
Over time, the sister worlds split from each other,
and humans forgot about the elves.

Centuries passed, and the elven world thrived until a beautiful and selfish witch came into power. Using her magic to dominate rather than to lead the elven people of Domhan, she cast a spell to keep men from ever assuming power. The old gods twisted her spell, and no female elves have been born since.

Darker and darker the witch queen became, until many fled the great city. Those who remained were transformed into her army of shadow demons.

Without female elves to continue their race, the elves living in fear of discovery will die out while Domhan falls into darkness. The only hope is a prophecy claiming that the human world holds the key. Only with the three earthly women and the sons of Riordan can the Watchers' Gate be opened. Inside lies the magic that can stop the witch queen.

The time has come for the three elven brothers to follow the prophecy.

Prologue

The night before the oracle sends the sons of Riordan to the human world

LIAM

Because the prophecy has been found, and the oracle is deciphering it, my brothers, the bulk of our army, and I have been ordered to remain in the city in case we need to deploy. Other than locking myself in my rooms, the garden is the only place I can find some peace in the bustling castle. Lounging atop the high garden wall gives me some privacy. It's a clear night, and the stars are bright before the second moon rises.

I should be strong-minded enough to sit still and wait, but I'm bored and anxious. It feels as if I'm standing on the brink of something, and I don't like not knowing my future.

Sensing my older brother's approach, I jump down. It's a

little reckless, but my magic and my elven strength allow me to land with ease. Behind Aaran, our younger brother, Raith, jogs awkwardly to keep up.

Our father often yells at Raith to be more disciplined like me or studious like Aaran, but Raith is his own person. He's kind and funny but not suited to soldiering or command, at least not yet. As unpredictable as Raith is, it's impossible not to like him. Even Aaran, who is most like Father, sees that there is something special about our little brother beyond his lack of control with his magic or what falls from his lips at any given time.

"You're looking for me?" Since this is the place I often go for solitude, the answer is obvious, and I see no point in them pretending they didn't wish to disturb me.

Aaran nods and steps through an archway made of shrubbery to the seating area beside the wall. "The prophecy has been deciphered."

Tripping over the flagstone, Raith leaps in the air, does a flip, and lands on his feet between Aaran and me. His long red hair flops into his face, and he brushes it back. "Oops."

With a shake of his head, Aaran sighs. "Try not to hurt yourself. We have orders."

"What orders?" My heart speeds, glad to have something to do besides wait.

"We are to go see the oracle in the morning." Aaran sits on the bench to my left. There are three in the small court, and it's familiar for us to meet here as we did when we were younger.

"Why not now?" I sit.

Raith lies on his back on the third bench, and his long

legs drape over the armrest. "Who knows why the oracle decides one time rather than another?"

Laughing, Aaran says, "He's right. They have their reasons even if we can't fathom them."

"What time do we go to the mountain?" It's a weakness not to be patient, but one I'm constantly working on.

"The mystery continues." Raith makes a spooky sound. "We're to go separately and in the order of our birth. Woooo." He wiggles his fingers in the air and laughs.

Unable to resist his enthusiasm, I chuckle too. "You should take it more seriously." I turn to Aaran. "What about the army?"

He shakes his head. "They only called for the three of us. I will go after we break our fast. Then they will send for you and Raith."

"I have a serious question." Raith points to the other side of the garden without rising from his reclined position. "Why is Dierdre hiding in the bushes?"

It's not that I didn't know that she was there. I just hoped she would leave when I didn't acknowledge her presence for long enough. "I assume she wishes to speak with me."

Aaran shifts to his side, leaning on his elbow. "I thought that relationship had ended."

"Months ago," I confirm, and a long sigh follows that I hadn't meant to share.

Raith's grin is sinister, which doesn't suit him. "Do you want me to scare her off?" He rubs his hands together, and a blue light sparks between his palms.

Laughing, Aaran lifts his hand and sends a spell to quash Raith's magic. "Leave her be. You and I will go inside and let Liam deal with his former lover."

Andrea Rose

With an unnecessary leap, Raith gets up and hugs me. "I think we should have a drink together tonight, but if"—he twitches his head at Dierdre's hiding place—"is going to take all night, we'll see you in the morning."

It's impossible not to be amused by him, but I force a scowl. "I'll meet you in the library shortly."

Aaran slaps my back and pushes Raith down the path toward the house.

When they reach the doors, I walk in the other direction. "Come out now, Dierdre."

Undeniably beautiful, Dierdre has long brown hair and bright hazel eyes. Her body is full and curvaceous, and she's a generous lover. She saunters toward me. "I thought your brothers would never leave." She wraps her arms around my neck.

I remove her arms and move back. "Why are you here? Our business together ended months ago."

"Business." She stomps her foot. "Is that what our love was?"

Stepping back, I cross my arms. "What we had was not love, Dierdre. You made that very clear when you began your affair with Kyle Mahony. Does he know you've come here tonight?"

"You should have proposed, Liam. If you had given me the position I deserve, I'd never have strayed."

"That was never going to happen," I say gently. "You will be happier without me."

Making a sour face, she pulls her shoulders back, which forces her breasts forward, calling into question whether her tunic can contain them. "My father said you would go to the oracle tomorrow. He wouldn't tell me what they'll ask of you. I was worried for your safety."

"You worry only for your own position, my dear. You should focus on Kyle. While what we had was a good deal of fun, it is in the past and was never going to give you what you wanted."

In two steps, she reaches me and slaps my cheek, digging her nails across my flesh. "You are a pig."

When her hand goes back for another swipe, I grip her wrists. "Go home before the guards are called to drag you home."

Softening, she drapes her body along mine. "You wouldn't call the guards on me."

I touch blood dripping down my cheek and send magic to heal the scratches. "I would and I will. Go now before I also send a letter to your current lover explaining your betrayal."

Narrowing her eyes, she growls. "I would have been a good wife to you. We could have ruled this land."

It's not as if I needed confirmation that I'd done the right thing in ending our arrangement, but her last sentence is perfectly telling. "My brother is the oldest. I am a simple soldier, and that is all I will ever be."

"Anything could have happened in the years of your mother's rule." Dierdre's beauty is soiled by the ugliness festering inside her.

"Go." I send a bright yellow light into the sky to alert the guards that there is an intruder.

Boots sound on the path.

Eyes wide, if she were a snake, venom would shoot from her mouth. "You really are a pig, Liam Riordan."

"I am. You are better off without me." When the three guards arrive, I say, "Please see the lady safely back to her father's house."

She stomps off with the guards behind her.

I make my way to the library.

At the cave, I ring the bell and wait for the portal to open. Once its swirling light appears, I step through to the antechamber.

My mother waits on the other end. She looks at my pack, weapons, and gear. "You've come prepared, I see."

"Father bid us all farewell when we broke our fast this morning, and Aaran didn't return. I assume I will be sent somewhere." I kiss her cheek. "You wouldn't want to tell me what this is all about, would you? Father said he knew nothing other than to make his goodbyes."

"Your father does not have the information, and I will let the oracle explain the needs of Domhan." Worry creases her forehead, and dark rings are under her eyes. She hands me a roll of green paper. "This is human currency. You'll need it."

Offering a short smile, I tuck the bills into my pack. "We'd better let them tell me my mission."

Side by side, Mother and I walk into the oracle's chamber. With only the dais lit and the rest in darkness, the room is hard to make out. Ten elves, all dressed in white robes, sit on a dais. A light shines from above me where I stand before them.

A Crown of Wind and Water

"What is it you would have from me?"

They speak as one voice, though none of their mouths move. "Second son of the Riordan. You must go to the world of humans and find one of the three prophesied to save our world. You will bring the woman back here, and six will travel to the Watchers' Gate. There, the prophecy declares you will find the means to defeat the witch queen and break the curse."

"I'm to grab a human woman? I thought humans had no magic. Why send me? Any elf could capture a human." Admittedly, I'm a little disappointed the task isn't more difficult.

Mother says, "I don't think we'll get much help from her if you force her to come to Domhan, a world she knows nothing about. You'll have to ask her to come."

"Why would she do that if, as you say, she knows nothing of our world?" I'll simply bring her here and convince her by any means to do as we say.

One of the oracle members blinks off the dais and lands in front of me. "The woman you seek has magic, but it lies dormant. She knows nothing of our world, and she will only help us if you can convince her our need is great. I offer you the song of her soul to guide you to Wren Martin. See that no harm comes to her, or all is lost, and we'll have to wait for another to come forth." She touches my temple.

The melody that enters my head is soft, sweet, and full of passion. It blends and balances with my soul's song in an alluring way. I have no idea who Wren Martin is, but her soul sings to mine in a way that is unsettling and appealing at the same time. I push the oracle's hand away. "I hear it."

She cocks her head. "The gate we create will stay open for a few minutes. It would be best if you could bring her back through right away, but if you cannot, I believe you have the knowledge of the old gates in the human world."

"I do." My brothers and I were all educated in the ways of humans and the history between elves and their magicless race. "I will bring her through."

The oracle closes their eyes and mutters words in the ancient tongue. A few feet in front of me, a pinpoint of purple light spins.

Turning to my mother, I give her a quick hug. "I will not fail."

She cups my head and brings my forehead to her lips. "I know."

The vortex widens and the portal opens. Through the small hole, I see her in a reclining chair with two people hovering over her.

Her song is louder, and she stares at me as she jumps from the reclining chair. The other two are frozen, and I know Wren and I are no longer existing in normal time. I step through the portal. "Wren Martin, by command of Elspeth Riordan, you must come with me."

"Who or what are you?" Her eyes sparkle the bluest blue, and her figure is petite, lush, and full. It seems impossible that this small human can save my world. Still, I was given a task.

"I am Liam. Come with me now." I step close and offer my hand to pull her back through the portal.

She is the most beautiful woman I've ever seen, but she looks at my hand as if I'm a viper. "No. Get away from me."

A Crown of Wind and Water

Frustrated and unreasonably hurt, I step closer to her and grip her shoulder. "I don't have time for this. You will come with me now."

Her foot connects with my balls faster than I have time to react. And I hit the floor hard enough to smash my kneecap.

Chapter One

WREN

I t's bad luck to go on my dream vacation and break a tooth. My Aunt Dot used to say that if I didn't have bad luck, I'd have no luck at all. She was a peach, old Dot was.

Still, even with a broken tooth and lying back in the dentist's chair, I'm in London, and Momma is with me. Life is pretty good.

The polishing tool buzzes. "Just about done here."

I adore Doctor Emmit's accent.

"What do you have planned for the rest of the day, Miss Martin?"

He stops polishing long enough for me to respond. "Momma and I are going to tour Westminster Abbey and take one of those double-decker bus tours."

Both the doctor and his assistant give me a fake smile before focusing on my incisor. After a minute, Doctor Emmit lifts the dental tool and pushes the overhead light back.

"There..." He freezes with his arm in an awkward upturned position and his other hand halfway to the console where he'd replace the tool.

Confused, I look to the assistant for some explanation. Maybe the guy has a condition. Hands reaching toward me, a warm smile plastered on her face, and her brown hair no longer falling forward from her ponytail, she has stopped moving as well.

"Is this a joke? Some bit of English humor to unsettle the American?"

No reaction.

A sound that reminds me of a tornado chugging closer begins, and the papers on the tray next to me blow around the room. My hair and the bib I'm wearing fly over my face.

Tearing the bib off, I push my curls out of my eyes and slip from the dentist's chair. I back up to the closed exam room door. The sheet I filled out with my medical history heads toward my face and I bat it aside.

"What in holy heck is happening here?" Maybe I'm dead, and this is the afterlife. Except that my mouth is still a bit numb, and why would that be the case if I'm dead? Plus, where is my body? I look at the empty chair with Doctor Emmit and his assistant still hovering over it. "Momma?" I grab the doorknob.

A spinning hole opens up in the wall in front of me. There had been a painting of an old-style dentist chair in the center of the wall, with transom windows at the top letting in some light from the drizzly London day. The hole widens and brightens while a figure grows larger in the center.

I should run, but I'm mesmerized by the fact that this is

happening, and neither of the other two people in the room seem affected or aware.

The man who jumps down from the vortex is tall and broad. Wearing a blue uniform of some kind, he has long, dark-blond hair bound at the back. He has a pack on his shoulder, a sword hangs in a scabbard at his side, and another knife hilt pokes out of his tall black boot. He winces before straightening and looking right at me. "Wren Martin, by command of Elspeth Riordan, you must come with me."

"Who or what are you?" I'll admit, he's beautiful. I mean, like a movie star but with a keen gaze and a roughness that is more military than Hollywood.

His eyes are sapphire blue, and they narrow as he steps closer. "I am Liam. Come with me now." He holds his hand out.

I stare at his open palm, then look him in the eyes. "No. Get away from me."

Jaw ticking, He closes the few feet between us and hovers over me. "I don't have time for this. You will come with me now." He touches my shoulder.

Instinct takes over. Still holding the doorknob, I kick between his legs as hard as my five-foot-two-inch body can. I connect squarely and jerk the door open.

With a yelp, he crumbles to the floor, holding his crotch.

The wind from the vortex pulls papers from the administration desk outside the exam room. The young man who checked me in is pointing to something on the computer screen while a woman with graying hair and kind eyes looks over his shoulder. Neither move. A woman in a white coat is holding a chart on a metal clipboard across the desk, her mouth open, as if in mid-sentence. Pink, yellow, and white papers fly around them, but none of them move.

Rushing past, I find my mother with four others frozen in the waiting room. One man is near the door leading outside. A woman with a little girl in her lap reads a children's book, but no words leave the woman's open mouth and the pages are flapping. An overweight man in a business suit looks as if he's dozing off with his head back and mouth agape.

Other than hair flying along with paper and magazines, no one moves or even blinks.

Taking my backpack from the floor, I grab hold of my mother's hand. "We have to go."

"She can't hear you." Liam stands in the archway between the administration desk and the waiting room. At first, I didn't notice, but now I can hear that he sounds more Irish than English.

"Momma, you need to wake up, and we need to go. There's a madman." I shake her arm. When she doesn't move, I grab the lamp from the table and raise it above my head while facing Liam. "Let her go."

He limps one step closer but stops when I raise the lamp higher. "I'm not doing this. It's the magic that pulled you and me out of time. No one can hear or see us until the spell is through. I really must insist you come through the portal with me, Wren Martin. This is your destiny."

It isn't nice, but I get a bit of satisfaction from his limp and the fact that I could knock down a big man with one kick. "Stay away from me. I won't hesitate to bash in that pretty head of yours if you come near me or my momma. My destiny is to enjoy a nice vacation before returning to Texas and my work."

A Crown of Wind and Water

Holding up his hands, he backs away a step. "The oracle of Domhan sent me to get you and bring you back so that you can save our world."

"I'm a jewelry maker, not a soldier. I'm small and can't do a single pull-up. What exactly do you think I can do to save anyone, let alone a world? You should go back to wherever you came from, and I'll pretend none of this ever happened since no one will ever believe me anyway." Keeping an eye on him, I shake my mother's shoulder. "Wake up."

"I don't make prophecies, Wren. I follow orders. I was sent to find you and bring you home." He strides toward me.

I smack him with the lamp. "If your orders include forcing me to go anywhere I don't want to go, you had better rethink your career choice." I hit him again and again.

He deflects the blows with his arm and hands, but there's still a gash on his wrist and one above his right eye. Stumbling backward, he touches the cut and then studies me. "You act as if forcing you to do something is a simple matter, though you've made it quite obvious that's not the case." He passes his hand over the wound, and the flesh mends back together in an instant.

I have a lot of questions, but none of them matter. "Momma, wake up." I touch her cheek and pray she comes back to me.

My mother blinks and stares at me. "What's wrong?" She grips my hand.

Liam says, "That should not have been possible."

"It's difficult to explain, but we need to get out of here."

Momma stands and gapes at the statue-like people

around us. Her gaze lands on Liam. "Fairy folk, just like Grandma always said."

Liam cocks his head and studies her. "I'm an elf, not a fairy. Have you heard of my kind?"

Before Momma can go into the details of my great-grandmother's stories, I tug her out of the dentist's office. "We need to get away from that…um…man."

"Why? He's easy on the eyes." Clutching her oversize black handbag, she stumbles after me, looking over her shoulder at him.

There's no arguing with the fact that he's very handsome, and if it weren't for his pointy ears sticking out, he would be a hunk of a man. However, he tried to abduct me, and that's a big red flag. "He just tried to get me to go through a vortex without my permission, Momma. We have to go."

The cars on the streets of London are all stopped, as are the people. Some are mid-stride, and others are sitting across the street on the bench in Hyde Park. A woman is gesturing, and her mouth is open as if she'd been talking to the man beside her. For his part, he looks bored with whatever she was saying.

Momma pulls her hand free. She turns right, then left. "What is going on?"

I turn to respond, but Liam has followed us out of the office, and my mother is directing her question to him.

"We are out of time with your world until the portal closes. I am Liam Riordan, and my orders are to bring Wren Martin back to my world, as she is part of a prophecy." His voice is smooth and commanding.

Offering her hand, Momma smiles. "I'm Birdie Martin,

and you can't just take a woman with you because you have orders, Mr. Riordan."

Taking her hand in his, his full lips tip up in something close to a smile, but without letting go of his soldierly sternness. "My mother is the rightful queen of Domhan, but a witch displaced her, and soon my world will be covered in darkness." He shifts his gaze to me. "I concede your point about my methods for accomplishing my goal. Clearly, Miss Martin is not a woman to be bullied."

"Kicked you in your tender bits, did she?" Momma shakes her head and draws a long sigh. "I raised her to be a lady, but also to protect herself. My grandma spoke of fairy folk who lured women away with their good looks and flowery words."

He winces, and so do I. "I don't know many flowery words, I'm afraid." Turning back toward me, he stares for a long moment. "Is there any way I can convince you to come through the portal with me?"

A loud, piercing screech forces me and my mother to hold our ears.

Liam says something in a language I don't know, but I can gather from his tone that whatever he said was a curse.

"No." I take my mother's hand and step toward the street.

The din of London hums back to life. Cars speed by, and I pull back before we're run over. The world is moving again.

"Did you pay the bill, baby girl?" My mother has been calling me that since I was a baby, and while I wish she'd use some other endearment in public, I can't help feeling warmed by the sweetness of it.

Now that I think about it, I was too distracted by the near abduction. I point at him. "Stay back."

He shimmers for a moment, and his ears disappear under his hair. His weapons also vanish, and his uniform changes to plain white pants and a blue jacket. Holding up his hands palms forward, he sighs. "My portal is closed, Wren. We'll have to find another way." He leans against the building next to Doctor Emmit's door.

"I'll just wait here with Liam while you pay." Momma stands on the other side of the door with her arms crossed and her expression determined. Like me, she's barely five feet, two inches tall. She has her blond curls cut above her jawline. If she narrowed her eyes at me like she looks at Liam, I'd be afraid. Of course, he stares right back, as if he encounters a Texas momma every day.

For a moment, I feel sorry for him. "Don't you dare hurt my mother. I'll hunt you down, and there'll be nothing you can say to make me help you."

Raising his eyebrow, he softens his expression. "Noted. I'll not harm Birdie, or you for that matter."

Despite it sounding like a sacred vow the way he said it, I'm not leaving my mother with a man who recently tried to drag me through a vortex or portal or whatever that thing was. "No. Momma, you need to come inside with me."

"She doesn't trust you."

He nods. "Trust must be earned, and I have not done so."

Damn him for sounding contrite. I glare at the pair and hold the door open for my mother to precede me inside.

The office is in complete chaos, with employees and patients picking up papers and magazines. It feels as if I should apologize, but I didn't make the mess.

A Crown of Wind and Water

At the administration desk, I force a smile. "I guess in all the fuss, I forgot to pay you."

The young man gathers a stack of papers. "Oh, Miss Martin, we didn't know what happened to you. Actually, we don't know what happened at all. It was like a great wind blew through. Is it windy outside?"

"Not particularly." I wait, and when he doesn't give me a bill, I say, "I know you have a lot to clean up, but can you tell me how much I owe you?"

Putting the papers aside, he clicks on his keyboard and prints out a bill, which I pay by credit card.

In the waiting room, Momma and Liam are standing near the door, chatting like old friends. His expression remains serious, but she's laughing.

This entire thing is too much. I storm forward. "Momma, we're leaving."

"I've invited Liam to join us for the tour of Westminster Abbey." She says it as if we met him at a party.

As soon as we're on the street, I face her. "You invited the man who tried to abduct me to go on a tour with us?"

"Don't put it that way. His people are in real trouble. He was following orders, and you're still here. No real harm was done." She grins at me.

I'd like to say this lack of worry over the state of the world around us was unusual, but the truth is, my mother never worried a day in her life about the dangers around her. She has faith that she'll always be safe.

I grew up in a different time, without her sense of peace and harmony. Still, I can see how the gruff soldier is charming in his way. If he's lying about the plight of his world, he's the best I've ever seen. No. I think he's telling the truth, but that doesn't mean I'm getting involved with whatever insanity happened in the dental office. I'm going to see London and Scotland as planned. "Y'all do what you like." I walk past them and head to the corner where I'll cross to the park. There's plenty of time to get to the Abbey.

There's no doubt in my mind that when the light turns, the two of them are striding behind me. I keep going past the wrought iron gate and into the lush green park with its meandering paths. I breathe in the bit of nature in the middle of the city and know I'll remember the soft scent of roses and sweet magnolias with a hint of a mustier floral I don't know, yet it's familiar. It might be zinnias or marigolds. The presence of city odors only makes the country air more remarkable.

Momma says, "We should find the statue of Peter Pan."

Too annoyed to agree with her, I stride forward.

"Who is Peter Pan?" Liam's voice is deep, and every word he says seems to vibrate along my skin.

I rub my arm, trying to banish the sensation. "He's a character in a book. It's fiction about a place where unwanted boys never grow up."

"Unwanted?" He sounds incredulous.

Momma sighs. "Yes. Unfortunately, that part is not always fiction, Liam. However, in the book, the head boy, Peter, makes his way to London where he convinces three children to go on an adventure with him. It's a darling story."

"My people cherish their children," he says flatly.

I round on him. "You have no orphans? This world you want me to save is perfect, other than it's dying because of a witch?" I want to not care, but I was made very empathetic, and I can't help feeling everyone's concerns deeply. Sometimes, so much so that I ignore my own.

The only sign that he's the least bit moved by my words is a slight tick in his jaw. He blinks several times and pulls his shoulders back. His voice is soft but full of gravity. "When an elven child is orphaned, another family usually raises them. Sometimes it's family and sometimes friends. In some cases, the royal family will adopt the child. My parents did so when I was a baby, though Nainsi was nearly grown at the time. She lives in your world now. To your other point, I'd be glad to tell you all about Domhan's troubles if you would stop running away from me for five minutes together." There was more bite in that last part.

I can't help the shimmer of satisfaction over making him angry. His cool exterior irritates the crap out of me. Staring back, I have a dozen questions about his world and his family, but in the end, one thing trumps them all. "Why is your adopted sister in my world?"

With a slight shake of his head, he bites his top lip.

It's impossible not to watch his mouth. I force my gaze back to his eyes, which are just as pretty as those lips.

The sound of water fills the silence as we stare at each other.

There's a subtle shift in his attitude, but I see the moment when he pushes aside his frustration and regains his soldierly composure. "My parents brought a party to this world ten of your years ago. Nainsi was with them. She met a man and fell in love. They live in someplace called Newfoundland."

Before I can ask more questions, Momma grabs my hand and pulls me around the fountain. She whips her London tour guidebook out of her purse and flips to one of the page tabs. "This is the Italian Gardens. If we go this way, we should see the Peter Pan statue and eventually Diana's memorial fountain."

I should stay silent and mind my own business. Liam is nothing to me. "If I had a sister I hadn't seen in ten years, I wouldn't be trying to abduct unsuspecting women in London. I'd be in Canada catching up with Nainsi."

He's a step or two behind me. "I was very young when she went to live with an aunt and uncle, though I would like to see her. However, my duty is to find one of the three human women from the prophecy and bring her to the Watchers' Gate. My brothers have been sent on the same task. Each of us was sent to find one of you and ask you to help us."

Acting as if I ignored the part about taking me away, I ask, "How much older is your sister?"

"At least twelve suns." He steps beside me and keeps pace with me while Momma rushes ahead of us.

When I stop, he faces me. "Your parents must have been very young when they took her in. Wait. How old are you?" I'm trying to be nonchalant, but my voice is incredulous as I attempt the math in my head.

A few strands of his dark-gold hair fall from the ribbon holding them back. My hand itches to push them back. Liam tucks them behind his ear. "I have lived only thirty-four suns. Elves live a great deal longer than humans. My parents were already married, and my mother was ruler of our people in all of Domhan when the witch queen started the war that left Nainsi orphaned at fifteen." He cocks his head. "I was little when she lived with us and remember her as a soldier and dear friend to my mother. She never came back to my world after falling in love here."

Besides trying to kidnap me, it's hard to find anything wrong with him, which is annoying. "How long will you live?"

He shrugs and turns to catch up with my mother.

I have to jog to keep up with his long strides.

Momma is staring at the bronze statue of Peter Pan playing his flute. His face is full of mischief, and on the stump beneath him are little animals and fairies. It's quite beautiful and reminds me of Momma reading me the book as a child.

Liam turns his gaze from Pan and the crowd around him and whispers, "Elves can live over two hundred of your years, Wren."

Two hundred. It's inconceivable to imagine living so long. Shaking my head, I pull my sketchbook out of my backpack, take a pencil from the front pocket, and make a quick sketch of Peter Pan. I'm not missing my lovely England vacation because of Liam or anyone.

Looking over my shoulder, he asks, "You said you make jewelry?"

"That's right. Not war." I shade in the shadows cast by the trees and shrubs surrounding the statue.

"You draw very well." He touches my bracelet. It's a gold band with a green marcasite stone in the center. "Did you make this?"

I take a step forward. He's too close, too warm, and smells too male. "Yes. Won't you just go away?"

"I can't do that." There's an apologetic quality to his voice, but I sense no wavering in his goal.

Maybe if I ignore him, he'll get the hint eventually.

That is not what happens. We go to the Abbey, and he follows. We take a double-decker bus tour, and Liam sits behind us. When we exit the bus, I give our tour driver some money, and when I turn, I see Momma pointing to the sign over a pub door.

Liam looks and nods.

Without having to ask, I know that she's invited him to eat dinner with us. I'm too tired to argue, and something about him is hard to dislike. It's more than his good looks, which cannot be denied. He's easy and comforting. I have no doubt that in a tough spot, that he'd protect us or die trying. Maybe it's because I've never had that in my life, and I'm almost certain my mother hasn't either, that I silently follow them into the English pub and sit opposite him at the booth as the waitress hands us menus. If I can't get rid of him, I may as well enjoy the sight of him.

The waitress blushes and says, "We have chicken pot pie and beef Wellington on special tonight. I'm sorry to say we're out of the mutton already, but it's popular with the local crowd and they've been here a while." She points at a large, loud group watching the sports news about a soccer match.

"Thank you." He looks at her name tag. "Mary. You're very helpful."

Even redder in the face, Mary giggles and steps away.

"Good lord. Have some pride, woman," I mutter.

Momma elbows me in the ribs. "Don't be ugly. She's smitten, bless her heart."

I close my eyes and remember myself. Forcing my smile into place, I say, "Sorry, Momma. I think the pot pie sounds good and a half pint of beer. I'll sleep like a baby."

"I agree." Momma slaps her menu down with a flourish. "This is a good ol' boy bar if I ever saw one."

"I think all the cowboys are across the Atlantic, but I see what you mean. Local pub with lots of character." It's just the kind of place we like to find when we go on vacation or head to Houston for a weekend getaway.

Still giggling and now watched by two other waitresses, Mary returns. "Can I get you something to drink?"

Liam looks across at me, then at Momma, but Mary only has eyes for him. "I think we're all decided on beer and pot pie."

Mary shudders as she draws a deep breath. "Pints or halves, ale or lager?"

"Half pints and ale, please," I say gently. My mother is right about Mary being smitten. If I don't say something, she'll pile all three meals on his side of the table.

As if out of a trance, she turns and gapes at me. "Of course. Yes, miss." She rushes away and joins the other two for a good giggle.

"Maybe you shouldn't speak to her so sweetly." A tiny knot of jealousy curls into my belly.

Cocking his head, Liam stares at the women ogling him, then turns to me. "I didn't say anything to lead her to believe I was looking for more than food and drink."

"You don't need to say it, Liam. You only need to smile." Even I'm not immune to his good looks as much as I'd like to believe I am.

His smile is slow and full, and all of his attention is on me. "I will try to keep my smiles to myself, Wren."

"You two, play nice now," Momma whispers as Mary brings over the beers.

Chapter Two

LIAM

By some miracle, despite a poor showing, I am still with Wren and Birdie a week later. They have rented something called a flat in the city of Edinburgh. If not for Birdie, I'm sure I would have been left behind with little means to follow.

From the moment I stepped through the portal, I've gone about my mission wrong, and thought I could command a human woman to do as I say through force or magic. My balls still sting from the memory of where she planted her foot the moment I touched her.

My mistake was thinking it would be easy. My mother told me to ask. Admittedly, I didn't believe her. How could a being void of magic be a match for an elven soldier?

After meeting Wren, my view has changed. She caught me off guard twice. After a week of watching her ignore me, it's difficult to want to put her life at risk. She is small and sweet. Her heart is kind, and her gifts lie in making jewelry, not fighting shadow demons. Yet the prophecy says she's vital to our cause.

I was sent to ask her, and I tried to force her. It was stupid and has stripped me of any trust I might have built with her. The only thing saving me is that her mother likes me.

Magically forcing her into a portal would make me as bad as the witch queen. The shame of that thought will stay with me for a long while. Somehow, I must convince her to travel to Domhan and assist in saving my world.

I'm not a diplomat. Hopefully, Aaran had more luck with the human he was sent for.

I sip an ale and watch as both Martin women dance with strangers on the street while two women play instruments and people put money in the box they have set before them. The weather has turned warm, and Wren is wearing short pants that hug her deliciously round bottom and expose so much flesh that my mouth waters at the sight of her. Silver earrings catch the light as she shakes her head, singing along and dancing with joy. Her bright blond curls bounce and are so different from elves' typical long, straight hair. My fingers itch to feel the texture of every strand.

Get yourself together. I close my eyes and take a deep breath.

As the song ends, Wren drops a few bills in the box. She and her mother laugh together as they make their way to the table. They sit across from me and pick up their drinks.

Birdie says, "Tell us more about where you're from, Liam."

"Momma, this isn't the place." Wren looks around at all

the people seated outside the pub called the Devil's Dance Card.

Birdie waves her hand in dismissal. "They're more interested in their drinks and the busker's music. No one is listening to us."

"Busker?" It's a new word for me.

"That's what they call street performers." Wren rarely speaks to me directly unless she's disapproving of something. She looks away quickly and takes a long pull on her ale.

The fact that she's friendly and sweet with everyone else we meet should bother me, but I can see her point of view. I'm not like her. I'm not like anyone else here in her world. I came here to change her life forever, and without permission.

"Domhan has different areas: marshes, meadows, deserts, and forests. There are mountains, rivers, lakes, and oceans. It's vast, with different kinds of people living separately."

"What kinds and why do they live apart?" Wren's pupils are small on this rare sunny day, and her stare is fixed on me.

Lowering my voice, I say, "Dwarves are greedy and live in the mountains where they dig for more riches. Fairies keep to their island and never bother with the rest of Domhan. Centaurs live in the forest and, by all accounts, are a vicious race. Giants live in high mountain caves and do not come down. Dragons have trapped themselves in time until the witch queen is defeated."

Birdie's eyes are wide, and her voice is soft with wonder. "Dragons and giants. My grandmother never said anything about those. I suppose she didn't know."

"You said your ancestor met elves in Texas? Perhaps they didn't tell her about Domhan. They were likely in this world to learn about humans. Elves don't usually come through. I'll have to ask my mother or a historian what brought them here so long ago. My parents came ten years ago looking for a way to break the curse." I'm deep in thought when I realize Wren's gaze is on me. I stare back.

"You didn't say why all these people you say live in your world live apart from one another? Why don't fairies mix with dwarves and dwarves with elves, and so on?" Her expression is deadly serious, and she's so beautiful it's hard to think when she looks at me so intently.

"Honestly, I'm not certain. I've never met a fairy or a dwarf, Wren. I only know what people say about each race and that they don't mix." A touch of shame creeps into my gut, and I'm not sure where it came from. This is just the way Domhan is, and it's certainly not my fault.

"Then you dislike all races save your own when you've never met anyone from the others? Do I have that right?" Her gaze is unwavering.

Birdie bites her lip, holding in a laugh at my expense.

"I never thought of it that way, but you're right. My prejudices are founded in old rumors and even older traditions. I will endeavor to be more open-minded." In one week, she has me rethinking a lifetime of beliefs. What kind of magic does this human hold?

"And humans?" She plops her empty glass on the table. "What is the overarching opinion of humans that all elves believe?"

A burst of laughter escapes before Birdie covers her mouth. "You're in big trouble now. I'm willing to bet this will be a doozie."

A Crown of Wind and Water

Wren has, in a few moments, made me feel like a schoolboy who spoke out of turn, and rightfully so.

"Elves think humans are weak and useless. Humans are believed to have no magic and no value to the elven way of life. Many believe that is why the old ones closed off the worlds from each other." I can't contain my chuckle. "However, I learned within the first minute of finding you that weak is the last thing you are, since you brought me to my knees with one kick."

How she manages to blush and look proud of herself at the same time is one of a hundred mysteries about Wren Martin that I yearn to uncover.

"Momma, it's getting late. Should we have another round or call it a night?"

Finishing her ale, Birdie swipes her hand across her mouth. "I'm plum tuckered. Y'all can stay, but I'm going back to the flat."

"I'm not letting you walk these city streets all alone. Besides, we've been running all over hell's half acre all day. I want to get into my comfy clothes and put my feet up." Wren follows her mother.

I walk with them back to the rental apartment. I've seen inns all over, but when I asked Birdie about this rental rather than a hotel room, she said she likes to have her own kitchen and more than one room to stomp in.

While the women go into the bedroom, I grab my pack and head into the bathroom. I take a quick shower and change. I'm going to bring this shower idea back home. It's a brilliant way of cleaning up without all the fuss of a bath.

On the second day in this world, I bought myself two pairs

of human denim pants and soft short-sleeve shirts. My uniform jacket made me look too out of place, and using a glamor for clothes is a waste of magical energy. I also purchased something called lounging pants, and I'm a bit too fond of them. It's like walking around naked while being covered up. The material is soft and stretchy. On the day before we left London, I went back to the store and bought two more pairs.

When I see the bedroom light go out through the space below the door, I make up the couch with sheets and a blanket and lie back. It's too early for sleep, and the television might keep the women from sleeping. I think of how I'll convince Wren to leave everything she knows to help Domhan, a world she knows nothing about.

Maybe the oracle can find another way to defeat the witch queen and break the curse. I'd prefer one that doesn't include putting Wren in mortal danger.

The bedroom door creaks slightly as the object of my thoughts steps into the living room. In a flimsy pair of pink shorts and a top that leaves her midriff exposed, she's all temptation, and I'm all frustration. "I thought you might still be awake."

I point to the still-light sky. "It's still daylight. I can't sleep yet."

"This is Scotland in the summertime. It will be light another hour." She sits at the edge of the other end of the couch.

Moving my feet to the floor, I watch her. "Are you unable to rest?"

"I don't want you to think I don't like you, Liam. It's hard to dislike you despite you initially trying to kidnap me." She blushes and looks at her hands as they twist in her lap, then fusses with her silver ring with its dark blue stone. It's one of her creations that she favors and wears much of the time.

"I'm flattered and glad to know you don't hate me." It takes all my will not to stare at her smooth, full thigh. "I find you brilliant, talented, and funny." I don't mention how beautiful she is because I need to protect myself from whatever is happening here.

Wide-eyed, she gapes at me. "Do you?"

"Yes. Why does that surprise you?" I sit with my back against the rolled arm of the couch and face her.

"I have refused to do what you want. I wouldn't think you'd have anything nice to say about me."

"One thing has nothing to do with the other. Besides, it's not what *I* want, it's what my world needs. I was ordered to come here to find you and ask you to return to Domhan with me. If it were up to me, I would leave you to live a happy life here." Too much truth might not be a good thing.

She smiles, which makes my heart leap. "So, you like me, but you also have a job to do."

"My world needs you, Wren. My liking you is beside the point."

"Not to me." She slips under the bottom end of my blanket and crosses her legs as she faces me. "I'm ready to know why you want me to come with you. Tell me about this curse and the prophecy."

"I'm not certain telling you about those things will benefit my cause." I long to pull her across the four feet that separate us and hold her against me. I want to breathe in the lilac scent of her skin and hair and whisper things that will make her want to writhe against me. Instead, I pull the covers over my expanding shaft and sit in the same manner as her.

There's that smile again. "Not telling me won't either."

She makes a good point. "Thirty years ago, a woman named Venora Braddish used evil magic to usurp the rightful elf queen, my mother. She took the great white tower and poisoned it with her dark magic. She turned good elves into shadow demons and forces them to kill in her name. She amassed an army, both elven and demon, for her cause. She ravages and kills, all while gathering magical power.

"The curse was only in part her doing. She cast a spell to ensure no elven man would ever come to power. Her purpose was to keep herself on the throne, as she thought one of her lovers might try to take her place. The old gods must not have liked her magic as they twisted the spell, and now there have been no female elves born in thirty years."

Wren gasps. "That's terrible. Humanity would be devastated. The damage would be nearly impossible to recover from."

"Elves live longer. We may yet recover if we can break the curse." It's something all Domhan prays for every day. "My mother took as many elves as she could across the sea and made a new capital close to the magic of the oracle. Their magic is strong and has protected us, but that time may be coming to an end."

"Tell me about the dragons. You said they are trapped in time. What does that mean?" She yawns and rests her head on the couch pillow.

"That is a sad story." I stretch my legs out and move them to the outside of the couch.

I expect her to stretch hers toward me, but she slides

down the pillows and curls into a ball with her head next to my thigh. "Why is it sad?"

Sliding my arm under her, I drag her along my side until her head rests on my chest. "You'll wake up sore from sleeping as you were."

"I'm not sleeping." She wraps her arm around my waist and relaxes. "Tell me about the dragons."

What is it about this human woman? Why can't I resist the urge to touch her? I toy with a few strands of her hair. It's as soft as it looks. "I will tell you if you agree to favor me with a story about your home in Texas."

"What kind of story?" She looks up at me without lifting her cheek.

It would be so easy to press my lips to hers, but if I kiss her, I'll be lost. I have orders to bring her back. It would be dishonest to make it more than that. "How do you live? What do you do all day? What is the land like?"

She sighs and closes her eyes. "We live in East Texas. There are a lot of pine trees and lakes. People like to fish and hunt. Most folks never leave the area where they were born. I've always wanted to travel. Momma and I live on the same property, but we each have our own home. It's nice to have her close and still have my own space. My house is small, but I like it. The land is flat and green. It's warm most of the year. I spend my days making jewelry, and it's turned into a nice business despite the doubters. I ship all over the country and sell at markets on the weekend. There you have it. My little life can be boiled down to a few sentences and reported in less than a minute."

"I suspect there is more to it. Do you have a man you spend time with?" Why did I ask that?

"No. I almost got married once, but that was years ago." She shakes her head as if coming to her senses. "The dragons?"

I'm doomed. Wren has me under some human spell, and I'll never get away from the effects. "When I was a boy, dragons were seen from time to time soaring above. They're highly intelligent and have a hierarchy not much different than our own. Trocar and Delana, a mated pair, ruled over all the dragons. Trocar is as big as the gates of that castle we saw yesterday and as black as night. Delana is only slightly smaller and white like a pearl from the sea.

"Shortly after Venora took the white tower, she must have been heady with power. She decided she could command the dragons with her magic. If it had worked, there would have been nothing to stop her from taking over all of Domhan and making every creature her slave.

"She went to the dragons' mountain lair and attacked. She cast her spell of forbidden dark magic. It would have enslaved every dragon to her service and blackened their bright hearts."

"No. What stopped her?" Wren's eyes are full of tears as she stares at me. One trickles down her cheek.

I catch it with my thumb and rub it between my fingers. My breath catches, and it takes me a moment to continue. "Trocar blocked the magic so that the full spell hit him and none of the others, while Delana used her magic to lock the rest of them in time. This way, Venora cannot reach them."

She grips my hand. "How will they return?"

I love how much she cares about events that happened in another world, before she was born. Studying her small fingers, I imagine the intricate work they do as she makes her fine jewelry. I trace each one and marvel at her neatly polished nails and the way the pink shines in the last light of day. "It's said that when magic comes back into balance in Domhan, they will return." I shrug and press her hand to my chest. "I don't know if that's true or if Venora can be defeated. It's just a legend now."

Her tears fall, and her pretty mouth turns down. "I thought I was the key to some gate that holds whatever can defeat her."

"Are you upset because you don't want to help me, or is it something else?"

As if she's come to her senses, she wiggles down the couch and stands up. "It's not that I don't want to help. I'm no soldier. I have no skills. I've told you. I'll just get killed in some war I know nothing about, and then what, you'll have to come back and find another artist from Texas to take my place?"

"I don't know, you protect yourself and your mother pretty well from what I've seen and felt. I would protect you with my life. However, that doesn't answer my question about why you're upset."

She wraps her arms around herself, which pushes her breast to the breaking point of her small nightshirt and makes me very uncomfortable. "Sometimes I can sense things. When you told the story of Trocar and Delana, I was filled with hopelessness, and it came from you. I didn't like to feel that when usually you're sure and determined."

"Magic." I stand even though my cock is stiff and has a mind of its own where she is concerned. "You sense my emotions?"

Her gaze drifts down then her cheeks turn bright red. "I

hardly need magic to sense them now." She turns toward the small kitchen. "If I've led you on, I'm sorry. I'll admit, I find you attractive, but any woman would. Still, you and I come from literally different worlds and I don't have sex with men when there's no hope of something deeper developing."

"I won't apologize for the state of my cock. You are very beautiful, and you were lying on top of me a moment ago. However, I think you'll agree, I've been a gentleman. Can you tell me if you have other magic?" I want to close the distance between us. I want to be less of a gentleman more than I want to take my next breath, but I keep my place near the couch.

Still bright red, she looks at me. "I didn't mean to make you uncomfortable. It's just nice to be held from time to time, and I'm tired and confused about how much I want you. I'm going back to bed."

Before she can cross to the bedroom door, I block her path. This is a dangerous road. "You want me?"

"Sometimes I have dreams and then they happen. It's been like that since I was a little girl. I don't know if I make things happen or if the dreams are premonitions. And, of course, some dreams are only dreams." She bites her lip and puts her palm flat on my bare chest.

Barely hearing her confession of another kind of magic, I cover her hand with mine. "I thought it was only me."

She shakes her head. "What does this witch look like?"

I shudder. "Venora is tall and has black hair. Her eyes were hazel, but evil has turned them mostly black. I think she must have been beautiful once, but now black magic has turned her features harsh."

"I've seen your witch queen in my dreams."

A Crown of Wind and Water

"What?" It comes out much louder than I planned, but I'm taken completely by surprise.

Wren's eyes widen, and I see the change from concern about the magic she holds and anger because I raised my voice. Fire returns to her face, and she crosses her arms. "Don't you shout at me. I'm not one of your servants, Prince Liam."

Birdie opens the bedroom door and blinks at us. She has an eye mask pushed up so that her normally orderly short curls are standing straight up on the top. "What's all the hollering about?"

"I'm going to bed." Wren turns, but her mother stands in the doorway, blocking her path.

Torn between letting her go and finding out about these dreams, I opt for my duty. "You cannot tell me that you've dreamed of the witch queen and then go to bed without explaining, Wren. I'm sorry for yelling, but your declaration took me by surprise."

"Goodness gracious, Wren darlin', why didn't you say something?" Birdie takes her hand and walks her to the small table that serves as a dining room. "Put a shirt on, Liam. I'm old, but even I'm distracted by all that." She waves a hand in the general direction of my upper body.

"I don't know why I didn't say. First, I didn't make the connection between my dreams and Liam's world. I've been seeing her in my sleep for months." She stares at her hands on the table. "Two days ago, Liam told you about the witch queen and her evil, and that night I saw her in my dreams. That's when I knew it was her and not something out of my imagination."

I do as I'm told and then join them at the table. Forcing down my urgency, I ask, "What did you dream?"

She shakes her head. "It's hard to explain. I was far away, or she was above on a butte. It was a dream, so things weren't clear. She had long black hair and pointed ears like yours. Her eyes were black like one of those creepy dolls. Her black gown looked expensive but tattered, and she wore a cape with a red lining. She screamed words I didn't understand and shot black lightning from her fingers. The wind whipped around me and lifted her off the butte. Her lightning went in all directions but hit my chest, and I woke up from the pain of it." Breathing hard, she presses both hands to her chest.

My heart pounds. The description is too close to reality to be a coincidence when, aside from a few moments ago, I'm certain I never described Venora to either Birdie or Wren. "What is a butte?"

"It's a rock formation, an isolated peak, with steep sides, and a flat top juts from the lower lands." Birdie speaks like a teacher, which I already know was her profession for many years before she retired.

"Is there a place like that in your world?" Wren's eyes plead for me to deny it.

"We have flat-topped hills. We call them table-topped. Where did the wind come from?" I've never seen a natural wind that could lift someone as Wren described.

Pale and miserable, she shakes her head.

Birdie combs Wren's hair back from her face. "What is it, baby?"

Her voice is soft, scared. "I think it came from me."

Magic again, but this only in a dream or vision. Forcing a

smile, I say, "Visions are funny things. They don't always come to pass. The future is unpredictable."

"Liam is right. Not everything you dream happens. You should rest now. We'll go to bed, and all you'll have is sweet dreams tonight." Birdie wraps an arm around Wren, and they walk to the bedroom.

"Wren." I stand. When she turns back, my heart is in my throat. She's so perfect. "Let me be clear, I would never shout at the people who work for my parents. I'm hardly a model son for a queen, but I'm not a monster."

There's a hint of a smile. "I know."

Chapter Three

WREN

Why did I tell him that I want him? Sometimes my mouth outruns all good sense. I've known Liam for eight days, and suddenly I'm considering going with him to some portal into another world with elves and dragons.

"You're angry," Liam says while we wait for Momma to get our tickets to the distillery tour.

"Not angry, no. I'm embarrassed and scared. I don't know what made me behave as I did last night. I hardly know you." I close my eyes and take a deep breath before I say something else better kept to myself.

"You have nothing to be uneasy about. As you said, sometimes people need to be held." He has the most beautiful lips, and when they hint at a smile, he's stunningly handsome. In fact, several women stare as they walk by our bench in the park across the street from the ticket office.

"Do women always gape at you?" I'm stupidly jealous, and I don't like it one bit.

"No." He crosses his leg over his knee and makes a growling sound. "Why didn't you marry?"

My attention is still on the three women who unabashedly stare over their shoulders long after they've passed us. I'm shocked by the change of subject. "What? Why are we talking about my broken engagement?"

"We're not. I just wondered why, if you were betrothed, you did not marry." He has his arms crossed, and his muscles bulge like the best arm candy I've ever seen.

"Cam couldn't keep it in his pants." I roll my eyes at myself. Why can't I say anything gently?

Liam's eyes narrow, and he cocks his head. I can practically see him translating what I've said into something he understands. "This Cam was unfaithful? Unfaithful to you?"

"You say that as if it's impossible." I can't help laughing at how incredulous he sounds.

He mumbles something.

"What?"

"For any man lucky enough to secure your hand, it should be impossible."

I would swear he's blushing, but I must be losing my mind. After all, it's ten in the morning and Momma has talked me into a scotch whiskey tour. "Thank you." What else can I say? It's the nicest thing anyone has ever said to me.

After an uncomfortable moment, he asks, "This whiskey they make here is famous, I gather?"

"Yes. Honestly, I've never really liked scotch as much as

our American bourbon, but Momma said we can't come to Scotland and not have a tour." Despite the strangeness of having an elf want me to go to his world, I've had a wonderful time on this vacation, and I'm not at all sorry to know Liam. He's perfect in many ways. "You don't have to come along. I mean, you're welcome, but we're not going to run off while on the tour."

"I'd find you." The matter-of-fact way he says it should be creepy, but instead, it's comforting.

"This is a big world. How would you find me?" I fuss with the little hem of my pink t-shirt. It's sunny but cooler today, so I'm back in my jeans.

"I can hear the song of your soul. The oracle gave it to me before I left so that the portal would track to you." He closes his eyes, and his expression softens.

"What is that? Are you listening to it now?" Great-grandma always said there are more things in heaven and earth than one woman can learn in a lifetime. I guess this is what she meant.

"Do you want to hear it?" He opens his hand, palm up.

I stare for a long moment before sliding my hand into his. "Why am I nervous?"

He draws a deep breath. "There's no need. Close your eyes and trust me, Wren."

I look around the park. No one is paying us any mind. Doing as he says, I close my eyes and try to trust him, but I'm not certain what that means. Then I feel the nudge of his thoughts at the base of my skull. It's a gentle prod to gain entry.

"Relax. I'll never harm you." His voice is soft and full of warmth and promise.

Swallowing down the moan that tries to eke out, I take a long, slow, deep breath and relax. Like a breeze, the soft hum begins inside my head. A moment later, I feel it everywhere; the hum mingles with a higher sound that weaves and dips. It's beautiful, filled with joy, and intricacies. "This is me?"

"This is you. It's the sweetest sound I've ever heard."

Connected as we are, and with my ability to sense feelings, I know he didn't mean to tell me that. "What does your soul sound like?"

Our internal link opens even more, and I feel his heart beating as if I were listening through a stethoscope. It's fast and strong, but then it evens out. A deep bass hum with a tenor melody mixing with my song.

"Oh my." Our songs together are like a dream of what heaven would sound like. We're in perfect harmony. "Liam."

He lets out a shuddering breath and releases my hand.

Without our songs, there is silence for a few heartbeats before the noise of Edinburgh fills the gap. I turn toward him. "That was amazing."

"It was." He pushes a wayward curl out of my eyes and tucks it behind my ear.

As his fingers meet my cheek, my skin heats. "Do you always hear your soul?"

"Only when I listen, which is rare." His gaze is intense and sends a thrill through me.

"If I could hear that, I would waste away, spending all my time listening." I already miss the music.

"I can teach you to hear your soul." His pupils are wide as he stares at me like I'm more than the woman he's assigned to bring home.

"I finally got them." Momma steps off the sidewalk into

the grassy area where we're sitting. She's waving the tickets in her hand. "We need to get a move on. The tour starts in fifteen minutes. I swear the lines in that place were a mile long. I thought we'd have to wait for the afternoon tour."

The moment gone, I laugh, as does Liam.

Momma looks at her phone, where she's tracking us on her map of Edinburgh, and we dutifully follow her the few blocks to the distillery.

Even though it was only a mile from our rental, we had to hail a taxi because Momma was three sheets to the wind after two shots of whiskey and a cocktail on an empty stomach. I could have used the walk since I feel a touch of a buzz from the morning tour. Meanwhile, one wouldn't know Liam had the same, as he easily lifts Momma from the cab and carries her up the steps to the rental.

I get the door and run to the kitchen for some water. "Momma, you need to drink this down or you'll be sorry when you wake up."

Liam carries her to the bed, and I manage to get her to drink the water before she passes out. I refill the glass and leave it on the bedside table. Liam uses magic to gently lift Momma and move the blankets out from under her. Then he tucks her in as if she were his own.

My heart does a bumpity bump. "We should let her sleep it off. She's put a shame on Texas women today. Most of us can hold our liquor."

"Your cheeks are pink, as is the tip of your nose." Liam gets two glasses and fills them with water. Handing one to me, he grins.

"Do you know how handsome you are when you smile? Is that why you're so stingy with them?" I take the water and drink half of it down before placing the glass on the coffee table and flopping on the couch.

He lifts my feet, then sits with them on his lap. "Elves are well-made by nature, and so I've never thought about my looks." He stares at me. "I won't deny that it gives me pleasure to hear you say such things. I'm a soldier and rarely have occasion for levity. I'm also the son of the rightful queen, and I take that duty seriously."

"Being a son is a duty? I've always thought of my mother as a blessing." It makes me sad to think his experience was something else.

"Where is your father?" His eyebrows draw together, making him look stern.

I sit up and pull my feet out of his lap. "He left before I was born. I never met him, and Momma hardly ever brings him up. I know he lives in Louisiana and works on oil rigs. They were only married for a year."

For a military man, he shows more emotions than he thinks. His eyes fill with anger and sorrow, and his lips pull into a thin line. "He lost a grand life, in my opinion. Birdie is a treasure, as are you."

"Thank you." I ease forward and cup his cheek. "I'm going to kiss you."

His gaze shifts from my mouth to my eyes.

Scooching closer, I press my leg to his thigh, then tilt my

head and press my lips to his. A flash of warmth smothers my entire body from just the kiss. I gasp.

Liam cups my head, brushes his thumb over my cheekbone, and makes love to my mouth. A long groan erupts from deep in his chest.

Sliding my tongue along his, I am on fire. I would crawl inside his skin if I could, just to be closer to him.

With one arm, he pulls me across his lap so that I'm facing him with my knees on either side of his hips. Leaning back, he takes me with him. He caresses from my upper back to the top of my jeans, then his fingers slip under my shirt and trace a path back the way they came.

I press my hips forward until I feel the hard ridge of his shaft straining against his jeans. My pussy aches for more of him and less material between us. Still, I'm hesitant to rush this kiss, which is rocking my world.

Breaking the kiss, he breathes fast and ragged. "You and I have a destiny, and I'm not sure this is part of that path. As much as I enjoy and desire you, Wren, I wouldn't wish to compromise you when you're not clearheaded."

This is the first time a man has stopped sex with me over my state of sobriety. I'm not sure if I should be upset or flattered. "So, if I were sober as a judge, you'd say yes?"

He pushes my curls back and groans as his cock jerks. Clearly, that part of him is as disappointed as I am. He closes his eyes for a moment. When he opens them, he is resolved. "I'll wait and see if you'd make such an offer without half a head."

Sitting up so that my breasts are at his eye level, I say, "Momma says a drunk man's words are a sober man's thoughts."

He heaves a short laugh and pulls me into a tight hug. "That may be true, but wanting something and acting on it are two different things, sweet Wren. I'm a man with a mission that includes taking you to an elven portal and into a world filled with danger. I'd hate to think our acts of passion would alter your decision making."

Pushing away, I flop back on the couch. "That's rich. Eight days ago, you tried to drag me through one of your portals. Now you have morals?"

"I'll not continue to apologize for that. I've already done so. It was a mistake. Now that I know you and your family, I would never force your hand."

"It's arrogant of you to think sex with you would be good enough to make me choose danger and possible death."

"Maybe, but in my mind, it's that good." He's not bragging in the way many men would. He puts his head back and closes his eyes as if it pains him not to follow through with what we started.

I think it would be that good too. Maybe he's right. This thing between us is scary and intense and should be put on a shelf. "You're right."

Letting out a breath, he relaxes. "Thank you. I don't know if I could say no if you persisted."

Gratified, I fail at trying not to look smug. "I'm glad to hear I haven't lost all of my feminine wiles."

Turning his head without lifting it from the back of the couch, he looks at me, and our songs filter into my mind. "I've never wanted anyone or anything more."

This entire thing is insane. I'm not fanciful. I make jewelry and sell it. I live on property my great-grandparents bought and passed down through the generations.

A Crown of Wind and Water

Nothing exciting ever happens to me. It took Momma and me two years to save for this crazy trip after she retired, and we are supposed to go home in four days. Suddenly, I'm considering following an elf through a portal into another world where I'll probably be killed by a witch queen. *Is all of that because I haven't been laid in a long time? God, I hope not.*

"What happens if you or your brothers fail?"

With a grunt, he adjusts himself. "The witch queen will continue to destroy Domhan until there is only darkness and all light magic is lost."

"So, she's a sociopath." Terrifying, but not the first I've heard of. "Once she's ruined your world, what will she do then?"

His stare is hard, and all the tenderness of a few minutes ago is gone. "Your mother was a teacher of history. What does a conqueror do after they've won a war?"

A knot grows in my chest as I consider all the people of this world who destroyed and conquered and what they did once they had "won." It's never enough. "They look for other places to conquer."

He nods and straightens, looking more soldierly. "There are other worlds. Venora has already taken Arcaina. It is visible from Domhan and was home to an early elven culture. They had not yet advanced to written language and had no magic, but now they are her slaves or shadow demons. She will continue to be a blight wherever she can learn the magic of a world."

My pulse races. Reaching across, I touch Liam's ear. It feels round, but I know it's just a glamor. He's not human. Venora will continue her reign of terror until she's stopped, like so many who were hungry for power before her. "She'll come here?"

"It's possible, and since she will learn of the prophecy, it is likely." At least he has the grace to look sorry for it.

My mother is sleeping in the next room after a great morning of fun and laughter, and granted, too much whiskey on an empty stomach. My friends in Texas are going about a normal Tuesday of work and family. Earth knows nothing of magic, light or dark. "Shit."

Liam cocks his head.

"This thing between us, the way I'm drawn to you, is it some magic spell?" It sounds stupid, but I have to ask.

"Not of my making, if that's your question." His grin is delicious.

I close the distance between us on the couch and take his hand. Every touch of my skin to his is like the first, and a thrill, like electricity, rushes through me. "I will go with you. I don't see how I'm of any use in a war, but if my going will save worlds, how can I say no?"

He seems to be waiting for me to say something else, or maybe he thinks he's hearing things. "You will go through the portal to Domhan?"

"We have a witch to stop, don't we?" It's a rare thing to surprise Liam, and I think I like it.

"Indeed, we do. Thank you." He kisses my hand. "I will protect you with my life."

The bedroom door crashes open. Momma's hair is standing out in every direction, and she has a smudge of lipstick across her cheek. Her eyeliner has nearly reached that same cheek. She gives each of us a hard look. "No one is going anywhere without me."

A Crown of Wind and Water

It's hard not to laugh. She looks like something out of an old drama movie.

Liam stands. "We weren't going to leave in the night, Birdie. Even so, this is not a pleasure trip. There are real dangers in Domhan. You'd be safer staying here. Besides, I plan to wait for Wren to agree when she's, how did you put it, 'sober as a judge,' before I accept the offer."

"What?" I blurt out.

Standing straight and strong as I'd expect from a soldier, he looks at me and shakes his head. "You didn't think I'd turn down your first offer and accept your second when you've had a few drinks, did you? As delightful as the first was, the second is more serious and life changing."

Momma moans and holds her head. "You two work this out while I finish my nap."

"Drink more water," I holler after her.

With a wave, she closes the door.

"I need a walk and some food." I get up and write Momma a note telling her where I've gone.

Liam follows me out. "I'll join you if you don't mind?"

We walk along the sidewalk. It's overcast but not raining. Summer in Texas is a whole different thing from summer over here. I've only been able to wear shorts once on the entire vacation. Not that I mind a break from the sweltering heat of home. If I wanted a tan, I'd have gone to the beach and still probably wouldn't have managed it with my fair skin.

It's nice the way he walks beside me without needing to keep up a constant line of chatter. He's a thoughtful man, which is a first for me. He was right, though, going to confront the witch queen probably shouldn't be taken lightly. "What will I face when I get to your world?"

He flexes his fingers. "I can't say for certain. The portal is not pleasant. The one I came through was made by the oracle, so it was fairly mild. I expect the one on the Isle of Skye is from the old gods and will be painful."

"Any good news?"

He smiles. "It won't kill you."

"Well, that's something. Where will it take us? I mean, will we have long to travel when we get to the other side?"

"It will depend on whether there is danger on the other side. The old gates have light magic that keeps those like Venora and her followers from using them. It was put in place to protect this world. There are other spells on the gates in Domhan to prevent us from portaling into danger."

"I'm going to take that to mean that you don't know where we'll land. What happens if the bad guys find us?" A shiver runs up my spine.

"I will do whatever it takes to keep you safe, but I can't make any promises. My world is dangerous since the witch queen began her reign." His gait is stiff.

The pho restaurant on the corner wafts delicious aromas down the street. "Let's eat here."

It's a nice place. Not fancy but clean and with fun Asian decor.

Once we're seated, and we order some tea, I look at the menu, but I'm preoccupied. "You said that Venora took the white tower thirty years ago. Have you known a Domhan that wasn't fraught with danger?"

"I have lived thirty-four suns, Wren. I don't have much

memory before we crossed the sea to escape death at her hands." There's deep sorrow lining his words.

My heart aches for him and the life he's had to live. "You could stay here where there is no dark magic."

"You tempt me more than I'd like to admit, but I have a duty to my people and my family." He looks at the menu and his eyes widen. "I think you had better do the ordering."

"It's noodle soup but better. Whenever I go to Houston or Tyler, I always stop for pho." I like that he trusts me, even if it's only to order food.

When the waiter comes back, I order beef pho for both of us and pour tea into the small handleless cups.

Liam sips his tea and smiles. "This is nice. Different from the tea we've had with other meals."

"It comes from the east. Different parts of the Earth have different cultures and foods. This restaurant features food from parts of Asia. I'll have to get a map and show you." Watching him try new things is almost as if I'm trying them for the first time again. I like it. "You've mentioned old gods several times. Who are they, and are there new gods?"

Gaze soft and focused on me, he smiles, slow and sexy as hell. "I think they are called old because they've been locked behind the Watchers' Gate for so long."

"They had a physical presence in Domhan at some point? Who are they? How many are there?" So many questions rush through my head.

"It has been many years since the Tuatha Dé Danann walked among the elves." The food arrives and his focus shifts.

"Holy crap," I blurt out as my mind spins with the familiarity of the mythological gods of Ireland.

The waiter blanches. "Something wrong, madam?"

"No. I'm sorry. It looks wonderful." I can't believe his old gods are the ancient Celtic gods. "You mean like Brigid and Morrigan?"

He studies the chopsticks and the spoon. Deciding on the spoon, he sips the soup. "Very good." Glancing at me, he says, "You know the old gods?"

"We need to find a library." I pick up the chopsticks and show him how to eat the noodles. The rest of the meal is spent laughing at his attempts.

Chapter Four

LIAM

We asked for directions to the library, but on the way, we passed a bookstore. Wren yelped. "This is better." Grabbing my hand, she dragged me through the door.

The smell of books reminds me of my school days. Back then, I couldn't wait to get out of the classroom and start my military life. I was young and thought strapping on a sword would be the beginning of the end for Venora. Arrogance did not get us the prophecy. That was found through education and exploration.

I follow Wren through the stacks like a pet fully enamored by his mistress. The description is not far off. It should be shameful, but I'm unable to care what anyone else might think. If the oracle or my parents disapprove, I will fight for Wren for as long as she wants me. Where did that come from? I need to gather my wits. It's clear I'm not acting like myself. Maybe my human has more magic than she knows.

"Here." She points to a section of books and snatches one off the shelf. Opening to the first page, she holds it out to me. "Look."

I take the book from her. The print is different than what I'm used to, but it is in the common language. The title page says *Celtic Gods and Mythos*. Below that, it reads *The Tuatha Dé Danann*.

She's already scanning for other books. When she has three, she takes the one from me and sits in a large chair tucked in the corner. Scanning each book, she is focused and serious.

"Shall I read one too?" I lean against one of the floor-to-ceiling shelves and watch her. Adorable, beautiful, and smart, she is everything. She must be stunning to watch make jewelry, though I can see this study of text comes from her mother.

Holding up a finger, she shakes her head. After three or four more minutes, she hands me a colorful soft-covered book. "This is what we need. I'll put the others back."

With no shame at all, I watch her bottom as she bends over to replace the books.

As she stands, she looks over her shoulder. "I guess men are the same in your world as here." Her tone is scolding, but she doesn't try hiding her smile.

"If you give a man a view like that, how can you expect him not to look?"

With a laugh, she snatches the book from my hand. "Come on." She pays for the book and rushes out of the shop. "We should check on Momma. I'm sure she's awake and feeling her head at this point."

The afternoon brings a light rain, and we jog all the way back to the apartment. As we dash through the door and climb the steps, the pink shirt she's wearing shows her undergarments and every inch of her beautiful body. A groan escapes me as she reaches the upper floor.

She looks back as she opens the door. My expression must tell the story. One look down at her tits, and she covers them with crossed arms. "I didn't think this shirt through with the weather in the country."

"You two are soaked through," Birdie croons from the kitchen.

A whiff of something on the stove reminds me of winter stew and makes me forget we ate noodles an hour ago.

"You'd better go change before you catch your death. I'm fixin' to eat something."

"We ate, Momma." Wren heads for the bedroom door.

"I reckon Liam will be ready to eat again in no time." Birdie smiles at me and seems no worse for her early morning whiskey tour.

I go to the stove and give the stew a deep sniff. "I'll not say no to a pot that smells this good."

Smiling widely, Birdie slaps my back and chuckles. "That's the way."

As soon as Wren is behind the bedroom door, Birdie pulls my arm. "Did she change her mind?"

"We have not discussed it, but she took me to a bookshop, and it seems there are still some similarities between our worlds." I grab my pack and head to the bathroom.

"Oh. I love a little research." She rubs her hands together.

I enjoy these Martin women. They are so full of life and joy. "I thought you would. It's in Wren's bag." I point to it on the coat hook near the door.

The worry over keeping Wren and Birdie safe in Domhan has me wide awake well into the night. When the bedroom door opens, I sit up straighter.

Wren stands in the doorway staring at me. She holds up a finger and retreats. A few moments later, she returns with the book we bought. Silently, she closes the door and crosses to the couch. "Why are you awake?"

"My mind is busy."

She tucks her wild hair behind her ear, but it immediately falls forward again, hiding her eyes. "I've been reading this book. Do you think the old gods are really behind the Watchers' Gate?" She flips to a page and studies the text.

Whenever she's near, my heart speeds up, and I want to protect her. As a soldier, I know that bad things happen. Still, the idea of losing her or Birdie has a knot growing tighter in my gut. "I don't know. That's what the tales say. As you told me earlier from the book, the people of Ireland believed that when the Tuatha Dé Danann became the hills of the land. We believe the old gods retreated behind the gate. No one travels to the northern island. The northern sea is treacherous. Who knows if the stories are true?"

A Crown of Wind and Water

"They had many sacred items like Dagda's harp. That could be what we have to retrieve."

I can't say that I love being sent on missions by the gods. Even in the stories of old, they manipulated elves to do this or that without explanation. I don't like it. "How will a harp help? I'd prefer the spear or sword."

Putting the book on the table, she looks at me. "You're upset?"

"I'm worried. My world is dangerous." I fail to adjust my tone, and it comes out biting.

She moves a cushion closer. "This world is dangerous. You almost were killed by a car yesterday. Momma nearly got stomped by a horse last week in the park. I almost drowned in the lake when I was ten."

Taking her hands in mine, I look into the watery blue of her eyes in the moonlight coming through the window. "I don't want you or your mother to be harmed. I couldn't bear it."

"You came here to take me to Domhan, Liam. What's changed?" She cocks her head. Her hair falls to one side, exposing the length of her neck and making me long to kiss that tender flesh.

Leaning forward, I press a soft kiss just below her ear. "I care now. It would be better if you remained part of an order to be carried out, but we have gone beyond that."

A soft sigh escapes her parted lips. "Have we?"

I draw back and watch until she opens her eyes, and her gaze meets mine. "If you refused me now, I would walk away. I'd tell the oracle they must find another way."

"Then you will return to your world and leave me here. We would never see each other again. I will never know if you lived or died in your war. The witch queen might make her way here and continue her reign of terror on this world. How can I want that?" She is all that is good and fine in any species.

"I don't deserve you caring about my safety. I'm a soldier. I have to go home and do what I can to protect my people. It's too much to ask me to put you in danger, Wren."

"I don't see many other choices, but I like that you care." She kisses me softly then sucks my bottom lip between hers.

Pleasure shoots through me like a wildfire. I pull her into my lap. "Are you certain this is what you wish to do?"

She wiggles her bottom maddeningly. "Are we talking about you and me or going to Domhan?"

Taking hold of her hips, I keep her still. I whisper against the shell of her ear. "You know, not that long ago, you kicked me in the very spot that you're now teasing."

"I remember. I didn't know you then. All I knew was that a strange man with pointed ears was trying to drag me through a swirling hole in the dentist's office. That seems worthy of a swift kick to the nuts." She runs her fingers over my bespelled ears.

When I shake off the glamor, my ears show their true form.

Rather than blanch, she caresses the tip and down again. "You're easy on the eyes no matter the shape of your ears."

It's taken time to get used to the constant stream of euphemisms. "I'm glad you think so." Taking her hand, I kiss her knuckles, then make sure I have her attention. "Be sure you know what you're getting into by jumping through a portal with me, Wren."

She sighs, and her shoulders slump. "I don't *really*

know. How can I know? I've never been in a war. I've never been the chosen one for anything. I could die. You could die. Momma could die. I get it." She dashes away a sudden tear and draws a sharp breath. "But if I don't go with you, your world and everyone you love will surely die, and one day, I'll have to fight the witch queen in this world."

Everything she says is true; I still want to protect her from the very thing I was sent here to do. "Venora might take a lifetime to reach this world."

"Then my children or grandchildren, if I'm lucky enough to have a family, will have to fight the battle I was too frightened to take on." She shakes her head. "No. I can't be the person who pushes off the inevitable for others to deal with. I will go with you, and my mother is not going to let me go without her. There is no changing Birdie Martin's mind once she's made it up."

I run my hand up her soft thigh and slip my fingers under the bottom of her little shorts. "I want to keep you safe. I should be stronger than this."

Covering my hand with hers, she pushes me until my fingers graze her wet folds. "I'm in no danger from you."

Breaking the contact, I get a groan of discontent from Wren. I laugh and adjust our positions, so we're both lying on the couch. "Your mother is only behind that door. Are you not concerned she'll storm out here?"

"She was so tired, it would take a four-alarm firetruck siren to wake her tonight. Besides, I'm a grown woman." Caressing my bare chest, she kisses my neck, then my jaw.

Kissing her lightly on the lips, I breathe in her scent of vanilla and berries. She's like a tasty sweet that I can't get enough of. "Grown or not, I doubt you want your mother to walk in on you with my head between your legs."

In a flash, she stands and pulls her shirt over her head. Her full breasts are beautiful and round, and her nipples are distended. "I'll risk it." She strips out of her shorts. In the sliver of moonlight peeking through the curtains, she's as beautiful as a goddess in the sacred pools.

One day I'll make love with her, and we'll be free to scream as loud and long as our passions demand. "You're the most beautiful woman I've ever seen." I run my fingers over her hips and along her ribs.

On an exhale, she lies beside me. "I thought you might tell me to go back to bed."

"No. If I am what you want, I am yours." It's a pledge I pray I can hold to for the rest of our lives, but for tonight, I'll let her believe this is only about pleasure. Taking her lips with mine, I slide my tongue inside, and she moans into my mouth as her tongue touches mine. Tentative at first, a few seconds later, she kisses me as if this will be our last kiss.

I intend to make sure that is not the case. I slow the kiss, sipping her top lip and then bottom. I kiss her chin and along the column of her throat. I linger at her pulse and listen to the songs of our souls harmonizing.

I open my mind to her, so she can hear the song as I kiss and lick my way down her chest. Taking her nipple into my mouth, I suck until she grips my hair and then I suck harder, letting my teeth worry the sensitive bud.

Biting my upper arm, she muffles her moans and cries.

Licking a circle around her areola, I mold her tit with my palm and fingers. I move lower to her abdomen and linger at her belly button.

A Crown of Wind and Water

On a soft cry, she opens her legs. The heady scent of her sex reaches my sensitive senses.

Sliding my hand between her thighs, I slip my fingers between her soft, wet folds.

She bites her palm, muffling her moan. Her bright gaze never leaves me as I reach the bottom of the couch and shift my knees to the floor.

Cupping her ass in my hands, I pull her to the edge of the cushion. "So pretty." I slide my thumb around her sweet pearl, teasing her. "So wet." I blow a puff of air across her.

She jerks her hips. "Liam."

I would love to spend hours teasing and tempting, but my own need grows uncomfortable even in the lounge pants I've grown so fond of. Slipping my thumb inside her, I lower my mouth and lick a path around before sucking her clitoris.

Her hips rise and fall with a constant, building cadence.

As I look up the length of her, her stare is fixed on me as she bites her bottom lip. Her cheeks are pink.

Drinking in her smell and taste, I know I'll never get enough of her. She's my greatest desire, and even if she's my downfall, she's worth it. Sucking harder, I feel her sheath clench as her orgasm shatters.

Eyes closed for the first time, she shifts her head from side to side and clutches my hair while pumping her hips against my mouth and taking my thumb as deep as it can go.

My cock is painfully hard as I wait for her to reach the other side of her pleasure. I lap up every drop of her nectar, then wait until she opens her eyes before I ease back. "Are you alright?"

"I'm better than that." Pupils wide, she moves her legs

over my shoulders and digs her heels into my back, drawing me to her.

I kiss her belly before standing and placing her feet back on the couch. Stripping out of my pants, I stand over her shapely body. My bedding is shifted and rumpled, and she's exactly as I wish she'd appear every night for the rest of my life. How have I survived my life this long without her? "You are everything, Wren. Whatever you think about me, know that I am yours for as long as you'll have me."

"Make love with me, Liam." She reaches an arm toward me.

Taking her hand, I ease down on top of her as she wraps her legs around my hips. Her hand slips between us and she wraps her fingers around my cock.

"By the gods. You'll drive me mad before this night is over."

Her caress is slow and soft as she directs me until I'm notched at her entrance, still wet and ready. Only then does she move her fingers out of the way. She caresses my ribs, then over my shoulder. Everywhere she touches, my body heats. Her legs tighten, and she tips her hips to take me in an inch.

Gaining control, I press inside her and have to stop and relish how perfectly we fit. Her body stretches to accommodate my size.

She moans low and deep.

I kiss her, muffling my own groan, as I pull back and slide home again and again. My body is on fire. I strain to keep my weight on my elbows and not crush her while plunging deep.

Her body tightens around my cock, and she gasps and

moans as another orgasm rocks her. Nails digging into my back, she makes the most erotic noises and locks her feet behind my ass, binding us together.

The first tingle of orgasm starts at the base of my spine while her body still pulses, taking me over the edge. Unable to help myself, I break free of her legs and fuck her hard and fast as I bury my face in the pillow to muffle my own cries.

Miraculously, she comes again, and between us, we groan, pant, cry out to various deities before collapsing.

Tugging the blanket, I cover our naked bodies and hold her close. I kiss the top of her head. "I think we were a bit too loud. I'm surprised your mother has not stormed out here with a weapon raised."

She laughs low and musically. "What weapon?"

"I'm sure she can wield a lamp as well as you can."

Another laugh before she sobers and stares at me, then touches my ears. "That was amazing. Do you think humans and elves can have children?"

I brush her wild curls away from her eyes. "I should have taken more care." I'm an idiot, even though the idea of our child growing inside her thrills me beyond anything I've ever hoped for in my life. "Yes. I think it's likely possible."

"We might be more cautious, but I'm not worried." She tucks her head under my chin and curls against me.

Holding her, I wish I could give her a life filled with comfort and safety. "Why not?"

"Because if I conceived, it would be a part of you that I would always have, even if our lives don't let me have you."

Running my hand over her soft hair, I feel as if my heart might burst. "We can't know what will happen. Perhaps our future is too unsure to make plans, but it doesn't mean all possibilities are filled with doom and loneliness."

She nods. "Anything is possible."

Before dawn, Wren returned to the bedroom.

I shower and dress before the ladies join me in the kitchen. "What is the best way to get to the Isle of Skye?" I ask around a mouthful of grapes.

Birdie grins. "I just happened to look it up yesterday, and there is a train that can take us to the highlands, and then we can take a bus over the Skye Bridge."

"Just happened to look it up, Momma?"

"Don't be ugly, or I'll mention that you were not in your bed when I woke in the night." Birdie opens the refrigerator and pulls out the bowl of grapes and another with blueberries.

Wren blushes but holds up her hands in defeat. "So, we need train tickets, but I think we'll need to trade in our rolling bags for backpacks."

It's a good point. "The wheeled bags will not be convenient in any terrain besides the city, and I don't know where we'll land on the other side of the portal. A pack like mine will be more practical."

"Shopping trip," Birdie sings, making Wren laugh.

"I feel the two of you are not taking this journey seriously. This is no 'vacation' as you call it. We will likely be walking into danger." I push aside my plate with grapes and cheese.

"That's no reason not to enjoy a short shopping trip, Liam." Birdie smiles at me, adding to my concerns.

Wren covers my hand with hers. "We understand. It's just in our nature to look at things in the brightest light until the situation calls for a more serious outlook or response. Don't worry. That said, I need to send a few emails about commissions that will have to be delayed or canceled." She goes into the bedroom and closes the door.

"These commissions are for jewelry?"

Birdie looks at the bedroom door and then at me. "Yes. I don't think she's had deposits, though. It's just a courtesy to let them know there may be some delay."

"What will she tell them?" Saying, *I'm going to another world to fight a witch queen* probably wouldn't be wise.

With a sharp laugh, Birdie says, "I don't know. She's clever."

"Indeed." I eat another grape, but my appetite isn't what it should be as worry has overshadowed everything else.

Lost in my thoughts, I don't notice Birdie staring until she clears her throat. "Are you in love with my daughter?"

It takes me a long pause to gather my wits. I'm glad for my military training as it gives me the ability to show little to no emotions in times of great stress. This is one of those times. "Birdie, as much as I like and respect you, my feelings for Wren will be discussed with her long before they're chatted about with you."

"Fair enough, but I don't want her crying 'til the cows come home." She waggles a finger at me.

"Cows? You're going to have to explain that one to me." I

thought I was getting the hang of the way they use language, but this one has me stumped.

"It means waiting for something, but it's futile." She dabs her eye and puts the fruit away, having only taken a few berries to eat.

"Did you wait a long time for Wren's father to return?" I can't fathom anyone leaving their family as he did.

All the joy is washed from her laughter, now laced with a touch of bitterness. "I was very young. It took five years for me to wrap my brain around the notion that he'd never come back, and even then, it was the divorce papers that made the point. I'd like to say it was my own good sense, but it took a legal decree to convince me that he didn't want me anymore."

"I promise that whatever happens with Wren and me, she will always know where she stands and where I stand. Any choices that are to be made will be hers, not mine." I place my hand over my heart, making my pledge hold the weight of my conviction.

"That is fair," she concedes.

Wren returns, waving the device I have learned is called a phone and is used to speak or write to people over long distances. It's very handy. "I have freed up my schedule for the foreseeable future and booked us on the train to Kyle of Lochalsh, which is the last stop before the Skye Bridge. We'll need to take the bus from there to the Isle."

"When do we leave?" Birdie asks.

"Tomorrow morning. They were totally booked for today, but we have to be at the station very early, and it's a seven-hour ride. It should be very pretty, though." She grins and sits on the stool next to me.

A Crown of Wind and Water

"We'll have today to get another look at the castle, buy some appropriate clothes and bags, and repack. I suppose we can donate what we don't need to take. I'm sure there are some shelters in the city." Birdie chatters on and on about what must be done before we head north.

I watch the two of them, wondering if the war I'm taking them to will change them and wishing I had another choice.

Chapter Five

WREN

On the train, I read the book about the old gods. "Could it be Dagda's harp behind the Watchers' Gate?"

Momma shrugs. "How does a harp help if we have no one to play the right strains?"

"Good point." I study the text where it says that he played the strain of sleep and never raised a hand in battle against his enemy. It sounds like a bunch of hooey, but I didn't believe in elves or magic until I met Liam. I need to keep an open mind.

"I'd rather have the spear or the sword if some treasure is behind the gate." Liam's gaze is forward, but it's obvious he's watching out for someone to attack us.

"You know about the four treasures of the Tuatha De Dannan?"

He nods. "It's taught in school. The old gods with sword,

spear, stone, and cauldron. The tales of Dagda and his harp. We're all taught these stories from a young age. I don't see how any of it helps. Venora is flesh and mortal. How will any weapon get us past her magic? If it were simple, the oracle would have found a way. They've had thirty years to look for a defense against the dark. Yet, year by year, the witch queen gets stronger and kills more of us. She turns good people into shadow demons and turns others into slaves. She bespells warriors to her army. We've slowed her, but most of the time, I think the oracle is at a loss for how to save the light."

I close the book. "You don't think you can win." A knot forms in the center of my chest and expands. "Why bring me to your world if you don't think Venora can be beaten?"

The deepest sorrow darkens his gaze. "I have seen the blackest magic come from the witch queen. She is more powerful than anyone would have expected. She uses terrible means to grow stronger. Every soul she turns into a shadow demon leaves the magic of its former elf attached to her. She'll continue to become more while we are dwindling. No female elves means that in perhaps fifty more years, there will be none to bear children. Time is running out for my kind, and I'm helpless to stop time.

"I bring you because you represent hope, and I've lost mine." He returns to watching the people on the train and the terrain outside the window as it speeds by.

If I could reassure him that everything is going to be okay, I would. The problem is that I don't think bringing an artist and her mother to another world will make much of a difference.

Momma says, "Maybe one of the other human women is a musician. Maybe the weapon behind the gate is something else altogether. Don't lose faith, Liam. Your people found the prophecy; that should mean something."

He offers a half smile. "It should, Birdie. The fact that we've already seen some of Wren's human magic is a good sign, too. Forgive me for sounding bleak."

"How do my dreams help?" I push aside thoughts of Morrigan and Nuada. My mind is swimming with Irish mythology. None of it is very helpful for stopping an evil elf or her armies.

"You have other magic."

"How can you know that? I had a dream. It might mean nothing." The notion that I can conjure wind that could lift a person is ridiculous.

His hair is pulled back, but one section always makes its way free, and it's damned sexy. He stares at me for a long moment. "You've already shown you can reach through time."

"I did what?"

He's making things up.

"In the doctor's waiting room. You pulled Birdie out of time so that she could leave with you. That should not have been possible. Only the oracle and dragons can meddle with time." His voice is low and intense, like he's imparting something sage.

"Interesting." Momma points to him. "You said you can't alter time and worry that you're running out of time. If time is a foe and Wren's magic is somehow twisted up with time..." She gets a faraway look and stares out the window.

"What does it mean, Momma?"

Drawing a long breath, she sighs. "I don't know, but

there's something there. We just need more pieces to the puzzle before we can put it all together."

Eyes wide, Liam looks to me for an explanation.

I shrug and open my book in search of any clue. Still, my mind wanders to the magic Liam says I possess.

It's after six by the time we take the bus over the Skye Bridge. There's still plenty of sunlight, and the beauty of the place can hardly be described. It's like a fairyland, and considering where we're going, it's kind of ironic.

"This place..." As soon as we're off the bus, I turn and take in the views. We're in a busy parking area and surrounded by stunning vistas. Craggy peaks, rolling hills, and the ocean. I can't take in enough of this beauty.

A man gets out of his car. Tall, with a large belly and kind eyes, he grins at me. "You should see the fairy pools. I just came from there, and it's magical."

Liam says, "We need to find a place called the Star."

The man whips out a tour book from his back pocket and flips to a page, pointing. "The Old Man of Storr."

Nodding, Liam takes the guidebook. "That's it. How do we get there?"

Happy to have our full attention, the man puffs up. "I'm driving up there tomorrow. You can ride with me." He points to his little electric cart. "I rented it. Hate to be hemmed in by tour timetables."

A Crown of Wind and Water

Liam nods as if he has any idea what the man's talking about. "I'm Liam Riordan." He holds out his hand.

The man grins. "Wally Snow. It's been my dream to come to Scotland, but my wife hates to fly. She left me at Christmas, so I booked this trip as soon as the ink was dry on the divorce papers. Traveling on my own isn't ideal, but I've met so many interesting people."

Momma grins. "You sound like you're from our side of the pond. I'm Birdie Martin. Sorry for your troubles, but we sure appreciate the offer of a ride."

Shaking hands vigorously, Wally laughs. "That's a Texas accent if I've ever heard one. I'm from Oklahoma. I've lived there all my life, and now I sell insurance to all the people I went to school with. This trip is a whole new world."

A short laugh escapes me as the irony hits.

"My daughter, Wren."

I shake Wally's hand.

"Wren and Birdie Martin. Are all the women in your family avian?" He smiles proudly.

Momma goes into a long story about how it's a family tradition, and Wally listens, happy for the company.

"Excuse me, Birdie." Liam pulls Wally aside.

My skin prickles as if a cool breeze blew through from Liam's direction.

In low tones, Liam speaks to Wally for several moments.

Wally blinks. "I can take you now."

Before I know what's happening, we're all four in the cart, motoring down a very winding road. Most of the traffic is coming the other way since it's getting near dinnertime. Momma makes them stop at a lodge on the way, and she runs in to get us some sandwiches.

I tuck two into my pack and watch as Momma puts several more into hers. She gives one to poor Wally, who seems focused on getting us to the Old Man of Storr.

When we arrive at the gorgeous outcropping of stones, I marvel at the view of the sea and the hills. It's rough country but more beautiful for its wildness. The grass is the greenest I've ever seen, and these mythical stones of gray and white jut straight up as if they were pushed up by the hands of the old gods I spent the journey reading about.

People are taking photos and rushing to get back to wherever they're spending the night. Soon, the parking area is closed, and the buses have all left.

Liam says something to Wally, who gets in his car and drives away without saying goodbye.

"What did you do to that man?" I demand.

"We needed to get here, and it's only a little spell that will wear off before he's a minute down the road. He won't remember having met us and will eat his sandwich and marvel at how he came upon the extra money I put in his pocket." Liam walks toward the Storr.

"That's not nice. You shouldn't manipulate people like that." Even to my own ear, my voice is grating.

Momma laughs. "It did get us here, and Wally was paid for his services. Just promise you'll never use such tactics on either of us."

"You have my word." He doesn't turn back until he senses I'm not following. "I have not and will not ever manipulate you with magic, Wren. I promise. We needed to be here at night, so no one sees us portal away, and Wally was alone and convenient. I don't like to use a person in that way, but he has been compensated."

"I suppose the fairy pools will have to wait for some other time. I have to go save a world." I use my sarcasm to hide my fear. This is madness.

When the last island police car comes, likely to check that the area is clear, Liam waves a hand, and I feel the prickle on my skin just as I did in the parking lot with Wally. The officer never looks in our direction before he drives away.

I rub my arm. "It's a strange feeling when you do that. Not terrible, but different."

"I don't feel anything." Momma watches the last of the sunlight dip beneath the horizon. "This place is wonderful."

Looking at me for a long moment, he raises one eyebrow. "Magic gives off a kind of energy that most people don't notice. It's interesting that you sense it." He climbs the rest of the way to the tallest stone. "I'm sorry you won't get to see all of this island, Birdie. Perhaps when you return."

I take hold of Momma's hand and squeeze. "Are you ready?"

"I have no idea," she says with a grin that stretches from ear to ear.

Liam takes my other hand. He waves his arm in a circle and speaks in a language I've never heard. A glowing portal swirls into existence between the largest stone and the one next to it. Wind whips around us and sends dust flying. "This will hurt a bit."

Bracing, we walk through together. I scream as my flesh is ripped from my bones. At least that's how it feels, though Liam assured me this wouldn't kill me. I'm having serious doubts about whether that was true.

Momma's screams are piercing, and I hold on tight to her hand.

My sight blurs, but I swear, a dragon flies past us, and there's an ocean bathed in purple light sparkling in the distance. It's impossible to tell if the dragon is flying closer to us or if we're barreling toward it. Either way, its red eyes and black scales are getting larger.

The sharp tingle of magic heats my flesh like a sauna turned up much too high. My blood may boil, and it makes me nauseous. I push against it. Freeing my hands, I pray for some way to rid us of the dragon.

"Trocar!" Liam's panicked voice sounds above the din of so much happening at once.

Momma's screams are far away.

I push harder, and the wind whips all around us.

Trocar tumbles through the air unnaturally. His legs and wings flail as he rights himself and roars out something that throws me backward.

Arms wrap around me as I pray harder to force the dragon back.

The ground pounds against my body, taking my breath. Grass and rocks crush between me and the hard earth. I gasp and grunt with every bruise.

Liam grunts, holding me tighter, shielding me from the worst of the landing.

The wind dies, and there is no sound but ocean waves and our breathing.

Jumping to his feet, Liam draws his sword, ready to face the dragon. "Are you injured?"

Am I? I ache in all the spots that hit the ground, and I'm more tired than before, but otherwise not hurt. "No." I rise and scan the sky. There are moons or something that look nothing like my world. "Where is the dragon?"

He shakes his head. Hair loose, the points of his ears show. With his sword at the ready, he's almost as foreign as the place.

The stones on this side of the portal are more like the standing stones found in England. Two are eight feet tall, and there's one capping them. Behind the gate, I see the ocean and its purple waves. I look around. "Momma?" My heart speeds. "Momma, where are you?" Panicked, I check over the cliff at the crashing waves but see only the rocks and water. At least she didn't fall. "Where is she?"

"Maybe she's back in Scotland?" He scans the land in all directions.

"She was in the portal." Maybe I blew her back. Oh god, she'll never forgive me. "I might have done something." I stare at my hands as if I'm seeing them for the first time. I wanted to blow the dragon away, and there was wind. Now, Momma is gone, and I have no way to know if she's safe. "What if she's injured or worse?" She could be lying on the ground at the Old Man of Storr with no one to care for her. I might have caused her injuries. Tears find their way up and out before I can stop them.

Liam continues to scan the land and the sky. It's nearing twilight, but the glow of the moons makes it light enough. Kneeling, he touches the grassy earth. "I think she came through." He stares at the moons or whatever they are. He crawls along the ground. "Look, Wren."

Rushing to his side, I see only dirt and grass. "What?"

He points to a patch of dirt that's indented. "This patterned footprint. We have no shoes like this in Domhan."

I wipe my eyes and study the print. It's rough and could be from the hikers we bought before we left Texas. Close to where she stepped, there's a deep animal print. "What is this one? Is it a horse?"

"Centaur." Standing, he looks to the woods in the distance.

"You said centaurs are vicious." My panic returns. "Where did they go? How did they get away before we saw them?"

Sitting next to me, he sighs. "The prints are old, weeks old."

"What? Centaurs were here before? They never saw Momma." At least she wasn't killed by crazy horse men. She could have found a village. "Do you think she's around here?" I get up. "We can follow her prints. She can't have gotten far."

Taking my hand, Liam holds me from leaving. "Birdie's prints are weeks old as well, Wren."

"What? That's not possible. She was right there with us." I point to the standing stones.

He cups my cheeks and captures my gaze. "Remember what I told you about dragons being able to shift time. I think that is what happened."

"You mean, Momma was sent back in time?" I spy the roofs of a small village not far away. "She could be there. Do elves live there?"

His eyes are sad, and he shakes his head. "I believe Birdie came through without being hit by Trocar's magic." He points up. "That's the planet Arcania. The other is our moon. Based on the orbits, I think it was you and I who were shifted through time. Probably three weeks."

"My mother has been in this world for three weeks all alone?" It's hard to breathe. I gasp and try again, but my knees buckle, and I crumple. "Is she even alive?"

Kneeling by my side, he kisses my forehead. "I don't know. I know she and the centaurs were here at about the same time." He studies the terrain. "Stay here. Don't wander off."

Wander? Is he mad?

Maybe he is, with the way he's running up and down the hill. On hands and knees, he crawls for several feet in one direction, then touches something before bringing his hand to his nose.

Momma is gone, and Liam has lost his mind. I may as well lie down here and wait for a dragon or something worse to kill me. I'm supposed to save a world, and I couldn't even protect my mother for one minute in this place.

"Wren." He stands over me. "I don't think your mother is dead. At least when she left this area, she was alive."

"I made the wind, but it wasn't enough." My sight is blurred with tears, and it feels as if an elephant is sitting on my chest.

Crouching next to me, he brushes my hair from my face. "Listen to me. The fact that you made magic is remarkable, but this is not the time to explore those gifts. You must get up and come with me. You're tired from the journey and the magic, which is normal. When your mother left this area with the centaurs, she was alive."

I pull myself to sitting. "How can you know?"

"The dragon clawed the ground." He points to a rough area where it looks as if the dirt was plowed. "The centaurs fought the dragon. I found dragon blood." He shifts his hand to another area to the right. "When Birdie left this field, she was not dragged or tossed over the back of a centaur. She ran among them toward their forest."

"You said they were mean creatures who kill on sight." It comes out as an accusation, but really, I'm just confused and terrified.

"That is what I've been told my entire life. But they did not kill your mother. Not on this field. I think they fought to save her, though I can't say why." He offers me a hand up.

The woods are miles away, but I start toward them.

Liam takes my hand and stops me. "We need help, and the centaur's woods is at least a day's walk. Clandunna is close and has an honorable leader. She will help us." He pulls me toward the village.

"Momma is that way, and you want me to go in the opposite direction. Now you really are asking too much." I snatch my hand from his.

"I swear, with or without Selina's help, we will go find Birdie in the morning. You need rest, and we'll need help if the centaurs are not hospitable." He says it as if the possibility that they are is unlikely.

"I can't leave her." More tears that I can't control blur my vision.

Pulling me into a hug, he says, "I know. I don't want to waste time either. Your mother is remarkable. She can make friends with anyone. Perhaps she's charmed the centaurs like she did the owner of that pub in London. She's been here for three weeks, sweetheart. A few more hours won't change her fate. Going into a possible altercation without planning and while you need to rest is foolish. I can't risk your safety."

That's what this is about. I push away. "Because I'm

some woman from a prophecy you're not even sure is real. I don't care about your oracle's orders. I need my mother to be safe and sound."

"I care very deeply about Birdie." His tone is harsh as he crosses his arms over his chest. "My duty is to bring you to the oracle and the Watchers' Gate."

"So, you admit it." I wish I could go find my mother by myself and get us both back to our own world where we belong.

He raises his arms out wide; he then lets them fall to his sides. "I do not need to hide the objective. You have known about it from the start. If that were all I cared about, we wouldn't even be having this conversation. I would find another portal that might get us closer to home and drag you through it."

I stutter with rage, trying to find words that will express my feelings, but nothing comes out.

He presses two fingers over my mouth. Softly, he says, "I will not leave Birdie. We will find her. She is not expendable."

"Thank you." I fall into his embrace.

Cawing, a white bird circles. Graceful and focused, it stays directly above us. Every few seconds, it caws, as if wanting our attention.

"A white raven." Liam's voice is soft, almost reverent.

"I didn't know ravens came in white." Maybe they're all white in this world. What do I know?

"They are rare and often a harbinger of good news." He watches the bird as if waiting for something. "My mother can see and speak through ravens. But it doesn't seem as if

Andrea Rose

this one is from her. It would have flown down and delivered a message to me."

"You can speak to birds?" The amount I need to learn here is beyond my current capacity for worry. I shake away those worries and focus on Momma.

"Only those who bring word or warning from another." Taking my hand, we head toward the village and away from the direction of my only family. My heart lodges in my throat.

Chapter Six

LIAM

The raven follows us down the hills, continuing to call out as we go. It's strange that a white raven would appear. I was certain it would be a message from my mother, but I sense no connection.

I've only been to Clandunna a handful of times, when I brought word from my mother or during regular patrols. We sometimes check with towns and villages for word about dark magic. It's a nice little community at the southern end of the continent. Sitting on a peninsula, it has the Gulf of Uaine on one side and the ocean on the other, with a river running through for fresh water.

The forest at the southern end of the point is small but one of the oldest in Domhan. Those trees have lived long enough to have obtained a kind of consciousness.

We're much farther from home than I'd hoped. The

Storr portal should have brought us near the Naomh River. It would have been an hour's ride to the oracle from there.

Now I'm weeks south, without a horse, missing one human, and three weeks later than when I left the Wren's world. Nothing has gone to plan, and the thought of Birdie in the hands of centaurs is sobering.

"Do they all go to bed early here?" Wren asks, looking at the empty central area surrounded by small houses grouped by family.

The raven lands on the back of a bench at the center of town. Its gaze is fixed on Wren.

She approaches the bird. "You're persistent. Have you a message for me?"

The raven caws loudly.

Cocking her head, Wren stares at it. "Huh."

"Does it speak to you?" My mother can send messages through ravens, and she can see through their eyes, but she's never met Wren, so it's unlikely a human woman would be able to receive the words.

"Not so much in words, but I think her name is Adhar." Raising her hand, she gently pets the raven's head. "You're very beautiful and unexpected."

Adhar preens and fluffs the feathers on the back of her head.

"It means air in the old language. If our new friend has no other message, let's see if anyone's home." I point to the largest house to the east. It belongs to Serena and Jax. She is the chieftain of this village. I take my sword in hand and head that way. "Where is everyone? Something isn't right. Stay behind me."

A Crown of Wind and Water

She points to the little woods south of the village. "What happened there?"

Several trees are blackened, and at least two look as if they've exploded. Whatever happened, it wasn't good. To kill ancient trees like those is a terrible act. "Those trees are many hundreds of years old. They have life and magic." I hear panic rising in the tone of my voice.

At the door, I pound as if I'm the invading force.

No answer.

I bang harder.

"Liam, look." She points to the other houses, the meeting area in the center, and the grassy area where children might be at play. "Everything is in perfect order. Maybe whatever destroyed the trees was the catalyst, but these people didn't run, and they weren't attacked here." She reaches around me and pulls the latch on the door, which swings open.

We step inside the tidy home. The living area is clean with several blankets neatly folded on a bench near an empty stand likely meant for some kind of instrument. The staircase is dark. The last time I was here, children sat on the steps listening to news from the capital. I remember their handsome faces peering through the wooden rails.

Despite several young sons living here, there are no toys anywhere. In the kitchen, not one plate sits on the counter or in the basin.

"These people cleaned, they packed what they needed, and then they left town." She stares down at the kitchen table where a shallow bowl sits. Dipping her fingers in, she disturbs the water. "Why would she leave a bowl of standing water when everything else is pristine?"

Rushing over, I pull Wren back a step. "I think it's a

scrying bowl. Probably not dangerous, but stay behind me, just in case. I might be able to contact my mother through it."

With my hand over the water, I search for magic and find the binding spell meant to keep foes from using the bowl. "It's locked."

Wren shakes her head. "That makes no sense. Why leave a device for communication and lock it?"

I wish I knew the answer. "It can be used to leave a message, but we'd have to know how to unlock it."

She touches the side, and the bowl rocks slightly. With a push, she spins it. "Explain yourself." Her voice is full of frustration, which I share.

"Whoever you are, you must live in the light if you've unlocked this bowl." Serena's soft voice echoes from the water. As it stops spinning and the water settles, her features become clear. Fair skin, blue eyes, and long blond hair all perfectly at ease. "We have left Clandunna and gone to Tús Nua. It's not safe here after the witch queen took the first of the prophesied. We will go and help with the coming war while our children are secure in the walled city. If you are in the light, you are welcome here. Use what you need and may the old gods be with you."

The image shimmies and disappears.

Pulling out a chair, I sit. I have a dozen questions for Serena, but the bowl gives no answers.

"Did she mean the witch queen took one of the human women? Could she have been talking about my mother?" Wren spins the bowl again as if it will bring the message back.

"This kind of message is only given once. Then the bowl becomes inert. I may be able to contact my mother in a sacred pool, or maybe if I revitalized the bowl." The problem is that it takes more magic than I'm willing to expend when I need my strength to go into a forest full of centaurs. "I think she was talking about one of the women my brothers were sent to find. Birdie's prints didn't come in this direction, and there were no elven prints at the battlefield."

"Maybe the centaurs destroyed those trees?"

"Centaurs are keepers of forests. They would consider it a blasphemy to violate an ancient tree like that." My heart is heavy. A human woman was taken and no mention of my brother. Which one had it been? Is either Aaran or Raith dead, or worse? I have to focus. "We'll accept Serena's hospitality and rest here. Tomorrow we'll confront the centaurs and find Birdie."

"You said they're vicious. You and I are going to get Momma back by attacking vicious horse men?" She pushes her hair from her face and wipes an errant tear from her cheek.

I must protect her. I'm going to have to get creative. "We can't fight them. We'll have to negotiate somehow."

Pushing aside the worry over things I can't control, I rise and take Wren's hand. "You have to rest. Do you want to go upstairs and sleep in a bed? It may be our last chance to do so for some time."

"You go up. I'm sure you're sick of sleeping on couches. I won't be able to sleep. I'll just stay here." She kisses my cheek.

There is no way I'm leaving her, even to sleep in the next room. I lie on the couch and pull her down beside me. "Try to close your eyes, Wren. You'll need your strength tomorrow."

Resting her head on my shoulder, she sighs. "Why not try to contact your mother if you can restore the bowl's magic?"

"Magic takes a toll, and it would take a lot of energy for the task. Scrying bowls are rare because they require a lot of magic to stay vital and useful. Serena probably left the bowl and the message, knowing her power would be needed for other things." I'm surmising a lot, but without facts, all I can do is try to make sense of things. "I think we can assume one of my brothers came through the same portal. It's possible she believed we might as well if it was safe."

"But it wasn't safe." She yawns.

"No. Light magic failed and that's not a good sign." I comb my fingers over her hair and ease her way to sleep with a relaxation spell that my mother used on my brothers and me when we were small.

Her head gets heavy as her breathing evens out.

It's difficult to stay awake. With another spell to alert me if anyone comes near the house, I let sleep take me.

Wren's heartbeat is fast like a bird's, but it doesn't beat against my chest. No. It's as if it's beating all around me.

Opening my eyes, I'm standing in water to my knees, but I don't feel the wet. As far as I can see is a flat still ocean. "Where are we?"

Wren's voice is filled with terror. "This is the dream, Liam. This is where I see your witch on the butte."

When I turn, she's behind me, staring back with fear in her beautiful eyes. I reach out and touch her, but while I see my hand on her arm, I can't feel her warm flesh. "I'm in your dream. How is that possible?"

Without looking at me, she walks past, still with her head tilted as if looking at something over my head.

An obsidian tower gleams in the sunlight and reflects in the water. It had not been there before, but maybe that's because I can only see through Wren's eyes. "Is that the butte?"

"In my last dream, it was golden brown, like those in New Mexico. It wasn't as clear either. Do you know this place?"

For as far as I can see, there is nothing but this shallow water. I take a step on the sandy surface and search for some clue about where this place is in the conscious world. I know for certain that I have never seen a tower of black stone anywhere on land in Domhan. Yet we are not truly on land. "Could this be the lost lands?"

She heads for the tower, and I follow. "What are the lost lands?"

"Far to the west, there was a continent that fell from sight. This was before the memory of anyone living. A thousand suns ago, the entire continent was lost to the sea." I've never set foot in that water. They say the spirits there will drag you under.

"Sounds like Atlantis." She keeps a steady pace toward the black monolith.

Unease makes its way into my gut. "I don't like the feel of this."

"No. It's evil." She seems calm and determined to get closer.

I splash forward, jogging to catch up with her and take her hand. "What is Atlantis?"

"A story about a continent that sank into the Atlantic Ocean. In some of the tales, the Atlantans continue to live beneath the water. No one has ever found real evidence that Atlantis exists." While she doesn't pull away from my touch, there is no warmth or feel to her skin.

"The lost lands are real enough. I've never seen them, but I know that no one has ever reported a giant tower protruding from the water." I try to squeeze her fingers. "I don't like that I can't feel you physically."

"But you feel me, right? In my head, I know we're still lying on the couch in the little house, but my heart feels you here with me in my dream." Taking her gaze from the tower, she stares into my eyes. There's worry and fear along with sorrow. I see nothing of the undercurrent of joy that is always within Wren.

"I feel you as if your heart beats inside mine. What will we find there?" I point.

"Momma, I think. Though she wasn't there before. At least I didn't have this driving feeling that I had to save her there the last time I had this dream." She breaks into a run, lifting her knees high to get through the water without falling.

"I see you, human." Venora's voice cuts through the air. The sky darkens. At the very top of the tower, she stands with her hands raised. Black lightning shoots from her fingers across the sky. She looks down at us and focuses her rage. "Give yourself to me, and I'll spare the woman you seek."

Lightning hits the water, making it erupt violently. It forms a wall blocking our way.

Letting go of my hand, Wren lifts her hands. Wind whips around, blowing her curly hair out from her head. The water whips away from our feet, revealing the skulls of those who *perished when the land was lost. She screams and forces her magic up the tower.*

Venora's rage is evident as the lightning shoots toward us.

As the wind reaches the top, the witch queen rises awkwardly. Her power shifts wildly.

A shard hits Wren, and I pull her back.

I gasp into consciousness. Half sitting, the weight of Wren against my side and shoulder keeps me from shooting to my feet.

She clutches at me. Her eyes closed, words stuck in her chest and throat as she thrashes.

"Wren, wake up. It's a dream. Wake yourself up." I shake her shoulder and kiss her forehead.

Her eyelids pop open. "Oh. The dream again. And you were there. Momma is in that tower. That monster has my mother."

Gently rubbing her back, I move us to sit. "You don't know that. It was a dream, and while parts of it might be real, other pieces might be conjured by your imagination and fear."

Turning to face me, a crease forms between her eyes. "You were there this time. Not before."

"I was there. I saw what you saw." It's not possible, but I traveled into her dreams.

"How did you do that?"

It would be simpler if I had a magical method. "That is magic beyond me, sweetheart. I have never walked in another's dreams or read anyone's mind."

"You got into Wally's mind."

Andrea Rose

How do I explain this? "I only made a suggestion and pushed it into him. I didn't read his thoughts or invade his privacy. I don't have those gifts and would be shy to use them if I did."

"Do you fear what you might find in my thoughts?" She rises and looks out the window into the predawn darkness.

Standing behind her, I wrap my arms around her. "It is an invasive and personal thing to be inside someone's mind. I could hear your heart beating all around me."

"That must have been unsettling." Her voice is full of empathy, laced with the residual fear from the dream.

"It should have been." I felt at home, and maybe that's even more terrifying. "I don't know how I came to walk into your dream, but I'm glad I was there to see what you saw and perhaps define a location. It might be best if we avoid the lost lands if we can."

"My mother is there." There isn't a shred of doubt in her voice.

"I saw no sign of Birdie, did you? Venora's threat may have been in vain. Besides, it was still a dream. The interaction from her side wasn't real. Or do you think she puts these thoughts in your mind?" Now that is a sobering thought.

When she turns, her chest is pressed to my body, and she cranes her neck to look me in the eyes. "I don't think so. Is that even possible? I've been having these dreams that come to pass for most of my life. Has she been in my head for decades?" She shivers.

Rubbing her arms from elbow to shoulder, I pull her into a hug and breathe in her flowery scent. "I don't believe the witch queen knew anything about you or the other prophesied before. I'm not even certain she knows now."

"So, what do we do?" She presses her cheek to my chest and wraps her arms around my waist.

This is comfortable. It's selfish, but I wish I could forget duty and the needs of so many and stay like this with Wren for the rest of my life. Impossible. I kiss the top of her curls. "Let's eat those sandwiches Birdie knew we would need and go find her."

Once we've broken our fast, I search for weapons and manage to find several knives and a child-size sword hidden beneath Jax's clothes in the back of a closet. Likely, he meant to keep them out of his boys' hands when he was not present to train them.

I take them all and tuck the knives into my sack. The sword is small but sharp and well-balanced. It would be better if I had the time to teach Wren how to use it, but for now, she's wise enough to know the hilt from the pointy end. "Strap this on in case you need to defend yourself."

With wide eyes, she buckles the belt low on her waist. "I have no idea how to use a sword."

"Hopefully, you won't need it." Packs slung over our backs and armed for whatever may come, we leave the safety of Serena and Jax's home. "We have a bit of a walk ahead of us. Up to the portal rise and then across to the forest. It will take most of the day." I have never wished for a horse more. Not only would it save us half a day, it would be an added layer of protection for Wren.

Adhar caws as we step outside the house. She takes flight and heads west but never too far ahead.

At the top of the rise, five centaurs stand in a row, all armed with bows and arrows, swords and spears, but they've not drawn their weapons.

The raven stands on a rock as if waiting patiently for us to catch up. While Adhar seems perfectly at ease, I'm less trusting.

Keeping my body between them and Wren, it takes an act of pure will not to draw my sword. Being outnumbered means diplomacy is in order. In a fight, I can't beat five beasts who are built to trample and are three times my weight. "We were just coming to find you in the forest."

The one in the center has wavy black hair and dark skin from the waist up. The rest of him is a pitch-black horse. His back is as tall as I am, with the man half of him towering over me. He cocks his head. "Were you, elf? It is never wise for elves to invade the centaurs' home." Even with the obvious warning and harsh tone, he's more cordial than I would have expected.

Having never seen a centaur in person before, I'm awed by their magnificence. "I agree, but our needs are so great, it was the only choice."

Wren steps beside me. "It would not have been an invasion. We're searching for someone. I am Wren Martin. My mother, Birdie, is lost."

The five centaurs speak together in muffled tones, and the bits I can hear are in their own language and foreign to me.

Reaching out, I take her wrist and pull her close. "You

shouldn't talk to them. We don't even know whose side they're on."

She shrugs.

The beasts are magnificent. I couldn't have imagined the majesty of these creatures. Two of the centaurs are similar in looks, with blond hair and pale-cream hair on the horse. They must be brothers as their facial features are so similar. The final two are equally fierce looking with scowling faces, but stand perfectly still. They may be half horse, but they share none of the skittishness of their animal cousins.

The central one steps toward us. "I am Corell of the Western Centaurs." He bows. Pointing to the two centaurs to his left, he says, "This is Jadar and Belloc." He gestures to his right. "These young ones are Wellon and Pallon."

The other four bow as well. Their eyes are red but not glowing as the fables say. I nod my head slowly but without taking my gaze from them. "I am Liam Riordan, second son of the Riordan."

Corell stares at me for a long moment before shifting his attention fully to Wren. "We have searched daily for you, daughter of Birdie Martin."

Fearless, Wren rushes forward, stopped only by my hand on her upper arm. "You've seen my mother? Where is she?" There's joy again in her voice.

I've missed that tone in the last few hours. Still, something doesn't feel right. "Is Birdie in the forest?" I point toward the west.

Sorrow fills Corell's eyes. "No. I wish my news were better, Wren. I will tell you how we came to know Birdie and how we lost her."

"Oh my god. Is she dead?" Gripping her chest, she crumples. "I thought I'd feel it if she were dead." She shakes her head, and tears run down her cheeks. She pounds her chest. "Nothing. There's nothing. I still feel her here."

I kneel and wrap my arms around her. My heart is near to ripping in two. I've failed in my duty, and I've lost a friend. Holding that aside, I comfort Wren.

Corell huffs a horsey sound, moves closer, and lowers his front legs. "Forgive me. I misspoke. The common language is rarely used among us. By lost, I meant, she is not with the centaurs any longer. I too feel she lives still." He presses his palm to the center of his chest.

Lifting her face, Wren hiccups. "Not dead?"

He shakes his head.

It's obvious that these creatures care about Birdie, and they've been searching for Wren. That's hardly vicious or warmongering in the way the old stories describe their character. "Can you tell us what happened?"

Corell backs up a few paces, and all five sit back on their haunches. With a heavy, trilling sigh, he begins. "When the dragon, Trocar, came, we defended our forest. The portal opened, and a human woman came through. Her arrival distracted the dragon. He breathed his magic, but she escaped the push and pull of time.

"There was a battle, and finally, injured, Trocar flew away.

"Birdie thanked us for helping her. She told us of coming through with two others and that one was her daughter. She wanted to know if we'd seen you. It was obvious to us that the magic had pushed you through time. If you'd been sent back, we'd know of it, but if you were pushed forward, then your time here had not yet happened."

Gathering herself, Wren sits up straight. "Did my mother go into your forest or did she take another path?"

Lowering his head, Corell says, "I almost wish she had gone her own way." He lets out a long breath. "We knew the elves here had moved on. We hoped you would come through and be reunited. She came with us into our trees and was our guest for more than half a moon."

"What happened?" I have a tightness in my belly that usually warns of battle or bad news.

"Five days ago, some of our young were playing at the far side of the forest. There is a beach there where they can run and play. It used to be a safe place, but the witch queen built her tower on the bodies of the long dead. She draws power from that cursed place. All the young had been warned to stay off the beaches."

Wren covers her mouth. "What happened?"

After a long silence, Wellon says, "Six foals were taken by the shadow demons. Our kind can't be turned, but they can be enslaved. They can be tortured."

"I'm very sorry." She brushes her tears away.

"Corell's son was among those taken." Wellon lowers his gaze at the sharp look from his leader.

Corell stares a long time at Wren. "The witch queen sent a message that she knew we harbored a human. She offered a trade."

"You traded my mother for the children." There's no anger in Wren's voice. She gives the centaur a watery smile. "I understand. You did what you had to do. Are they safe, the children?"

"I would not trade lives in such a way, daughter of Birdie. It goes against the light to sell a life even if it is to save six. We would have told the evil one no." His breath comes fast and hard, as if he's holding in a torrent of emotions.

"I don't understand." If they didn't make the trade, then where is Birdie?

"When Birdie Martin heard of our young in the hands of the witch queen, she was deeply saddened and angry. As soon as the trade offer came, she said she would go to save our young ones. She wouldn't listen to reason. I told her the witch queen would turn her into a soulless wraith who lives only to do evil at the witch queen's command. I tried to talk her out of making such a decision. She went to the witch queen's shadow demons, and the young were returned."

It might be the only time I've heard of Venora keeping her word. I wonder if she worries the centaurs will come out of their forests. She wasn't ready for a long standoff against forces so large, even with her evil magic.

Wren stands, and before I can stop her, she walks to him. She wraps her arms around his neck and hugs him. "My mother's entire life has been about caring for children. You could not have changed her mind."

Tears streak like small rivers down Corell's face. After a long minute, he hugs Wren back then drops his hands. "You are as kind as your mother. I ask your forgiveness, though I don't deserve it."

As though realizing she's created an awkward moment, Wren steps back. "You've done nothing to warrant forgiveness. However, if you need it, you have it. Can you tell us where this black tower is?"

I stand and clear the emotions from my throat. "Will you help us rescue Birdie?"

"I do not know if such a thing is possible, Liam, son of

A Crown of Wind and Water

Elspeth." Corell stands and runs his hands over his face, wiping away his sorrows. "My son is safe, as are the others. If you have a way to save Birdie, the centaurs will listen."

"If you can tell me everything you know about the black tower, perhaps we can make a plan together, Corell of the Western Centaurs." Part of me expects him to decline.

Adhar caws loudly and wings west toward the woods.

Chapter Seven

WREN

Even though I'm from Texas, it's been a minute since I was on a horse, and that one was half the size of Jadar. He is not a horse. This is a man and a draft horse, and there's no saddle and no reins. I have my arms wrapped around Jadar's naked torso. My cheeks are so hot that I may explode.

High in the blue sky, Adhar circles as if keeping watch. I shudder at what she might be worried will attack us.

Beside me, Liam wears a wide grin that he's trying to subdue as he rides Belloc as if he's been bareback on a centaur all his life. His hands are resting easily on his thighs as they gallop past and crash into the river.

I close my eyes and hold on tight as we thrash through the shallow water, then up the bank on the other side.

Jadar laughs. "You are afraid?"

"Yes. If I fall, I'll break my neck." I spare an unfortunate glance at the hard ground rushing past. My stomach roils, and I force my gaze ahead to the trees, which are getting closer and closer.

"My gate is even and steady. You will not fall," he assures me.

"My balance is not steady or sure, Jadar. I do not doubt your abilities. It's my own I worry over."

He laughs again, and his shoulders shake. The warm brown of his skin is almost the same color as the hair of the horse part of him.

"I have the impression your people liked my mother." I can see we have a long ride ahead. It's better to pass the time with conversation than worry about falling to my death.

"Birdie Martin is the first human I had ever met. She was full of life and flowery speech. She is a kind soul, as I can tell you are." He slows to a trot as we enter an area with rocks and low bushes.

"Why do your people allow the rest of this world to believe you are a warmongering race who will kill on sight?" I should probably hold my tongue, but it's not in my nature. When I want to know something, I ask. I'm not saying that's never landed me in trouble, but most of the time, I learn something.

A low chuckle rumbles under my hands where I'm clinging to Jadar's torso. "You are much like your mother with your direct way of speaking." He moves to the left to avoid tall brush. "Centaurs keep to themselves. Our herds have grown strong in the forests and the plains, distant from elven cities and villages. Many centuries ago, we were enslaved by the elves. We won our freedom and retreated to the forests."

This history is not unfamiliar. I suppose there are good

and bad parts to any history. "Do you fear the modern elves would attempt to enslave you?"

"We are many and strong. Never again will the herd be strangled by the yoke of slavery," he rages.

"Forgive me. I just wonder why all the various peoples of Domhan keep separate rather than join to stand against the witch queen." I hold my breath, hoping I haven't insulted the centaur.

He cocks his head and returns to a gallop. "There is history that keeps us apart, but I believe time is the cause."

"Time?" Like the dragons shifting time? What does that have to do with the apparent prejudices festering in Domhan?

His chest rises and falls on a huff. "So many suns have passed since an elf came into a centaur's woods, and we have also kept to ourselves. Time creates the widest chasms."

"I see your point." My attention drifts back to my nightmare. Nothing on this journey looks anything like the visions. I'm tired, emotionally and physically drained from the events of the last few days and the lack of restful sleep last night. I rest my cheek on his back and close my eyes. These centaurs are truly beautiful. This world may be worth saving even if I'm not the one to do it. I need to find my mother. That's my only quest. I'll figure out the rest once Momma is safe.

We slow as we near the tree line. The sun and whatever that other orb is are starting their path west. I must have slept for a few hours. It's a miracle I'm not dead on the ground somewhere. I suppose I have Jadar to thank for keeping me from falling.

To the left is a sheer cliff down to the ocean, and behind us is the wide plain. The forest is dense and the light through the canopy is dim.

Liam drops to his feet and reaches his hands toward me to help me down. "Are you alright?"

My knees and hips are sore from sitting in the same position for so long, and it takes me a moment to gain my footing. "Just stiff."

"I'm surprised you could sleep on the centaur's back." He keeps his hands on my waist while I'm unstable.

"It would seem Jadar is a safe haven for a human woman from Texas, and I feel much more rested with no nightmares." I grin at Jadar.

"Hmm." Liam sounds annoyed. "I'm pleased you got the needed sleep." Still, he doesn't sound glad.

I spare a thought for him being jealous. Part of me thinks that's sweet, and another part says he should use his energy for more useful emotions. I'm about to tell him so when the forest comes alive with a dozen or more centaurs. I yelp out of instinct, but immediately put my hand over my mouth and feel my cheeks heat. Since meeting Liam, every moment feels like a surprise and a strain on my senses.

The centaurs stare at me and Liam with equal interest as they lead the way through the dense trees.

Corell says, "We are going to our home. Son of Elspeth, you will be the first elf to set foot in the Western Centaur dwellings in memory. Daughter of Birdie, you are the second human, perhaps ever, to see such a place."

"Do you worry we'll be disrespectful?" Liam asks. He threads his fingers through mine.

Everyone is so much bigger than me that I have to jog to keep up. "Are there rules or customs we should be aware of?"

"You enter with me. I, with my mate, lead this generation. You are the son of a leader. I assume you know how to behave." Corell gives a half smile and trots ahead.

A minute later, the forest thins, and sun shines into a wide area that serves as the centaurs' village. There must be over a hundred homes built in rows like streets. Some are in the shade, and others are fully in the cleared spaces. They are open, with roofs that overhang wooden floors. I would call them porches, but it is clear they are used as living rooms. Centaurs are playing with the young and doing needlework.

A large crowd gathers at the center where a fire burns. Males and females in armor that covers from their chest to where their bodies become equine. Some hold spears, and others have swords strapped to their side. Behind the soldiers stand hundreds of centaurs, unclothed. Females are as bare as the males.

It takes me a moment to adjust to so much flesh and the contrast with the armor shining brightly in the late-day sun.

The crowd parts for Corell, and we follow.

Liam is stiff, and his jaw ticks. His hand sits gently on the hilt of his sword, but he doesn't wrap his fingers around it or do anything to indicate aggression.

To the right is an enormous kiln putting off heat that I

feel from a hundred yards away. A dozen centaurs are working to pound out weapons and armor.

They were planning to go to battle before they found us. Were they going to try to rescue my mother with or without me? So many questions about how they live and why they care about a human woman. I know she saved their young, but these people have kept to themselves for centuries, and it's mostly kept them safe. They can avoid that beach and stay clear of the witch queen.

Adhar caws from a tree, but I can't find her in the leaves. Still, for some reason, I find her presence comforting.

Corell walks into a large meeting room. It's not enclosed, but the floor is wood and there is a roof. Large cut logs hold the twenty-foot ceiling in place but leave adequate room for centaurs to walk and mill about.

Hundreds of hooves on the wooden floor make me wish it was polite to hold my ears. I restrain myself, but I'm sure I cringe before I can stop myself.

Jadar leans close to my ear. "It's loud for us as well. Give it a moment and everyone will settle."

I smile at him and nod.

Corell stands at the front and turns to face the assembly.

Jadar indicates a large box where Liam and I can sit.

Once we're seated, the centaurs sit back on their haunches, and the clomping stops.

Jadra and Belloc sit behind us. Wellon and Pallon sit facing us with a wide gap between them, where the entire gathering can see Corell.

A female with a glittering chest plate made of silver and pearls sits behind Corell. She gazes intently at Liam and me. When Corell calls for silence, she focuses on him.

A Crown of Wind and Water

"We have found the daughter of Birdie Martin," Corell says.

The crowd erupts with cheers and applause while staring at me.

My cheeks heat.

Corell holds up his hands, patting the air to call for silence. Once the cheering dies down, his expression turns grave. "As Birdie told us, her daughter travels with an elf." He gestures to us. "This is Liam, son of the Riordan."

The crowd erupts in mumbled mutterings.

"Quiet. These two are foreign to us, but Birdie gave herself to save our own, and thus she is one of us. I extend that same bond to her daughter."

Many centaurs nod in agreement with the statement.

I stare, trying to fathom the idea that I'm now part of a centaur tribe.

"Objections?" Corell calls above the din.

The crowd silences as the female behind Corell stands and strides to his side. She is stunning, with bright ruby eyes and long blond hair. Her coat is snow white, though her hooves are black, as is her tail. She's striking. "Of course, the daughter of she who saved our son and the other young should be honored in such a way, but you have brought an elf into our midst, mate." She points at Liam. "What does he want of us?"

Taking her hand, Corell eases the rudeness of her pointed finger. "Farress, while we have lived separate and safe for so many long centuries, it is clear the threat to Domhan is also a threat to our kind. As Birdie is our kin, we will help to fight for her freedom."

A cheer rises, and Farress gives a short nod. "It will be as you say. The armor and weapons will be finished tomorrow. The blacksmiths have been tireless while you searched for the daughter."

"Wren," he says softly.

My name is repeated through the hushed voices of the gathering.

Farress bows her head toward me.

I stand and do the same for her. Right or wrong, it feels as if some gesture is needed.

"What would you like from us for your comfort, Wren Martin?" Farress steps toward me, but not so close that I need to crane my neck. She could have done so for intimidation purposes, but instead, she accepts her mate's decision and is now the hostess.

My throat is dry, and my knees shake slightly. It feels as if I've been presented to the queen and must think of something clever to say. I know at some point I'll need food and a place to sleep, but that's not what I want at the moment. "I'd like to meet the children who were taken by the witch queen if that's possible."

She stares at me for a long moment and myriad emotions pass over her lovely face. From surprise to indignation and awe, she runs the gamut.

I stutter. "If...um... that's not permitted, I understand."

Cocking her head in a similar manner to her mate, she smiles. "I expected something for your comfort, but your request is not forbidden." She looks at one of the centaurs over my shoulder.

The crowd begins loudly exiting the pavilion.

When the noise dissipates, she says, "Why do you wish to meet our young?"

"It would comfort me to see the faces of the children and the reason for my mother's sacrifice." Clearly, Momma thought these people were worth her life. I like them, but I need more. I want to know what I'm risking everything for. My feelings for Liam aside, this world should be worthy of Birdie Martin's life if we've already risked that and more.

She gestures to us to exit out the back. "Are you soft of heart like your mother?"

"Both Martin women are kind as well as brilliant," Liam says.

My cheeks feel as if they might burst into flames at any moment. A whirling wind creates a dust devil to my right. Whatever this is, I must learn to control it.

Taking my hand, Liam smiles.

Farress and Corell walk with us to a large house with a grand porch, complete with an oval table that King Arthur's knights would have been proud of. No chairs, but that makes perfect sense considering the way the centaurs seem comfortable to sit on their haunches. The house sits half in the woods with the front looking out over the village.

"Your mother stayed with us. I hope you will do the same." Farress clomps onto the porch. She walks to the open door and says something in a guttural language before returning her attention to me.

"Thank you. You are very kind." I sit on a box that Corell brings to the table, which is too high for me, but I'm glad to be off my feet and wish I had appreciated the soft couch in the village more.

Liam sits beside me, his thigh touching mine as if we've spent years together. It does feel as if I've known him all my life, and considering we're literally from different worlds, that's something. His back is straight, and his tone is diplomatic. "Corell, can you tell us about the tower in the lost lands? What is it made from? How long has it been there?"

Sitting across the large table beside his mate, Corell threads his fingers through hers. "We started to sense the rise of dark magic from the west a few months ago. From the seashore, you can now see the top of the tower, though it's a two-day hard ride from the shore. It's made of some kind of black stone, smooth, and catches the sun rather than reflects."

I stiffen as the description mimics what I saw last night. How is it that my dream was so accurate about a place I have never seen?

Liam's hand on my knee calms me. He nods. "Wren saw such a place in her dreams. It was tall enough that even with magic, it should have taken far more than a few months to construct."

"You speak as if you saw it too," Farress says.

"I walked into Wren's dream." Liam's voice softens as if he's not fully certain he should divulge the information.

Not sure of the significance beyond it being impossible, I remain silent and take in every expression and all the information.

Farress's ruby eyes widen. "Is dream walking one of your elven gifts?"

Jaw ticking, Liam pauses for a long moment. "Not until I brought Wren to Domhan."

"Then the human from the prophecy awakened this gift." Farress focuses on me. "What kind of magic have you been gifted with, Wren, daughter of Birdie?"

With both leaders of the centaurs staring at me across

the table, my tongue feels too fat for my mouth. "I... Um...." I take a deep breath. "Humans don't have magic. We can't alter the course of another's thoughts, and we don't shoot lightning from our fingers or whatever other things elves can do. I sometimes dream things that come to pass, though not always exactly as I dreamed them. Since meeting Liam, I've created wind a few times, though I can't control it. It just comes when I pray and the need is great." I hold my breath, hoping I haven't said anything wrong.

Liam's hand tightens on my leg.

Covering his hand with mine, I take another shaky breath and try to calm my nerves.

Farress and Corell look at each other for several moments.

I wonder if they have silent communication. Can they read each other's minds?

Finally, Farress looks at me. "Humans have no magic, and yet you do. This is likely why you are in the prophecy." She looks as if she has more to say, but her cheeks flush and she demurs.

On a chuckle, Corell clears his throat. "To enter another's dreams is an intimate connection. It is very rare in centaurs and reserved only for those who are..." He stares away as if searching for the word.

Taking a deep breath, Liam stiffens. He lets it out and says, "Mates in the old way. Fated by the old gods."

"Yes." Corell grins and pounds his fist on the table, pleased to have the information translated even when he couldn't find the words in the common tongue.

Farress's blush deepens, and my cheeks and neck are warm. She smiles. "Matings of this kind are not as common as in the age of the old gods. Though they do still happen from time to time." She gives Corell a knowing look.

With a quick squeeze of my hand, Liam pulls away. "Perhaps it's more useful to focus on the tower and what Venora has planned to use it for. Do you know how many entrances there are or how large the circumference is?"

"It is larger than our village from side to side and a perfect circle. I saw no doors." Corell shakes his head. "It was two days of hard riding. We exchanged Birdie for the foals. They were not there one moment and there the next, and Birdie was gone in a moment. I would have left soldiers, but there is no cover. On the ride back, we found floating debris and left two centaurs there to watch. It's in water and extremely uncomfortable, and damages our hooves after a while. Farress has sent replacements for them twice while I rode to find you."

"No doors." Liam's voice is barely above a whisper, and his eyes are downcast while he thinks. "It's an obelisk."

Both centaurs look as if they've been provided with an epiphany. They gape at him.

"There has not been an obelisk in Domhan since the ancient age, and even then, it is only theory and myth." Farress sounds doubtful, but there is fear in her narrowed gaze.

"Um... Not to sound ignorant, but what is an obelisk beyond a tall structure? Obelisks have four sides. I thought this was round." Everything that's going on and the fact that the tower in my dream doesn't match the technical description of an obelisk is what's bothering me. I may actually be cracking up.

With a hint of a smile, Liam looks at me. He's so close; if

he leaned in, he could kiss me. He turns away too soon, as if he thinks better of our proximity. "You're right, of course, Wren. However, in some of the darker mythologies and dogma of the ancient age, the towers were built around the four-sided obelisk."

"What's the purpose?" I wish I had a dozen books at my disposal right now so I could learn all the information about this ancient age of Domhan. I'm better with books than people.

The three of them stare a long time at each other. Finally, Liam says, "To focus power. Those in the light brought power from the sun and stars. The wielders of dark magic drew their power from the demon realm within Domhan. It's called Coire."

"Hell. She's drawing her power from hell?" I blink several times. Maybe this is all a dream and I can wake myself up. None of this sounds real. It's fantasy, horror, but not truth. Yet Momma is gone, and I'm sore from riding a centaur for the better part of a day. Clearly, either my dreams are more graphic than ever, or this is the new reality. "My mother is in a tower designed to draw power from hell," I mutter, but the effect is the same. My gut tightens, and my eyes fill as emotions swamp me.

"We're going to find her and bring her home, Wren." Liam is making promises that he can't possibly know will come to pass.

Even so, his words comfort me, and I dash away the tears.

Chapter Eight

LIAM

Jadar brings six foals to the front of Farress and Corell's house. "These are the foals who were saved by Birdie Martin."

The young centaurs all look thin and diminished. Even though I've never seen centaurs before today, I feel the young would be full of laughter and life. The four colts and two fillies standing before us are afraid. Still, the fact that centaurs have had female children since the curse is not lost on me.

They should, at the very least, be curious about an elf and a human in their midst.

I step forward to question them.

Wren puts her hand on my upper arm and steps in front of me. She looks at each centaur child individually until he or she meets her gaze. "My mother would not wish for your fear and sorrow. She made her sacrifice, as she would for any child of any species. It is who she is and why she is so beloved. I'm happy you are safe. I pray we will rescue my mother, but even if that is not possible, your lives should not be marred by her sacrifice. I hope you will see how lucky you are and use your time to be of service to others."

She's magnificent, my Wren.

The filly with black hair, dark skin, and a black horse wipes a tear from her cheek. The other has red hair and a roan horse, and she pats her back in comfort, where they stand close together.

A colt who looks very much like Farress, with a white horse and fair skin and hair steps forward. "I am Dollan, son of Corell. We are honored by your mother's sacrifice. We will live to make her proud. How can we help the daughter of Birdie Martin?"

His parents pull their shoulders back and beam at him.

I give Dollan a short bow. "Can you tell us how you were taken and everything that happened after that?"

Dollan's already light complexion pales further. "I will tell it, though it isn't easy, and if my language fails..." He looks at his father.

"I will help you," Corell says.

Swallowing hard, Dollan sits, as do his friends.

I sit on the short stoop leading up to the living area.

Wren takes her seat beside me.

"We like to play in the sand by the ocean. We've been warned since the tower rose that it might be dangerous. My father told us to keep to the forest." Dollan lowers his head. "That day, we went farther down the beach. It was a nice day with a bit of wind and a drizzle that kept the sand firm.

A Crown of Wind and Water

When the shadow demons came, it was fast, and the sound they made hurt our ears."

"Go on, son," Corell encourages.

"We ran toward the forest, but they were faster. There were at least twenty of them, and they lifted us high in the air. My stomach lurched as the ground grew smaller. I thought they were going to drop us, but they brought us to the black tower."

I feel the fear from these children and don't wish to make the memories too vivid, but there are things I must know. Keeping my voice soft, I ask, "How did you enter the tower, Dollan? Did a door open on the side or at the base?"

Shaking his head, Dollan winces. "It was as if they flew us straight through the evil thing. It hurt and burned at the same time. Then the pain stopped, and we were in a room. There was no light. We found each other and huddled on the floor rather than succumb to the total darkness."

Farress's voice is strained, and her arms are wrapped around her waist. "Centaurs have excellent eyesight even in the dark of night. Wherever the witch queen held them must have been pitch."

"Did they hurt you?" Wren asks gently. "I mean, beyond the entry and what must have been terrifying."

"Without sun or moon, we lost track of time. We were neither fed nor given water. It was as if they planned to starve us. No one touched us once we were in the tower." Dollan's voice cracks.

"They were there for two days." Corell looks ready to go into battle. His fists are clenched at his sides, and he stomps a hoof, bringing up dust.

Two days without any contact with light or basic needs. "The witch queen never came to you?"

They shake their heads.

"What happened when you came out of the tower?" I ask, looking for some clue, anything that might help.

Dollan shrugs. "There was no pain. One moment we were in the dark, and the next, blinded by sunlight and lying in the waters of the lost lands. We didn't know what had happened until later, when Father told us of Birdie Martin's sacrifice."

The filly with red hair stammers, "I-I am Lassa. May- maybe it's not important, but there was a sound. The tower hums, and the humming is constant. When we were transported, the sound grew loud enough to hurt my ears."

That could mean there's a power source. What would Verona need power for? What is she doing in that cursed tower? "It wasn't the same noise the shadow demons make?"

She shakes her head. "No. This was deeper and steadier."

"I appreciate all you have told me. You have been very brave." I need time to think about what we know and what we don't know, but the longer we leave Birdie in Venora's hands, the more unlikely it is that we get her back.

"Thank you." Farress hugs her son and leads the children away.

I hate that I must ask my next question. "Wren, how long can your mother survive the conditions they described?"

"If she was able to keep her backpack, she had at least one sandwich and a few bottles of water. She probably had a few protein bars stashed in there, too." Sorrow fills her eyes and breaks my heart. "The darkness would not be great, but she's strong. Maybe five days, depending on how much water she has and if she has rationed it. Maybe longer." Shoulders sagging, she looks ready to break.

As much as I want to comfort her, I have to stay focused on the task. "Corell, am I correct in believing you planned to attempt a rescue regardless of finding Birdie's daughter? I see weapons and armor being made and mended."

He nods, and his tail flicks against his side. "We planned on trying to find you for three days. Tomorrow was our timeline to return to the tower. We could not forsake her after her sacrifice. I told her I would find a way, and she told me to get the children to safety."

"We'll continue with your plan." I bow. "Somehow we have to get Birdie out without giving anything or anyone in return."

"She'll want me." Wren's voice is soft but strong. "The witch queen doesn't really want Momma; she wants me. She needs to stop what you and the elves are doing. If the prophecy is followed, she could lose. She's afraid, maybe for the first time."

Gut in a knot, I nod. "I cannot and will not trade your life for your mother. I care deeply for her, but that trade will not be made, Wren."

Fire flares in her eyes. "Find another way, then, elf." She stomps inside the centaur's home and doesn't look back.

Corell lets out a long breath and sits on his haunches. "She is much like her mother. You have a lot to deal with, son of Elspeth."

It's clear he's teasing me, but he's not wrong either. "How do I teach Wren to use her magic at will?"

"First, you must find the source of her magic. How is it

realized? Until then, I don't see how you will teach control." The centaur leader watches his son walk through the center of the gathering space.

The boy's gait is slow, his chin tucked, his tail hangs still, and his fists are tight at his sides. As the son of a leader, he should hold his shoulders back and his head high.

"Dollan is strong. He will recover. He needs time and to know that the one who caused his distress is no longer the greatest power in Domhan." It's painful to admit that Venora rules my world when it was my mother who lost that power.

"You want me to say that the centaurs of the west will join forces with elves in the coming war?" Rising, Corell paces away from me. His tail swishes hard against his side. "Keeping to ourselves has kept my herd safe for many generations."

"That was true in the past." Farress returns and sits close to her mate. "Venora Braddish took our children. She has declared war on the centaurs."

"You have the right of it, sweet one. We will not let her actions go unchallenged." Corell threads his fingers through Farress's.

Venora made a tactical mistake. She woke the anger of the centaurs, who had always been neutral and disliked elves.

"She's panicking." I speak mostly to myself. Another thought distracts me. "How did the witch queen inform you of her desire to make a trade for Birdie?"

They look at each other, frowning. Sorrow fills Farress's eyes, though she sheds no tears. "She dropped an elven slave on the beach."

"What happened to him?" My temper rises at the

thought of the centaurs sending a slave back into the clutches of evil.

"He came to us near death and did not survive." Corell meets my gaze. "We did not kill him, and we would have done all that was possible to save him."

My temper is under control, and I take a deep breath. "What happened?"

The color drains from Farress's face. "The elf's name was Kieran. Shadow demons came en mass. Our patrol stood their ground ready to defend the village, but the demons did not attack. Instead, they dropped Kieran from a height that, without magic, he could not survive. His bones were broken, and he bled from within." She pauses and takes several slow breaths. "He told us where the children were and that the human woman would be taken in trade for the foals' safe return."

"How long did Kieran live?" My fury roils under the surface. Cruelty and evil are the calling cards of the witch queen. Elves are disposable, as slaves, shadow demons, and converts.

"Only a few hours." Corell's voice is strained. "He was made as comfortable as possible, but moving him would have been agony, so we brought the comfort to him on the beach. We eased his pain with what magic we possess, and Birdie spoke to him, which seemed to bring him peace. As soon as he was gone, Birdie insisted we make the trade."

Despite the necessity of it, I feel Corell's shame. I want to assure him that he did the right thing, but there is only one answer to that. "We will get Birdie back. I'm not sure exactly how that will happen, but by the old gods, we will find a way."

"I hope you are right, Liam," Corell says.

"If an elf and a centaur can sit together and plan a battle as allies after centuries of separation, the old gods are surely with us." I stand and offer my hand.

Corell rises and grips my forearm in the way of soldiers.

We look into each other's eyes, and there is mutual respect.

The hour is late when I find Wren lying atop a soft mattress in a private room. The bed must have been made for infant centaurs, as it is far too small for an adult. The room is otherwise sparse, with hooks on the wall and a table with a mirror over it.

I ease down next to her with my body close but not touching. Listening to her heart with my keen hearing, it's easy enough to know that she's not asleep. My arrival made her pulse race. "If you think my choices are because of a prophecy, you are wrong. The longer I know you, the more I think the oracle is probably correct in their belief that you are special and more powerful than we yet know. However, it is my feelings which force me to protect you, Wren, not my duty."

She rolls to face me. In the moonlight, her eyes shine bright blue. Her hair is a halo around her beautiful face. "I will not accept that my mother must pay with her life to keep me safe."

I brush her curls from her cheek. "I did not say I would

forsake her, only that a trade for you would not be made. Centaurs cannot be turned into shadow demons. I don't know if humans can or not, but we need Birdie free and out of danger before we meet Venora."

With a nod, she asks. "How do we do that from a tower with no doors?"

It's a fair question. "I'm hoping the centaurs who watch the obelisk have seen enough to know how to enter." I take a deep breath. "There are some things we need to discuss. Should we talk now, or wait for you to be rested?"

"I can't sleep." She sits up and faces me with her legs crossed. "What is it?"

Facing her, I sit the same way with my knees grazing hers. "Two things, but one is not strictly relevant to saving your mother."

Her throat bobs, and she takes a deep breath that pushes her breasts high, stretching her shirt and making my mouth water. "Start with the one that is relevant, please."

How has she gotten so deeply embedded into my heart in such a short time? "You can create wind, but we don't know how you control it, and so far, you've not conjured it without imminent need. If you could tell me what you feel when you bring the wind, maybe I can help you with control."

Her curls shift as she tips her chin and looks over my shoulder at the wall. "I feel scared for someone's safety. In the portal, I saw you, my mother, and the dragon, and I knew we were in trouble. I prayed for someone or something to save us from the dragon."

Is it the prayer or the fear that motivates her magic to

action? "Did anything like that ever happen to you in your world?"

She bites her bottom lip and lets the plump flesh slip through her teeth. "When I was nineteen, some girlfriends and I went to Gulf Shores for spring break. That's when schools take a break in the better weather. It was my freshman year in college."

I nod my understanding but say nothing so as not to interrupt her.

"We were at the beach. I was working on my tan and enjoying the sunshine when I heard a scream." She closes her eyes for a long moment. When she opens them, she's calm. "Maggie was knee-deep in the gulf. She was screaming and pointing. Dana and Julie were being dragged out to sea by an undertow. Dana's head went under." Tears fill her eyes.

Keeping my voice even, I smooth my hand over her shoulder. "What did you do?"

She dashes away the tears. "I stood up, and while I felt afraid, I also felt like I could save them. I prayed that they'd be safe on shore. The wave that pulled them under pushed them to the surface, along with the lifeguard who'd swum out to get them. A few seconds later, the wave deposited all three in shallow water.

"I ran to help Maggie pull them to safety. I never told any of them or even Momma, and for a while, I told myself it wasn't me." She blushes. "But I always knew I had somehow pushed the water to do what I wanted."

My mind is working fast. "Wind and water are powerful elements, Wren. Your control needs work, but I wonder if you couldn't keep the shadow demons at bay with the wind. At least long enough for us to get into the tower."

Eyes wide and mouth agape, she looks terrified. "What if I can't? I've never done magic on purpose."

Honesty is always best. "Then I'll be turned into a shadow demon, and the centaurs will likely be dropped from a height that will kill them."

"No. You can't expect me to risk that. I don't know how to make the wind. It comes when I'm afraid that something bad is happening. It comes when I pray for a better outcome." She grips my hands and pleads as if I'm holding a sword to her heart.

Leaning in, I press a gentle kiss to her lips. "I'll not force you to do anything, sweetheart. It's an idea that might work, but if you don't want to try, we'll find another way." I kiss her hair. "Prayer is like making a magic spell."

"Not for humans. Prayer for humans is to ask god to help or for giving thanks." She curls into my lap and leans her head on my chest.

Holding her like this is more than I have ever asked for. "Do most humans have the response of the elements that you do when they pray?"

"I don't think so." After a long pause, she says, "If I hadn't been there that day at Gulf Shores, I believe Dana and Julie would have died." There's embarrassment in her tone.

"You saved them, and that's all that matters. These gifts you were given are not arbitrary. You were meant to save them, just as you're meant to save Domhan." I rub her back in a wide circle, and she relaxes.

"That feels nice, Liam. Being here with you, like this,

feels right. I just need my Momma to be safe before I'm willing to go further with this quest of yours."

Kissing her again, I whisper. "I know. I understand. We'll find a way."

With a sigh, she snuggles closer. "What is the other thing you want to talk about?"

I should have left that for another day. "The dream. My being in your dream or you taking me into your dream means something to my people."

"That we were fated to find each other?" She says it casually, as if she doesn't believe it.

I wrap my other arm around her bent knees and hold her tight. "My parents are true mates. They knew the moment they saw each other that they would always be together. They were only eight at the time, so there was a long friendship before it turned into romantic love. They can speak to each other with their minds. They know if the other is safe when they are apart. It's very intimate."

"I imagine it is." Her skin warms under my fingers.

I wish it were light so I could see the pink of her blush. I've become a fool and a poet in a few weeks of knowing this woman. "Being inside your dream was very personal, don't you think?"

"Yes. I heard your heart beating and the warmth of your skin. It was as if we were one person with two minds. It should have been awkward and uncomfortable. I should have felt intruded upon or even violated, but it was as if I had come home after a long journey." She wraps her arms around my neck and kisses my cheek.

"It was the same for me. Only..."

Leaning back, she looks me in the eyes. "Only what?"

"I don't see the future the way you do. How does this thing between us not result in broken hearts?" Mine is already feeling more than it ever has in my entire life.

"I have no idea." She yawns. "My dreams haven't shown me that."

Could she look that far ahead while asleep? Can she direct her premonitions, or are they only what the gods wish to show her? Too many questions and no answers. "We should try to sleep. Tomorrow will be a long, wet day."

Chapter Nine

WREN

Once again on Jadar's back, this time with a soft blanket between me and the centaur, I'm far more comfortable, but I wish there were a saddle. I can understand the strangeness of saddling a centaur.

My random thoughts continue as I busy my mind rather than think about what I can or cannot do to help save Momma.

"You should not worry so much." Jadar gallops through the shallow water.

"How can you tell I'm worried? You're facing away from me." More confident, I only hold him at the waist. He's wearing armor, so the ride is less embarrassing compared to the first time.

He slows as the water level deepens. "Your muscles tighten with the trending of your thoughts."

My heels drag in the still waters of the lost land. It's not like Atlantis, as that mythical place is not visible, nor has anyone ever found proof of its existence. In contrast, the lost lands are just under the surface of the sea. Sand has covered whatever was here before the sinking, but there are places where the water is deeper or shallower, and even a few spots where there are sand bars. "I was thinking that I don't have the strength to save my mother from whatever evil holds her."

"You are wrong. You have been chosen by the old gods for the task of saving our world. Perhaps this is your first test. I have no doubt you will succeed." He breaks into a gallop across a long stretch of sand.

"I wish I had your confidence."

"I shall believe in you enough for both of us." He turns his head and grins at me. His dark, handsome face and bright white smile could light any room he entered.

Who would have thought a centaur would be so charming?

Belloc gallops over with Liam on his back.

Liam's gaze is intense. "Are you alright?"

"Fine. Worried. Fine." Both are true, but I'm leaning toward the worried side.

Belloc says, "The water will get deep. The party will have to swim a short distance."

"Can you swim, Wren?" Stress is etched on Liam's handsome face.

More than that, I feel the tightness of his chest and the strain within him. I take a deep breath to push away the sense of his emotions. I grip Jadar tighter as my head feels light.

Both centaurs stop, and those behind us as well.

A Crown of Wind and Water

A shout goes out, and the centaurs riding ahead circle back with Corell at the lead.

Liam's feet hit the water with a splash. A moment later, his hand is on my leg. "Wren? What is it?"

I clear my head and the mix of his fears and mine eases. "I'm sorry." The army of centaurs watching me makes my cheeks heat. "I can swim."

"You can hold on to me and I will pull you through," Jadar promises.

Jaw ticking, Liam spares a glance at Jadar. He offers his arms to help me down. "If you need a moment, we can wait until you feel safe to ride."

It's a good idea, and I let him help me into the water. It's cool but strange. The sand is soft but doesn't go deep. Instead, I feel land beneath. "I'm alright."

"Did you have a premonition?" Liam keeps his hand on my back as we walk a few feet away from the centaurs.

"No. It was you. I sensed your worry." Lowering my voice to a whisper, I add, "Your jealousy. I felt the strain of being responsible for me and for my mother. It was as if our hearts were pounding together. I felt disoriented, as if I was looking through your eyes."

"I'm not jealous," he grumbles.

I look at him, knowing he's lying.

"Perhaps a little, but I'm a grown man. I can control my wayward thoughts." He places his hands on my shoulders and looks into my eyes. "I felt it too. A moment where my thoughts were mingled with yours."

A million questions, none of which will help save Momma, fly into and out of my head. "It's distracting and bad timing."

"That much is certain. I will put up a block at least until we are ready to think about more than saving Birdie and getting to safety." He looks a little sick as he closes his eyes.

As if the radio static has been shut off, I hear only my own thoughts again. It was not that I knew what he was thinking. No. It was more that his mind was static. Perhaps because I don't know how to listen yet. I find myself grasping for that noise now that it's gone. My heart sinks.

Walking me back to Jadar, he says, "It's not permanent, sweetheart."

It still aches to be cut off from him, even though I hadn't realized there was that connection until a moment ago. Shouldn't it take time to have something before I miss it?

Liam lifts me onto Jadar's back.

Once he's back atop Belloc, he waves to Corell, who starts the march again toward the black obelisk where Venora holds my mother.

"Tell me if I must stop." Jadar's voice is stern and filled with worry.

"Of course." I clutch his waist as we crash through the water.

Ahead, the ocean grows dark. One by one, the centaurs enter the deep water and swim.

I grab hold of the strap between Jadar's armor plates as we enter the deeper area. I can swim well enough, but it's good to have a handhold to keep me moving. I kick my legs, so he doesn't have to drag me along with his weight.

I'm out of breath in a few minutes. I really should get more cardio into my routine. Luckily, the deep water doesn't go very far, and soon I'm once again atop Jadar's back. My lungs hurt, and catching my breath is not easy. It's shameful since the centaur did most of the work.

Feeling more useless than ever, I force my breathing to slow.

"Are you alright, up there, little savior?" Jadar laughs as he runs easily through the shallows.

"I'll live and don't call me that." I'm certainly nobody's savior or the vision in a prophecy. Still, somehow, we're going to save my mother, even if I have to give myself to do it.

Even with Liam's mind blocked from mine, I know he'll never allow that. The thing about Texas women is we don't always do what the men around us want.

"How much farther is it, Jadar?" I lean against his armored back and hold on.

"There are many miles of this cursed place. Try to rest."

Tired of my own thoughts and doubts, as well as the endless sight of still water, I give the tower my attention. "What can she do with an obelisk if that's what's inside there? And why would she hide it?"

Jadar's arms pump on either side. "She would draw power from the demon realm to bolster her magic. It's dark, dark spells that have been forbidden since the time before the old gods. She breaks all of Domhan's laws by building such a thing. Perhaps that's why she conceals it. I don't know. Its appearance at the edge of the horizon was a bad omen."

The farther west we ride, the taller the black tower grows. A chill runs up my spine.

Laughter, female and horrible, echoes in my ears. "What is that sound? Who's laughing?"

Slowing his gate, Jadar looks over his shoulder at me.

Concern is etched in the strong lines of his masculine face. "There is no laughter, Wren."

I shake my head, and the sound slips away. "I think I heard the witch queen."

"Can she hear you?" Tone sharp, he rides faster to converge with Corell, Belloc, and Liam.

How would I know that? "I'm not sure."

When we reach the others, Jadar tells them what I said I heard.

Rather than delay further, Corell shakes his head. "Let's get to the watchpoint. Then we can decipher this new information."

"And if I'm accidentally giving the enemy information?" My stomach is in knots.

Liam shakes his head. "You have a gift of premonition. There's no reason to believe your gift is shared by Venora or anyone else. It's more likely that you relaxed for a moment and heard some piece of the future."

I let my breath out and relax. He's right. I've never heard someone in the present. It's always been the future that I hear and see. I nod and force a smile so he knows I'm alright.

Even though the centaurs all seem outwardly calm and unconcerned about this journey and what I heard, they ride harder.

I have to hold on tight despite the smoothness of Jadar's gait. Trying to relax, I hope my bottom holds out long enough to get to this tower and that I'll still be able to stand when we arrive.

A Crown of Wind and Water

It's long past dark when we reach the watchpoint. I don't know what I expected, but I'm glad the debris field of fallen trees, branches, and leaves is stuck on a large sandbar. Even so, it's not exactly the Ritz.

As expected, it takes me some time to get my legs back under me. I'm sore from the neck down.

The tower is big enough that it blocks out one of the moons. Well, I guess the other is a planet. At least, that's what someone said. To me, it looks like a purple moon.

My fear for Momma is not relieved by being closer to her. The black monstrosity makes me nauseous. It seems to ooze evil. It's the same way I feel when I see a sociopath on the news, and they tell of his or her crimes.

Liam finds me near a huge, waterlogged tree. "Come." He holds out his hand. "Corell is questioning the soldiers on duty. You'll want to hear."

Threading my fingers through his, I walk to the group of centaurs seated in a circle.

I whisper, "Can't she just look out of her tower and see us here?"

"There is magic in place to prevent our detection," Liam says, kissing my head in a way that is very familiar and nice.

"Come sit," Corell says.

Belloc brings over a semidry log and places it for Liam and me to join the circle.

Corell nods once we're still. "I have news that the witch

queen is indeed inside the tower. She flew via her shadow demons and landed at the very top of the tower. So, there is at least one way in."

"Not a very convenient entrance." I should stay silent, but my brain and my mouth are not always on the same page as my good sense.

All heads turn to stare at me.

Liam smiles. "No. Not helpful for us to enter. Maybe we don't need to go inside at this moment."

Frowning, Corell says, "How do we bring her to task if we don't go inside? We should find a way in, get Birdie out, and destroy this abomination."

I like the sound of that.

"Our goal is to save Birdie Martin. Destroying the structure, while it would be nice and satisfying, is not imperative. We don't know what it is. We have no idea what kind of monsters she has inside. If this is an obelisk, there could be fire demons or worse behind the walls." Liam's voice is strong and calm. He's every bit the son of a leader. Looking at each centaur one by one, he gauges their expressions before focusing on Corell.

"I don't disagree," Corell begins. "How do we get Birdie out even if we don't destroy that thing, which looms too close to the lands of my people. Do you have some plan in mind?"

Turning toward me, Liam looks conflicted. "You will have to agree to this."

"If it brings my momma to safety, I'll agree to anything." My voice is clear and stronger than I feel.

His lips barely register a smile that doesn't reach his eyes. "We have only one choice. The only thing we have that the witch queen wants is Wren. To get her to come out of the tower and show us Birdie, we have to show her the prophesied human woman."

"You would trade a life for a life?" Jadar stands and stomps his hooves.

It's sweet the way the centaur has taken to me. I'm half afraid he has a crush and half flattered that it might be true. "I'm willing to save my mother no matter the cost, but I don't think that's what Liam has in mind, Jadar."

"I want to provoke the witch queen. Venora is vain in the extreme. My parents have told me many stories of her exploits. I think we can enrage her enough to win this battle. The destruction of the tower will have to wait for another day."

Wellon's long blond hair is pulled back in a queue, and his thick arms are crossed over his chest. "And what if she sends her shadow demons to take revenge on our homes?"

"Farress will have the village secure." There's pride in Corell's voice. "She'll expect retaliation if we succeed, and she'll be ready. The centaurs cannot be turned."

Letting out a long breath, Liam slumps his shoulders. "Perhaps not, but you can be enslaved, and you can be killed. I don't want either of those things for your people. I would much prefer our friendship to continue and to fight by your side in the coming war."

"Elves and centaurs have not fought side by side since the old gods walked the land of Domhan." There's wonder in Belloc's voice.

"Yet we are here together in a single cause." Liam rises. "I don't know how it came to be that neither elf nor centaur broke the silence of these centuries, but I do not wish to return to ignorance. My people think yours are vicious killers without moral sense or caring. Now that I know this to be a lie, I'd be proud to fight with and for the centaurs."

Wellon says, "We were taught since birth that elves care only for themselves and would not lift a hand to save a centaur were they to find one dying in the river. I know now that this is not true. There is no haughtiness in Liam, son of Elspeth Riordan, though you are the only elf we've ever known."

With a laugh, Liam confesses, "I know a few elves who are ignorant and some who are haughty. I know many more elves who would be extremely happy to know centaurs are nothing like we have long believed. My mother would welcome you at her table and in her home."

"This is dangerous for the centaurs." Corell stares into the darkness.

Crossing the circle, Liam stands in front of Corell. "It is not my business. I apologize if I overstep. Can you give your mate a message to head north?"

"You ask a lot. If it were just for me, I would agree and risk everything to help." He sighs. "A moment."

Liam returns to my side while Corell closes his large, red eyes.

"What's happening?" I lean toward Liam and whisper.

Voice hushed, Liam speaks into my ear. "Corell and Farress are true mates and can speak with their minds. They also rule the Western Centaurs together. He'll not make such a decision without her full agreement and while ensuring the safety of his people."

"How can you know all of that?"

He stares into my eyes. "Because it's what I would do in his place."

My heart expands inside my chest, and I cannot look away from his gaze. I swallow hard and try to wrap my mind around how perfect he is while remembering why we're sitting in this damp, horrible place, in a strange world, with very little chance of survival. "How will we get Momma out of there without getting all of these centaurs killed or me taken by Venora?"

"Magic, sweetheart. You're going to have to use your magic." He shares his sexiest grin.

"You've lost your mind. I don't even know how my magic works. Why don't you use your own magic? Do you have magic besides mind control over unsuspecting humans?" My anger rises, but it's more fear than rage.

"I do. You and I are going to work together. Magic is something we have to learn, but it's also innate. I'll hide the centaurs and create a distraction. With my help, you can make this work, but you're going to have to trust me the same way I trust in you." In front of a dozen centaurs, Liam cups my face in both of his hands. "I have complete faith in you, Wren. Your magic is exactly what this situation calls for."

"Is this all some crazy leap of faith about oracles and prophesies?" There's no hiding my sarcastic tone.

Smiling even brighter, he kisses the tip of my nose. "I doubted the oracle and the prophecy until now. We all need to believe for this to work." He turns his attention to the centaurs, who are all watching.

"Do we even know if centaur magic and elf magic will meld?" Pallon sits beside his brother, shaking his head.

"Let's find out." Liam opens his palm facing the sky. He mutters something I don't understand. A golden ball of light forms in his hand. It's like a small universe with swirling light and shadow. Rising, it hovers over his flesh, then moves to the center of the circle. Liam looks at Pallon. "Make my magic larger. I give you leave to alter what is mine."

The words feel important.

Pallon stares at the golden ball of light. He says something in the centaur's guttural language.

The light grows larger and brighter, doubling in size.

Corell cocks his head. "Good." He makes a grabbing motion with his left hand and the light disappears. "Farress agrees that we must join in the fight for Domhan. She will move the centaurs north and hopes to meet us by the river after we have retrieved Birdie."

"I am honored, and my people will be grateful." Liam bows his head.

Worry mars Corell's handsome face. "Since you plan to make a showing and gain the witch's attention, I assume we shall wait for daylight."

"Yes." Liam meets the centaur leader's gaze. "The shadow demons are not as strong in daylight."

"They carried our foals away before the sun went down." Jadar's tone is matter-of-fact.

"We can only use the knowledge we have, my friend. Shadow demons are less likely to mount a successful attack in daylight. It's strange what happened with the young. Perhaps in time, we'll better understand the dark magic."

"I wonder if that will be a blessing or a curse." Jadar stands. "I will take the first watch."

Belloc walks with him to the perimeter of the magic that shields us.

Returning to sit beside me, Liam says, "He's not wrong."

Corell lowers to the sand in a position that reminds me of

how a cat might rest. "No, but we have little choice if we are to defeat the evil and send their souls to rest."

Sliding to the soft sand, I lean against the log.

Jadar trots over and hands me the blanket that had been my cushion during the ride here. "This will keep the damp away."

"Thank you." I stand and lay the blanket on the sand.

Smile firmly in place, Liam sits beside me, leaving no space between us. "I think Jadar is enamored with you."

"Are you jealous?" I'm teasing, but I can't help noticing the way his jaw tightens.

"More than I have any right to be." He watches as the centaurs circle the perimeter.

Changing the subject, I ask, "Why is there no breeze here? I've never seen a place so still."

Looking around, he shrugs. "I'm not certain. Perhaps the lost land and the curse of its sinking have stolen the wind."

"Sounds ridiculous." I lean my head back on the hard wood and close my eyes. "Maybe the loss of land caused some kind of odd weather pattern." It's a much more sensible idea, even though not much has made sense since I arrived here.

"You may be right. I suspect it's this lack of air movement that brought Venora to this place. The demons she creates would have an easier time moving about with no wisps of wind." He eases my head up and slides his arm under so that I'm lying on his biceps.

Much more comfortable, I sigh. "And the evil. Even I can feel it."

"Yes. This is a dark place." He pulls me close and kisses my hair.

I open my eyes as I lean against his strong side. Centaurs sleep in a circle around us. "Do you have to give permission for someone to affect your magic spell?"

"Not strictly, but with it, the bond is stronger. Also, it's polite." He smiles, meeting my gaze. "I'm sorry this is the way you came into my world. I wish I could have shown you the beauty and wonders of Domhan."

"Perhaps those are yet to come." Trusting that Liam and the centaurs will keep me safe, I sleep.

Chapter Ten

LIAM

I've been a soldier for my entire adult life. For more than fifteen suns, I have trained and fought. I have faced Venora's army and her creatures on the battlefield more times than I can count. Yet walking across the shallows of the lost land toward the black tower, I'm more afraid than at any time I can remember.

As a soldier, I am prepared to die. I am not willing to watch Wren come to harm.

Focusing on the magic that shields the centaurs, I feel their strong yet rough magic bolstering my spell. It's my first time feeling the energy of centaur magic. They are nothing like I expected, leaving me ashamed of the prejudices of my people.

Both Martin women immediately called out the ugly way elves view the other species who share our world when we've made no attempts to know them.

"Are you alright?" Wren asks as we get close enough to see the smoothness of the seamless stone rising from the sand and water. It's as if the tower were cut from one piece of black glass that sucks in the sunlight rather than reflecting it.

"I worry that I'll not be able to protect you." I'm relieved that I closed my mind to her, as I worry my fear will be reflected back to me.

"We follow the plan. The point is to get Momma back and stay alive. Nothing more." Her voice is tight, and a slight whip of wind disrupts the stillness.

"Easy, sweetheart." I keep my voice soft and soothing, even as a thrill runs through me at seeing her magic pushing to get free.

I stop far enough away that we can see the top of the tower. The evil emanating from it makes bile rise in my throat. I've never felt anything like it.

Wren whispers, "When this is over, if I never see that horrid thing again, it will be too soon."

"Ready?" I wish I felt more so.

"As I'll ever be. Though I feel like a cornered cat." She pulls her shoulders back and stares up the side to the top. "Venora Braddish, I am Wren Martin of the human world. You will return my mother to me unharmed."

The first shadow demon floats out of the tower. It's soon joined by many more.

"They know we're here." My instinct to draw my sword is so strong that my fingers itch. Reminding myself to stay with the plan, and that a blade is of no use against shadow demons, I call my magic and hold the golden ball tight in my hand.

From high above, Venora's voice fills the air. "Another

puny human woman who thinks she can best me. I am the ruler of this world. None can command me."

"I only want my mother. Send her down safely, and we can talk about whatever you want." Chin up and voice clear, Wren shows none of the fear she must be feeling.

Pride for her courage swells inside me.

"Who is that with you, human? Is that another of Elspeth's spawn? Shall I tell you what I did to your brother, Riordan, or would you prefer to be surprised when you meet him on the other side?" Even at the distance of an eighty-foot-tall monstrosity, her eyes meet mine, and the venom she feels toward my mother reaches me.

Hearing that one of my beloved brothers has fallen cuts like a knife deep in my soul. Still, I hold my emotions at bay. She wants a reaction. She uses fear to manipulate people. "My mother is the true queen of Domhan. My brothers and I have always been willing to die to serve her."

"You will make an excellent shadow demon, and I will revel in absorbing your magic. I can already taste the sweetness of your power, like liquor one can't get enough of." She points to the demons flying in a circle around the peak. "Bring him to me."

They swoop down and their shrieks rise to a deafening pitch.

I call the golden light, and when they close in, I put myself between Wren and the evil and throw the light while calling for fire.

My magic streaks across the air toward the shadow demons.

A wave of centaur magic blasts into the gold, and it erupts so brightly, both Wren and I have to shield our eyes.

Two demons are shredded to nothing, and their essence falls to the water like ash.

"Not possible," Venora cries. "What have you done?"

Wren steps to my side. Her voice is gritty and commanding. "Give me my mother back right now."

Face twisted with hate, Venora reaches through a magic wall. Her hand disappears for a moment. She pulls Birdie into the daylight by her hair.

Birdie squints against the sunlight. Probably blinded for a moment before she focuses on us and the long fall she faces if Venora lets go. She locks her gaze on Wren and screams, "Run!"

"Never," Wren says under her breath. "Send her down here unharmed or you will regret ever being born."

Venora's laughter is sickening as she hangs Birdie half over the edge of the parapet. "I make no deals. The only way this useless human lives is if you trade your life for hers, chosen one." The last two words are biting and disdainful.

"Why don't you come down here and get me?"

Gripping the hilt of my sword and conjuring another ball of fire, I swallow my desire to grab Wren and run to keep her safe. Instead, I whisper, "Don't take it too far."

"You are so small. Do you think I have to lower myself to reach you? That tiny human mind has no imagination." A bolt of black lightning shoots from Venora's free hand. Sulfur fouls the air. Magic powered by the demon realm stinks of it. These are lessons from my youth.

Rather than attack her quarry, the bolt is headed straight for me. I leap out of the way, and the water explodes around us.

Unharmed, but wet, we barely catch our breath before

the shadow demons swirl toward us. There must be a hundred of them. It's a wonder their shrieking doesn't deafen us all. The closer they get, the more grim the impending outcome. It's the effects of those who have lost their souls and their magic to the witch queen. I must fight the sense that there is no good in the world.

When they are nearly on us, I scream, "Now, Wren!"

Venora shoots another bolt of her dark magic toward the ground.

Wren's cheeks turn bright red. The water around her feet pushes back as the wind swirls around her. She screams, and the wind gusts upward as she pushes her palms toward the demons. The demons struggle against the gale, but it blows them back.

Changing her focus to Venora, Wren sends the wind up the side of the tower.

Venora stumbles back from the edge, similar to what we saw in the dream, her lightning shifts and arcs away, harmlessly hitting the water in the distance. She looks at Wren with black eyes. "You want her, you can pull her broken body from the lost lands before my army kills your false heir and brings you to me." She throws Birdie over the side.

Birdie's screams fill the air.

Even with my mind closed off to her, Wren's horror, rage, and fear wash over me.

I use my magic to slow Birdie's fall, but I know it won't be enough.

Wren stretches her arms wide and brings them together, her palms slapping above her head. The water rushes forward and up until it meets Birdie's flailing arms and legs.

Centaur magic binds with mine to further slow her descent.

As the water falls back to the land, I snatch Birdie into my arms before she can crash.

Still thrashing and screaming, Birdie takes a moment to realize she's safe. Her face is swollen and bruised, and her shirt is torn at the shoulder. She grips me like I might not be real. "We have to get out of here. She's hiding them." She points west.

Fifty yards past the tower, the water churns. There is only one thing that can make water move that way. The marching of troops through the shallows. The horizon shimmers, and one by one, elven soldiers dressed in black with a red V signet at the chest appear and march toward us.

Venora's horrible laughter hurts my ears.

With Birdie's arms and legs clinging to me, I grip Wren's arm and back up. "We have her. Time to run."

Wren turns, and together we rush past the centaurs.

I toss Birdie onto Wellon's back.

She screams but hangs on to the centaur.

Once Jadar plucks Wren from the water and puts her on his back, I swing onto Belloc.

Lightning pierces the air, and the stench of sulfur comes with it. It strikes the water to our left, forcing us right.

Looking back, I let the shield magic fall as I'll need my strength for the battle to come. A thousand troops rush toward us.

A black cloud of shadow demons swoops across the sky. Several lift a centaur, and when they reach a fatal height, they drop him.

A Crown of Wind and Water

My gut knots. They outnumber us ten to one. We cannot win in a full battle.

"All who defy me will pay the price." Venora's voice rattles the sea. She hurls a fireball east across the lost lands. There is no doubt of its destination. The magic needed to create such a missile is disturbing. She should be weak from the conjuring, but she stands on the parapet and watches gleefully as it explodes in the forest where the centaur village is.

That maniacal laughter fills my ears.

Several centaurs stop their retreat and shoot arrows into the enemy line.

They are exposed to the shadow demons, who rush in and pick up two more and drop them. Their bodies break on the ground beneath the shallow water.

"Retreat! Retreat!" A shadow demon whisks by me, and a chill runs up my spine. A mad idea, not fully formed, wakes in my mind. "Belloc, get me close to Wren."

Without question, Belloc rushes dangerously across the galloping centaurs until we're next to Jadar and Wren.

Her eyes are wide as she clutches the centaur's armor in a death grip. Seeing me, she screams, "They're dropping the centaurs to their deaths." The horror of it is clear in her tone.

"You have to get us out of here."

"What? Me? How?" She looks around as if the answer will be found somewhere in the charging centaurs.

"The same way you caught your mother with the wave. It will have to be big, and the wind must push the shadow demons back as well. I'll help with my fireballs."

Wren stares at our retreating troops. She focuses on the

water, then closes her eyes. Her lips move without any sound.

The rushing away of water leaves us on dry land, and the centaurs increase their speed, which puts some space between us and the oncoming army.

I turn on Belloc's back and throw balls of fire at the shadow demons.

The centaurs' magic sends a charge across my skin, making the hair on my arms stand on end.

The fireballs expand and explode, destroying several of Venora's stolen souls.

As the water rises behind us, it pulls many of Venora's soldiers off their feet and washes them farther away from us.

Forming a wave, the water flows back in a rush, scooping us up with a hundred centaurs and carrying us northeast toward land. The power of Wren's wave is more than I could have imagined. It's many minutes before we begin our descent, and she sets us down gently. We're miles from where we started, perhaps more than a day's ride. The tower looks small, and it's too far to see if the witch queen still watches.

If Venora has enough power left after destroying the centaur village, she could send another missile, but I think she expected her soldiers to best us in battle. "I think we've gotten away."

"It's a miracle," Belloc says but keeps running through the shallows of the lost lands. The beach is in sight, and no one will feel safe until we reach solid land. "Now to get out of this cursed place."

Wren sits with her shoulders slumped.

"Wren?"

"She's well, just tired." Jadar's voice is full of concern, but he gives me an honest nod to let me know she's in no danger for the moment.

Birdie's left eye is swollen shut, and her face is bruised. Her cuts and dried blood will need tending. She stares from Wren to me. "Did my girl do that?"

"She saved you and then us all. Wind and water are at her command in a way I've never seen in an elf. This is a different kind of magic." I hate to say that I owe the oracle an apology for not believing in their prophecy, but the last few days have made me a true believer.

We continue at a steady pace, but slow from the breakneck gallop as our shadows grow long. The entire party is nearly falling from exhaustion. Where we land is mostly marshes, but we find a dry knoll and stop to make camp.

Wren and Birdie fall into each other's arms, both crying.

Corell steps beside me. "If nothing else goes right, we have done a good thing in bringing mother and daughter back together."

I nod. They are a family, and knowing one of my brothers may have fallen makes me yearn for that closeness.

As if she heard my heart, Birdie looks up from the embrace with her daughter. She holds an arm out to me. "Liam, come here."

Walking into her embrace, I wrap my arms around both

of them. Watching Birdie fall from that parapet was one of the most horrifying moments of my life.

"How did you do it?" Birdie asks. "How did you save me from that fall?"

"I didn't save you, Birdie. It's the greatest miracle that you survived, and I couldn't be happier, but I cannot take the credit." I tighten my arm around Wren's back.

She keeps her head down.

"But you caught me. I know you caught me." Birdie pulls back and looks at me. Her one uninjured eye is wide.

I press my fingers over her battered face and channel enough magic to heal the damage. The swelling immediately reduces, and the black and red flesh fades to a healthy pink.

Birdie's expression eases as her pain subsides. "Thank you. You wouldn't have anything for a few broken ribs, would you?"

"That ride must have been torture." I cringe just thinking about the pain she endured because of me. "Come, I can try to heal it."

Jadar hands me the blanket from his back.

I place it on the sandy grass for Birdie to lie on.

Her movements are slow, and her face twists with the pain from something so simple as stretching on her back. It's a testament to her strength that she made no complaints on the long ride. "You didn't answer my question."

I close my eyes and place my hands over her ribs. Heat emanates through her blouse.

Her hand covers mine.

Opening my eyes, I meet Birdie's gaze. "I meant what I told you. Wren used her magic to save you, and the wave that carried us away from the tower was also her magic."

A Crown of Wind and Water

Wren kneels next to her mother and combs Birdie's hair off her forehead.

Before Birdie can speak, Wellon trots over, his expression full of concern. "You are injured? What can I do?" He curls his legs under him and leans in, looking for something to do for her.

Patting his cheek, Birdie smiles. "I'll be fine. This was not your doing. When that witch realized I wasn't the one she was looking for, she threw me against a wall with her nasty magic. The ribs cracked then. Lord knows what Liam will find as far as them being placed as they should. It's been a hell of a few days."

She's right about that. I'm not the greatest healer, but I can visualize the injury, and her bones have begun to heal out of place. "You're going to need a stick or something to bite down on."

Several centaurs gather around. Corell says something in their language, and Pallon rushes away. "We are with you, Birdie."

"Corell. It's good to see you. Are the children alright? She didn't hurt them, did she?" Her eyes widen. "The fireball. Oh no." Tears stream down her face. "The village."

"It's alright, Momma." Wren kisses her mother's cheek. "Don't get riled up."

"The village was empty," Corell says. "We knew there would be vengeance once Venora saw we had moved against her. Farress leads the rest of the Western Centaurs north."

Birdie lets out a long breath and winces. "I'm so relieved." She looks around at so many staring down at her. "I can't believe all y'all came to save me. Thank you."

Pallon returns with a stick with a diameter of about an

inch. "This is the best I could find. There are few trees in this region."

Taking it from him, I say, "It will do. Thank you." I force a smile for Birdie. "Your ribs have begun to heal badly. The process to make them right again will be painful. I'm sorry, but there is no help for it."

Birdie nods, and when I offer the stick, she puts it between her teeth.

Holding her mother's shoulders, Wren asks, "Is there no other way?"

"Not out here. We still have five days to journey. These ribs will pain her the entire way if I don't get them fixed now." My gut is in knots. "I'm sorry."

Even with the stick in her mouth, Birdie gives me a smile. "Do it."

"Wellon, I will use my magic to set the bones properly. Once that is done, you can gently add to my power for the healing."

Wide eyed, Wellon nods vigorously, and his hands open and close with his distress.

I grip his shoulder. "Gently, Wellon. If we heal her too quickly, we could do more harm than good."

The centaur takes a deep breath and lets it out. "I will only add what you allow. I understand." He touches Birdie's shoulder. "You will be well again."

"Hold her, Wren. The ribs have to break to be set, and that's going to be painful, even with my magic to ease the way. I'm not a natural healer. If my brother Aaran were here, this would be a simple thing." My heart and pulse are racing. I'm more of a field dressing kind of healer. In battle, I can stop bleeding until a true healer can be reached. This is delicate work.

Wren touches my shoulder. "We trust you, Liam."

The soft tone of her voice, with her clear gaze, calms me. I press both hands to Birdie's midsection and close my eyes. Three ribs have begun the healing process, and all are out of place. Willing my magic forward, I pray to the old gods for strength in gifts that are not mine. I send power to the misaligned breaks and feel the pop of each one as it cracks at the healing point.

Birdie's screams are muted by the stick she's biting.

I have to push aside my worry over her pain. It can't be helped, but with my magic flowing through her, I feel the sharpness of it and grit my teeth. I don't have the strength to use magic to ease pain and still have enough to heal her when the sun is nearly gone from the sky.

The worst is over. I move the bones into place. As I begin the healing, I open my eyes and look at Wellon.

His sharp magic thrusts against mine, hard at first, but then he gentles the flow and boosts my power. One by one, we mend the bones, then heal the bruised tissue around them.

Once I'm sure it's done, I say, "We've done it, Wellon."

His tail flicks once, but then he lets out the breath he'd been holding and stops the flow of his magic.

I do the same and find a teary-eyed Birdie staring up at me. "How do you feel?"

After lifting herself to sitting, she hugs me and then Wellon. "You are both miraculous. It's as if they were never broken." She pokes the spot. "No pain at all."

Exhausted, I slide from my knees to sit. I wish there were

sunlight to reenergize my magic, but it will have to wait for morning.

Birdie stands. "I'm going to want to know more about your magic, baby girl." She points to Wren for a moment before she walks off with Corell and a few other centaurs.

They recount everything that happened from the time Birdie went to the black tower.

Resting on my elbows, I lean back and watch how full of life and joy she is. What a crime it would have been if she hadn't survived. A rush of relief fills me, as if I had just snatched her from the waters and tossed her atop Wellon's back.

Wren lies next to me in a similar position. "You look tired."

"Don't you want to listen to the stories?" I point to where the centaurs are building a fire to sit around for the night.

She shakes her head. "Momma is in her element. She must really love the centaurs. I like them too. I wonder what Venora is doing and why she didn't follow."

On the long ride to land, I had a lot of time to think about that. "Magic has a price. She gathers her strength from the demon realm, but there is still a price to pay, and one must recover. I'm in the light, and my magical strength comes from the sun. Tomorrow, I'll regain what I've lost. How Venora recovers, I don't know, but that fireball she used to destroy the centaur village will have cost her. She's powerful, but not smart enough to conserve her energy for better use. She might have won that battle had she preserved her resources.

"So, we should be grateful the enemy is unwise." Wren rests her head on my shoulder.

The fire blazes and then recedes to a warming ember. The centaurs use magic to heat stones. It's a handy trick.

Birdie tells them about her ordeal and how Venora tried to extract magic from her. The pain she describes is enough to make me want to vomit.

"It's not your fault, Liam," Wren whispers.

"My only purpose is to protect you, and as I brought her here, I must protect Birdie. I never wished for her to become a pawn in this war. I don't want you to be either. If you asked me to, I would find you a portal back to your world. I would find a way to get you home." I'm the worst soldier for offering this, but my heart can't bear what I've asked of these humans. They are too precious for this world.

Her voice is soft and kind. "What would your mother say when you arrived at the castle without the human woman from her prophecy?"

"I don't care."

"Of course, you do." She points to Birdie. "Does that look like a woman who is ready to tuck tail and run?"

Adhar swoops down and lands on the ground just in front of the blanket. She looks at us, cocking her head from one side to the other.

"Where have you been?" Wren asks the bird. "I'm happy to see you're safe."

With her little legs, she scratches at the sandy soil until she's made a little nest, then she lies in it and closes her eyes.

"I'd be willing to bet we're safe for the night." I watch the bird go to sleep in the midst of a large party of soldiers and warriors. "I think she's a familiar."

"You mean like a black cat for a witch? I've never really understood the concept." Wren wraps her arm around me, and we lie back onto the blanket and the soft ground beneath.

Threading my fingers through hers, I close my eyes. "A familiar is an animal guide of sorts. They often know when danger is coming, and they also can help guide their master to the right decision."

"Are they always birds?" Her voice is soft and sleepy.

"No. They can be other animals. I've never known anyone who's had a familiar. It's rare in this time. I only know what I was taught from books."

"I think Venora lied about your brother." She yawns.

"What makes you think so?" The idea of one of my brothers being gone is too much to contend with. As a soldier, I can push my emotions aside for long periods. When Wren and Birdie are safe, I'll let those sorrows out.

She shrugs. "I'm not really sure. It's more a feeling than a knowing. It felt like she was lying to distract you. Maybe to enrage you since that's how she responds to adversity."

What she says makes perfect sense. Still, I push aside hope as well as mourning. What I don't squander is the wonderful feeling of falling asleep with Wren in my arms.

Chapter Eleven

WREN

It's not yet light when I wake up with the distinct feeling of being watched.

Arms crossed, and her hip jutted to one side, Momma stares down at me. She looks ready to burst out laughing or scold me.

I can't tell which. The funny thing is, I'm not at all embarrassed. I could never feel shame over what's happening between Liam and me. He may not be human, but he's good and kind, and always does what's right, even when it's not what his mission calls for.

Liam's arm is slung over my waist.

With a resigned sigh, I ease his hand up and over my torso. I get up and walk far enough away from the camp that we won't wake anyone.

Momma wastes no time. "I knew you two were getting chummy in Scotland, but this looks more serious."

"Why? We were just sleeping." I toe the sandy soil and watch the dust carried off by a breeze. It's nice to have a bit of wind after the unnatural stillness of the lost lands.

"That's just it. You were sleeping. Once you were safe, you went to him for comfort, and he was more than willing to provide that service without any promise of sex. To me, that means you're either good friends or there's deep feelings involved between you. Care to tell me which it is?" Momma watches me, and I know she's looking for lies or signs.

There's no point in avoiding a subject with Birdie Martin. If she wants to know something, she will find out. "He's a good man."

"No one here will argue with that." She raises her eyebrows and waits for more.

"Momma, I don't know the answer. He's a good man. I'm probably falling in love with him. And we're from two different worlds. He's not human, and I'm not an elf. Where can this lead besides heartbreak?" My throat closes, and I swallow down the emotions clogging it. I sit on the ground and cross my legs.

Dropping down beside me, Momma says, "We never really know how anything will end, Wren. Maybe we'll all die tomorrow. Would you wish you'd never met Liam if you knew that was the outcome?"

Would I? The idea of never having met Liam is too sad to bear. "No. I wouldn't want to give up knowing him even if that were the inevitable outcome. It might well be, based on the last few days."

"Saving a world ain't easy." She smiles and slaps my knee.

My gut is in knots. "I don't know what I would have

done if I'd lost you, Momma." I lean into her embrace. "There was a moment when we first arrived and Liam knew that we'd been shifted forward in time, where I thought he'd drag me across the country to his home and leave you to your fate."

"It would have been the logical thing to do for a soldier following orders." She keeps one arm wrapped around me and plucks at the grass with the other. "I was resigned to dying in that horrid tower. I hoped you'd one day find out what became of me. I prayed you would understand that I couldn't let that witch hurt those children if I had the means to prevent it."

Nodding, I say, "It was exactly the kind of thing I'd expect you to do. I always know you'll do what's right, even if it's not what I want for you."

"But Liam is another story?"

"He surprised me when he agreed we had to go after you. He surprised me when he was cordial and diplomatic with the centaurs. He surprised me when he believed in me and my abilities so much that he let me fight the witch queen. I guess I don't know him at all if everything he does is a shock." It's hard to breathe as I admit that the man I might love is a mystery to me.

Momma releases me and lifts my chin to meet my gaze. "You know, baby girl, you've not had too many good men in your life, and that's probably my fault. I won't apologize, though. If I hadn't made all the mistakes that drove your grandma crazy, I would never have gotten you." She grins. "You know what I'll do in every situation because you've known me your entire life. Liam is new and pretty darn shiny. You don't have to anticipate his responses. He's here and now, so watch and see what he does. Don't expect the worst just because other men have been low-down dirty dicks."

I laugh. Momma does have a way with words. "I can hear his thoughts. Well, I could, and then we decided it might be better if he locked that part up so we don't get distracted."

"This magic thing is interesting. You can move water and hear Liam's thoughts?"

"I can move wind, too. That's how I blew away the shadow demons. I don't even really know how I do these things. Though I can feel the energy filling me before it happens." I wish I could explain it better.

"It's miraculous," she whispers, and her eyes are far away.

"Momma? Are you alright? The things you endured, if you need to talk, I'm always here for you."

Her smile is sad. "I appreciate that, Wren. I may take you up on that offer at some point. It's just a bit too raw at the moment. Right now, I'd like to push it aside. Maybe when we get where we're going, I'll tell you everything." She chuckles. "Or maybe there's an elf psychologist who I'll spend a week or so with."

I want to help her. I can see there's pain and more behind her eyes. Momma is the kind of person who is so full of joy that her pain can sometimes be stuffed away for a long time. "Maybe so."

To the east, the sun crests the horizon.

"Do they have a sun over there, too?" Momma points west across the lost lands.

A ball of red moves toward us, growing larger, and it

doesn't rise into the sky, but pushes fast and with purpose. "Liam!"

The camp wakes at my scream.

Liam rushes to us. He looks in the direction Momma is still pointing. "Kron from Coire! Get ready."

"What is it?" I squint, trying to figure out what the fiery thing is.

"It's a fire demon." He grips his sword in his right hand and one of those golden energy balls in his left. "You need to stay back, Birdie."

"I'm already going." Momma rushes around the centaurs and stands beside Wellon.

"How do we defeat it?" It's still too far away to see exactly what it is, other than it appears to be made of fire or lava. It glows bright orange and moves steadily toward us. "Can we outrun it?"

He shakes his head. "It's moving faster than you think. By the time we reached the river, we'd be exhausted, and it would have caught up. We must make our stand here."

Finally, the shape of the demon becomes clear. A round body, with spindly legs like a giant spider. "I hate spiders."

"Can you push it with the water?" Liam sends his magic across the lost lands, and as it hits the demon, it explodes.

Pausing, the demon rears up on several legs before continuing toward us. If the magic had any effect, I'd say the spider got bigger.

I'm about to say so when Liam fires off another round. This one grows with centaur magic, and the explosion sends water and sand flying in every direction.

Adhar screeches above us. Her warning is also too late.

The Kron is double its original size.

"Stop. It's feeding off the energy." I grip Liam's arm and push past the barrier he put up to block my thoughts. *You cannot defeat it this way.*

The muscles in his arm ease as he looks at me. For a moment, he looks as if he may argue with me, but then his eyes soften. "What do we do?"

You've gotten yourself into shit now, Wren. "I don't know." I look from him to the demon barreling toward us with flames bursting from its center and steam rising from the water. I push down the sense of utter panic rising inside me. I'm just a jewelry maker. But that's not true. I'm more than that now. Maybe I've always been more than what I believed. Everything in my new reality seems like a dream-slash-nightmare that I should be waking up from.

The centaurs continue with a barrage of arrows that barely slow the demon.

I slip my hand into Liam's. He is solid and strong. He's the most generous, wonderful man I've ever known, and he needs me.

Letting the tingle of magic rise inside of me, I pray that water will douse the fire within the demon. I close my eyes and imagine the shallow water drawing toward the spiderlike creature from this world's hell. When I open my eyes, I thrust my hands forward.

The lost lands shimmer. The damp wetlands beneath our feet crackle as the moisture seeps away.

At least ten feet tall now, the demon's legs were easily managing the two feet of water, but now that level is at least five feet, and it's slowing the monster down.

"Yes, Wren. You've got the idea." Liam squeezes my hand, and his bold magic flows through me, adding to mine.

My heart pounds, and a bead of sweat rolls along my hairline. I imagine the water rising higher and enveloping the beast.

Foot by foot, the waters of the lost lands rise around it. When its legs can no longer keep its body above the growing waves, it flounders.

The centaurs stop their assault and cheer my accomplishment.

"How do I kill it?" A sharp jolt of doubt rushes through me. "Will it drown?"

Liam transfers my hand from his right to his left. He steps behind me so that his front is firmly against my back. He puts his right hand under my arm, where I'm directing my energy toward the water. "Somehow, you are the key to this, my love," he says softly in my ear. "Inside you is the knowledge of how to defeat this demon. Pray for the result you want. I will go with you wherever your magic takes us. I am with you. Don't be afraid."

And there he is. His mind, at the edge of mine, making me see my potential, lending me strength without forcing my hand.

No demon or witch is going to take him away from me. I'll die first. With the water still rising, the monster is slowed, but not stopped. I can't hold it like this forever. It will make its way ashore and burn everything in its path. Eventually reaching us or some other innocent beings.

Lifting my hand an inch higher, I pull Liam's hand to my heart and tighten my grip. "We can do this." Unleashing all the growing magic within me, I see the waves crashing over the demon before it actually happens.

Liam gives me his magic and a stream of blue light, just like that of his missiles, pours from my outstretched fingertips. The magic light cuts through the water and slices the drowning monster in two.

Rather than sink or even bleed, the demon reforms into two smaller spiders that glow under the wave.

Heart sinking, we stop the flow of light magic. I push aside my disappointment and think of how I must protect these centaurs, my mother, and Liam. If I don't stop this, no one will.

A wash of Liam's pride fills me. His voice is soft in my head. *You can do this.* "You can do anything," he says aloud.

I think it's the wonder in his voice more than his belief in me that strengthens my resolve. Killing anyone or anything has never been part of my life. I'm no soldier or warrior. Still, when you threaten those I love, I will defend them.

I form an image in my mind of the demon obliterated. It hurts none of my friends. In the aftermath, I visualize Venora's pale face as her magic is defeated. "She's manipulating that thing. She's using her magic." I draw myself to my full five feet two inches and focus on the two creatures that have nearly swum to the edge of my water wave. Pulling the water closer to keep them immersed, I focus on Liam's light—the magic tingles inside me.

This time, as the blue light cuts through, I push the water inside, blending my magic with his. Rainbows shine through the stream, and when it hits the beasts, it doesn't cut them. Instead, it fills them until they reach their capacity, and light explodes inside them, destroying the dark magic.

A Crown of Wind and Water

A flash of Venora's face and her shock burst into my mind for an instant. Her already pale skin is almost gray from her evil efforts. A second later, she's gone from my inner vision.

A cheer rises from the centaurs as Liam pulls me tight into his warm hug. "How did you know?"

Turning in his embrace, I crane my neck to meet his gaze. His skin is pale, and his eyes lack the fire I've grown accustomed to. "Know what?"

"How to destroy it?" He brushes my wild curls from my face and tucks several strands behind my ear.

I cup his cheek. "Are you alright?"

"We used a lot of magic. I'll be fine." He rests his hand over mine.

Momma runs over and wraps her arms around us both. "I've never in my life seen anything like that. Those monsters never had a chance against the two of you joined in battle. I thought my heart would plum jump out of my chest when it became two. What kind of world is this, where a demon can just pop up out of hell and attack good people?"

"The kind where evil is close to winning the battle," Liam says as he releases me and takes a step back. His shoulders slump, and he turns toward the sun.

"Son, are you alright?" Momma touches his arm, and her eyebrows draw together.

"Magic always has a cost, Birdie. I need to rest for a while." He struggles to climb the small, dry knoll.

I rush to his side and wrap my arm around his waist.

After a short hesitation, he leans some of his weight on my shoulders. My pulse is racing. "You gave too much."

"It was necessary." Even his voice has lost some of its normal strength.

Jadar eases Momma out of the way and takes Liam's other side. "I will lend you some of my magic to speed the healing process."

The tick of pressure in Liam's jaw eases after a moment. "I would be grateful for the help, friend."

We help Liam sit in the grass where our duffels and backpacks are stacked, and I kneel beside him. "Why didn't you stop before you gave too much? Why didn't you ask for help?"

Sitting like a cat at rest, Jadar lowers himself so he can reach Liam. "Your mate is right. You could have taken power from a centaur to supplement your magic." He places his hands over Liam's chest and closes his eyes.

My skin tingles with the warm and forceful centaur magic.

Fear of losing this elf tightens in my chest. I've fallen in love, true and lasting love, for the first time in my life. I could have lost him today. I could lose him at any moment. Part of me wants to run away and forget any of this ever happened, but that is no longer an option. I won't abandon Liam, these centaurs, or Domhan.

A tiny voice echoes in my mind, warning me that one day, I'll go home to Texas, and my heart will break into a million pieces, just like those demons exploded with too much light magic.

After a minute, Liam's skin brightens, as do his eyes.

Jadar pulls his hands away. He grins. "The rest the sun will restore."

A Crown of Wind and Water

Shaking Jadar's hand, Liam says, "Thank you."

I had been so focused on Liam and my worries that I never noticed that several centaurs, including Corell, gathered with concern for Liam.

Corell nods, and they disperse. Corell says, "We should be safe to rest here for a short while. You can recover your strength while the sun is high."

Remaining seated, Liam takes slow, even, deep breaths. "One hour. Then we'll need to move on. The lost lands are full of darkness. We shouldn't remain this close for too long."

In agreement, Corell steps away and gives orders to his centaurs to rest for one hour.

Momma steps close. "Will you be alright, Liam?"

With a weak smile, Liam says, "Yes, Birdie. I'm fine."

For the briefest moment, Momma's eyes fire up the way they do right before she's about to give me a long lecture. She kisses his cheek and sits with Corell and Jadar. I guess she decided he's been through enough.

"I think you should explain to me how magic works." I settle in beside him, and he wraps his arm around my shoulder.

"I don't know how your magic works. All I know is that it's linked to your desires and prayers. At least, that's my guess. I'm no oracle." Stretching his legs, he crosses his feet and leans back on the duffel bags.

"What about your magic? Why did you get so weak? I felt my own energy failing, but once I stopped expending the energy, my body was fine." Like the true teacher's daughter, I need to understand everything.

"Maybe your magic and your body are separate. For an elf,

that's not the case. We are wrapped and weaved with our magic. Small things are not an issue, but there are spells that wear us down. Today, I pushed a little too far, but I could not have let you stand alone. I'll admit, I should have asked the centaurs for help, but this friendship with them is new, and I didn't think of it in the moment." He closes his eyes and holds me tighter.

"So, if you push your magic to its limit, it could kill you?" The last two words come out shaky.

"It is possible." Liam opens his eyes and turns his head to meet my gaze. When he speaks again, his voice is soft and just for me. "I heard your thoughts and worries, sweetheart. I have no desire to lose you either. You are a gift that I never expected to receive in my life. Leaving you or seeing you leave me would break me."

Emotions well up within me, and a tear slides over my bottom lid. The future has no choice but to rip us apart.

The future is a tricky thing, my love. He kisses my forehead, letting his warm lips remain there an extra moment.

I release the worry of tomorrow and warm into his affection.

Adhar lands three feet away with a disgruntled caw. She hops close to Liam's side with something in her mouth. She bobs her head and warbles some message. In my head, I hear *hand.*

"I think she wants you to open your hand." It's still odd to hear or sense the thoughts of a bird. Somehow, Adhar gives me a sense of order when she's near.

"We'll have to do some study on familiars when we get home." He opens his hand a few inches above the ground in front of Adhar.

Cocking her pretty white head, she steps up and drops

something from her mouth. It's a small brownish berry. Strange.

Liam's eyes widen. "Where did you find this?"

She nudges his hand with her beak.

"What is it?"

Looking from the berry to the raven, his voice is filled with wonder. "It's a leighis berry."

Unfamiliar with the name, I wait for more.

Liam studies the fruit as Adhar flaps her wings, agitated with his delay.

"I don't know what that means, but she wants you to eat it." I reach across and pet her head, trying to soothe her.

"Leighis berries are scarce. So much so that this is the first I've seen outside of a drawing in a book. It's said they have remarkable healing properties." Liam's voice is filled with wonder.

Corell and several others have stopped what they're doing to listen and watch.

"Do you think you should eat it?" As much as this bird has come to mean to me in the short time since she attached herself, I'm not sure of her motives or alliances.

"Would you eat something Adhar gave you because she insisted?"

Considering the question, I move my arm away from my lap, and Adhar hops onto my forearm and stares into my eyes as if she too is waiting for the answer. I scratch the feathers at the back of her head, and she lowers her crown for more attention. "I would. I believe she's here to help us."

Without another word, Liam pops the berry into his mouth, chews it twice, and swallows.

I stare at him, waiting. Honestly, with the events of the last few days, I'm not hopeful.

With a little pressure on my arm, Adhar spreads her wings and lifts into the air.

"How do you feel?" The suspense creates a knot in my gut.

Head lowered, he stretches his arms and legs, then presses his hand to his chest. "I feel fine. Actually, I don't know if I've ever felt this good in my life. Not one ache." He stands and twists his waist one way and then the other. Rolling his shoulders, he shifts his head from side to side. "If the things written in the books are correct, leighis berries can only be found on the far side of the Cumbachdach Mountains. The giants of those mountains are said to covet the berries, and rarely is one seen in the elven cities. Where in Domhan did Adhar find one here?" He looks across the terrain.

"They grow on bushes?" I can't help wishing he'd come back and sit beside me, but I subdue the thought before he senses it.

"Yes. Low brambles with long thorns. They tend to prefer shaded areas near the midmountain elevation." He shrugs. "At least that's what the books say."

Scanning the terrain, I don't see any mountains. "Well, either the books are wrong, or Adhar is more than she seems."

"Perhaps we shouldn't tarry here. If the raven sped your recovery, it must be for a reason." Corell gives orders to the centaurs to move on.

Offering his hand to help me up, Liam's smile is private

and just for me. "I, too, would prefer to lie here beside you for a while."

I move to grab my duffel, but Liam pulls me into his arms and holds me for a long moment. "One day, I will relish the moments we can tarry, and hold each other, and make love, Wren."

"The things you say, Liam." After a quick squeeze, I push him away and sling my pack over my shoulder.

Chapter Twelve

LIAM

The ride to the river will take two days if we ride hard during the day and rest only at night, but I fear that's a grueling pace for Birdie and even tough on Wren. They are my responsibility, and for the first time in my life, that means more than just keeping them alive. I want them healthy, and as happy as possible. My entire way of thinking has shifted since they came into my life. If I could spare Wren this journey, I would. Safe in the human world is where she should be, but even the idea of her leaving me burns a hole in my heart.

Honestly, I never considered I could feel anything so intense for anyone. Even so, I've closed off our mental connection. Now that I know she can break through the walls I've put up, I know that if she needs me, she can reach me.

Curiously, she's managed all that she has these last few days, never having used magic before.

We stop in a young wood. The trees here are only forty or fifty suns old. Compared to the forest where the centaurs lived, where the trees had stood for hundreds or maybe a thousand suns. Trees like those can communicate with each other. Their souls have evolved. These young trees are silent but afford good cover, and there's a stream nearby where we can wash and replenish our supply.

Several centaurs have gone hunting. Birdie insisted on going with them, claiming she is a fair shot with a bow and arrow.

I set up bedrolls for Birdie and Wren, then hesitate before setting up my own a few feet away. There are more critical things to worry about, but every moment away from her is torture.

Walking to the stream, I find Jadar standing with his back to the water about twenty feet away. He blushes. "Wren wanted to bathe."

My body's instant reaction is no surprise. "You can go. I'll keep watch."

Jadar looks more relieved than I would have thought. Perhaps he knows this is one woman who is not for him despite his attraction. He trots toward the camp.

I hold my desire in check and step closer, keeping the row of low shrubs between me and my view of where she's splashing. "May I join you?"

There is a louder splash, then silence.

"I can remain here if you prefer privacy, love." Even if my desire screams something else, it must be her choice, this attraction between us.

A Crown of Wind and Water

"I thought Jadar was keeping watch." Her voice is soft but without fear.

"He's gone back to camp." My blood rushes through my ears and to other places as well.

The water gently splashes. "You can join me."

I round the shrubbery. She's on the opposite side of the small but deep stream and facing away from me. Her bare shoulders peek out of the water, smooth and pale against the shadows on the water as the sun begins to set. I untie my boots and toe them off before stripping out of my shirt and trousers.

"Why did you send Jadar away?" She keeps facing away from me.

"I didn't want to be put to shame by the sight of an aroused centaur. They are half horse after all. He looked ready to die from being so close to you and knowing you're naked." I step one foot into the water.

"That's not true." She spins, and as soon as she sees me, her gaze shifts to my painfully hard cock. Cheeks bright red, she doesn't look away, but her stare moves back to my face.

I sink into the cool water and swim toward her. "Are you telling me you never noticed that the very handsome, young, warrior centaur has a crush on you?"

She stays in place, probably because her feet touch the bottom, and if she comes toward me, the water is too deep for her to stand. "Jadar knows that you and I are...together."

Her hesitation tightens my chest. "Knowing it and stopping his attraction may be two different things. He looked very relieved to be allowed to get away from your naked and *unavailable* body." I stress the word to make sure she knows I have no doubts about our status.

She takes one step toward me, and her shoulders sink beneath the water. "I have not encouraged him."

"No. I know. I also know that you are beautiful, brave, powerful, brilliant, and irresistible. I hardly blame the man for wanting you." A few feet away from her, I stand on the soft sandy bottom and step closer.

When I touch her upper arms, she looks at the water rather than meet my gaze. "What's happening between us is as terrifying as it is wonderful."

I wrap my arms around her and back her up so that it's easier for her to stand. "I know. I also know that it's gone too far to back away. I don't think I exist without you anymore."

Pressing her cheek to my chest, she wraps her arms around my waist and caresses my back with those soft fingers. "I'm glad I'm not alone in that."

"You're not alone in anything, Wren. I'm with you in all ways." Despite the cool water, my shaft is still on alert, and with her in my embrace, it's pressed thick and hard between our bodies.

"I thought cold water had the opposite effect on men?" She runs her foot along my calf to my knee, bringing her center closer.

I slide my hands down her back, squeeze her full, luscious ass, then grip her thighs and lift her. My cock splits her slit making me groan with need. There's a lot of satisfaction when her initial yelp of surprise is followed by a mewing and rubbing for more. "You are more enticing than the cold water is a deterrent."

"Is this a bad idea?" Her crystal-blue eyes are full of worry mixed with need.

I walk us to the creek bed and place her atop the steep embankment. "You're right, this will be more convenient."

Cocking her head, she's holding back a smile. "That's not what I mean."

I kneel on the damp sandy soil and place her thighs on my shoulders. Looking up into her sweet face and seeing both worry and longing there, I choose. "I know what you mean, but I can't let you go. Not now, Wren, not ever." I bury my mouth in her sweet center and press my tongue to her sensitive bud.

Placing her hands behind her on the soft grass, she lifts her hips and digs her heels into my back.

Tasting every inch of her, I come back to the pearl that makes her bite her bottom lip to keep from crying out. "One day, we'll make love in a place where you can scream as loud as you want. I want to hear you cry my name."

Opening her eyes, she stares into mine with desire burning in the depths of her. "Liam."

"Anything you want, my love." I lick her and suck until she's lifting her ass from the grass to get closer and feel more.

I slide two fingers inside her wetness and my cock jumps painfully as she lets a soft cry escape, her body clamping around my digits while she pumps hard and fast with her release. As she relaxes, she opens her eyes. "One day, I'm going to return the favor, but right now, I need you inside me, Liam."

The love in her voice as she says my name shoots into my heart like an arrow set aflame. Releasing her thighs, I stand. Whatever she sees in my expression, she backs away from the edge and gives me room to climb out of the creek. I cover her body with mine. Our damp skin rubs together.

Wren bends her knees to accommodate the width of my hips and opens herself fully.

Notching my head at her wet slit, I press inside slow and steady, and it's like coming home. This woman, her body, everything about her was made for me.

She moans with the stretch, and I cover her mouth with a deep kiss. Her tongue meets mine at every sweep as if this is a dance and we are perfectly matched. Holding still, I wait for her to move her hips and let me know she's ready for more. She tips her pelvis to take me deeper, grips my hair with strong fingers, and mews into my mouth. Her other hand scratches along my shoulders, her nails scraping my biceps.

I pull out to the tip, then press forward, filling her again and again, until our bodies are moving as one, and light in her eyes is all I see. Breaking the kiss, with my elbows holding most of my weight, I hold her head in both hands and stare into her magnetic eyes. I need to see her come.

Her core pulses, and her mouth opens, though nothing comes out. Passion and pleasure reflect back at me. She pulls me over the edge, and I moan against her lips as I spill my seed deep inside her. I can't pull out. As wise as that would be, I can't bring myself to leave her perfect body.

As the orgasm ebbs, I break the kiss and pepper small ones along her jaw and cheek. "I love you, Wren. You are my home. I will do whatever I must to keep you safe and stay at your side."

"Liam." The corners of her lips tip up, and she closes her eyes. "Don't make promises you can't keep." Despite her words, she lifts her hips, giving us both an extra shudder of pleasure.

A Crown of Wind and Water

My cock is so sensitive to her flesh, I ease out of her. Wren's cry is soft, and I can't tell if she's tender or missing the connection as much as I do. However, staying buried inside her until I'm hard again is not an option, even if it's an alluring prospect—*one day*.

Wordlessly, we climb down the embankment and swim across the creek. I wash quickly and help Wren, which nearly sends us back to the beginning. With a laugh, she restrains herself and lifts her exquisite body out of the water. She dries without taking her gaze from mine.

I remain in the water until she's clothed, hoping the coolness and the fact that I was sated a few minutes ago will be enough to quell my need. "You are driving me crazy, and I think you know it."

Her sweet smile and round eyes make me laugh. "You just had me. Surely, you don't want me again."

I step from the creek with my cock in my hand. It's satisfying when her eyes widen at seeing how much I still want her. "There is nothing that will stop me from wanting you, not even having you."

I expect her to back away, but she stands her ground, and when I reach her, she drops to her knees and replaces my hand with both of hers before running her tongue around the head.

"Wren, you don't have to..." I caress the crown of her head and along her jaw.

With a hint of a smile, she sucks me deep into her mouth until my cock hits the back of her throat before she pulls back with tight suction.

My knees nearly buckle as pleasure swamps me.

Again and again, she draws me in and lets me out,

keeping constant pressure. Her soft fingers wrapped around the base hold firm as she massages, and with the other hand, she cups my tight balls.

It's the most erotic sight, and it takes all of my strength to hold my orgasm, but that can't last. "Sweetheart, if you don't stop, I'm going to come down your pretty throat."

Her low moan hums along my flesh, and passion flashes in her eyes.

Threading my fingers through her hair, I lose control. No one could resist the way her pleasure hinges on mine. It would take a god to resist the longing and the vibration along the flesh of my shaft. I'm no god.

On her next release, her teeth scrape my sensitive flesh. Her tongue sweeps across my head and she sucks me deep, opening her throat and taking an inch more.

The tingle begins at the base of my spine. My legs shake. Nothing but her mouth, her body, her crystal eyes, exists in my world as I lose my thin control. I spill my seed for the second time and when I try to pull back, Wren's pretty mouth tightens around me, and she grips my ass to keep me in place.

She swallows again and again, not letting one drop free.

The camp is close, and I have to stifle the calls of pure ecstasy erupting within me. My chest aches, and I swallow down every groan. "Gods above," I whisper as the last shiver of pleasure rushes through me.

Letting me pop from her red lips, she stands. "I hope I did that right."

She must be joking. Stalking forward, I grip her upper arms and back her against the nearest tree. The bark is rough, but it's a young tree and not yet sentient. Glad she hadn't yet put her shoes on, I unbutton her jeans and pull the zipper down before stripping them down her legs. "You do everything right." I grip her breasts with both hands through her shirt—the nipples pebbling under my palms.

Her gaze shifts to my already recovering cock. "Already? Are all elves like you?"

"I hope you never find out the answer to that question." I can't even imagine Wren with anyone else. The notion makes me feel ill.

"You're quick to jealousy? I would never betray you, Liam." She brushes my hair behind my ear and trails her fingers along my jaw.

I lean into her hand and kiss her palm. "I know and yet, the idea of it makes my blood burn. Everything with you is different."

She cocks her head. "How?"

"I've never felt possessive or wanted to be possessed. No lover can compare to how I'm compelled to be at your side." I run my thumb over her nipple.

"Just my side?" With a wicked grin, she turns to face the tree, grips the trunk, and lowers her torso until her ass is high. She steps her feet apart, exposing her wet folds.

A low growl rumbles through me. This woman may be the death of me, but there is no help for it. If this is how I'm destined to perish, I'll die a happy man. I slide my fingers through her wetness and dip inside. Her sheath is soft, warm, and silky.

She moans and leans back for more.

My cock jerks and my balls ache despite having come twice in so short a time. Every moment when I'm alone with Wren is an opportunity for pleasure that I won't refuse. I tease her bud and thrust two fingers inside her again and again until she's fucking back into me in earnest and her bottom lip is tight between her teeth.

I replace my hand with my cock while sucking her sweet juices off my fingers. "By the gods, you're like nectar I'll never be able to resist."

She peers over her shoulder. "I hope not."

Thrusting inside her, I bury myself to the hilt. Gripping her hips, I take full advantage of the position she's given me. She's pure perfection, and I won't last long, but every stroke is everything a man could want. Tight and soft, her sheath grips me as alluringly as her mouth did.

As I slide forward, she slams back, taking me deeper. "Fuck. Liam. Harder."

At her command, my balls tighten. I give her what she wants, what I want. Pounding inside her until I can't bear the pleasure, and her body contracts around me. Again, I fill her with my seed. It's reckless, but I need to give myself to her. I long to see her grow with our child. The idea of anything else seems pale and dishonest.

Clutching her hips, I fold over her back and trail kisses along the back of her neck. "At some point, we'll have to join the others and eat something."

She groans and wiggles her ass, teasing where we are still intimately connected.

It takes all of my control to ease free. I wrap my arms around her and turn her in my embrace, kissing her hair and breathing in her flowery scent. "I could live on a steady diet of just you for the rest of my life."

Resting her cheek on my chest, she wraps her arms around my waist and lets out a long sigh. "Yes. Let's stay here and starve to death but have incredible sex until we die."

If only it were that easy. "I'm afraid we'd be found, and there is still the problem of the witch queen to deal with."

On a groan, she steps out of my hug and nods. "Yes. I guess we'd better do something about her, but when this is over, I will need you to myself for an extended period of time without interruptions."

"I promise." It's an easy vow to make. How this works out without heartbreak, I have no idea, but I'm willing to do whatever is necessary to stay with Wren, if she'll have me after what I've put her through and what is yet to come.

Once we're cleaned up and dressed, it's long past dark, and we weave our way through the trees to the camp. A small pile of rocks glows with magic-created heat. It's less dangerous and more efficient than a fire, not to mention harder for our enemies to see.

Birdie is already asleep on the bedroll I laid out for her.

My bedroll is unmoved, but Wren's has been placed beside mine. I lean in and whisper, "I didn't want to presume. I had put your bedroll next to your mother's."

Even without much light, I can see her cheeks glowing pink. "I suppose Momma approves."

As soon as she sits on the thick blanket, I join her. "Would it matter if she didn't?"

"Yes. It would matter to me, but it wouldn't change anything." She leans her back against my side.

Jadar carries two leaves filled with roasted deer meat. His gaze averted, he hands the food to each of us. "We saved you some food." The young centaur, who is usually so full of life, looks as if he'll never meet our eyes again. I don't know if it's because he knows we were making love, or if his attraction to Wren is causing him shame. Either way, it's not necessary.

"Thank you. We've worked up an appetite." I laugh.

Wren's cheeks burn red. "Liam. My word."

Surprise registers on Jadar's face. He looks at Wren, then at me with wide eyes before bursting out with a full, deep laugh. Without comment, he backs away, rejoining the other centaurs as they begin to find their beds for the night.

My stomach growls at the scent of well-cooked deer. I eat quickly, then go to a bucket set out for hand washing. Returning to Wren, I bring the bucket for her to wash, then return it for everyone's use. I toss the leaves we're forced to use as dishes into the woods.

Lying beside her, I let my hand rest on her hip. "Was the food enough?"

"Yes. It was good. Why did you embarrass Jadar?" She curls her upper arm under her head.

"He was already embarrassed. I just let him know we have nothing to hide. He has a crush on you. He knows you are not available. He wasn't sure how to act, and he was shy about his reaction to knowing you were naked in the stream. I gave the situation less gravity." I squeeze her full hip and pull her back to my front, letting my hand settle over her abdomen.

There's a long pause before she relaxes against me. "Very diplomatic. Will you be king one day?"

I laugh louder than is appropriate. Several centaurs turn to see what could be funny. I lower my head and relax. "No. If we don't all die in this war, and the curse can be broken, my brother Aaran will be next in line for the elven crown.

However, my mother will live a long time, and there is the curse that currently keeps men from ruling."

"Yet you have cultivated diplomatic skills." She yawns.

I kiss the back of her neck. "I like to put those around me at ease. I have good instincts about others. It is useful, even for a soldier."

Rolling to face me, she opens her eyes. Panic in her tone, she says, "I wasn't implying that your profession was less important than your brother or mother."

She's the most beautiful woman I've ever seen. Her soul is as lovely as her face, maybe more. I brush her hair out of her eyes and tuck the wild curls behind her ear. "I know, sweetheart. I'm not offended. My brother is an excellent diplomat as well as a good man. I am confident that he'll make a fine king if the curse is lifted. As it is, no man can rule Domhan, and if Aaran tried, he would likely perish very quickly."

She rests her head on my arm. "Tell me more about this curse. Because it seems counterproductive to have no females born, but no males may rule."

I lie back and pull her so that she is tucked against me with my shoulder for a pillow. "The witch queen cursed the land to keep any male from ruling the elves. She likely meant to protect her crown from the lovers she takes. However, the old gods can twist this kind of dark, evil magic. No elven women have been born in these last thirty suns. If my mother were to fall, there would be no one in her line who could rule while the curse exists. A younger female elf might take up the battle against the witch queen."

"When Venora took the white tower, how did the elves in the light escape?" Wren relaxes.

"Mother saw the evil coming. She tried to stop Venora, but half the army was turned into shadow demons, and the rest were forced to retreat. It was clear then that my mother had allowed Venora to become too powerful. She'd underestimated the dark magic and the lengths to which the witch queen would stoop to increase her power." It's not easy to keep emotion out of my voice.

"Your mother made a mistake." There's no judgment in Wren's tone. She squeezes my hand. "No one is perfect, Liam. She saved all she could."

That is true. "I've heard the curse has affected other races as well, though not for as long. I think the dark magic is pushing outward."

"Most of the very young centaurs are male. I heard the women lamenting over it in the village before we left. I didn't think anything of it at the time." She yawns again.

"Sleep, Wren. Tomorrow will be a long day." I wrap her in my arms and hold her and push aside a past that I was too young to alter. My mother did the best she could under terrible circumstances.

"Let me hear our songs?" Emotions, whose source I don't know, tighten her voice.

Opening my mind, I allow her song and mine to merge, then filter it into her welcoming essence.

"I love you, Liam." On a long sigh, she closes her eyes, and her head grows heavy.

Kissing her forehead, I'm filled with the joy of all things Wren. "I love you, too."

Chapter Thirteen

WREN

It takes a full day to reach the river, but I'm told that in the south, the Naomh River splits in two, and the villagers will have taken the eastern fork while we are on the western fork. It will be three more days before we reach the main source, then another two before we finally reach Tús Nua and Liam's home.

Adhar flies above us, keeping watch. The tug of a connection to the raven niggles at the outskirts of my attention.

Jadar is quiet compared to his usual teasing.

Perhaps I should break the ice. "Do you know much about familiars, Jadar?"

His shoulders pull back, and he holds his head an inch higher. "It is unusual for a centaur to have an animal who serves them, but I have read about them in the village scrolls."

"What do the scrolls say?"

He's at a smooth canter, and it doesn't seem like carrying me makes his work any harder. He speaks as if we were both at rest. "Familiars are animal guides or partners. They are said to be sent by the old gods or at least with old magic. The reason one person is chosen to be the subject of a familiar is not certain, but it is considered a great honor. Even Adhar may not know why she was compelled to find you."

It makes no sense. "So, she'll follow me around for the rest of my life or hers. What is the purpose?"

"The scrolls say that a familiar will merge with the subject over time. You should be able to sense things from Adhar."

I search the sky and find my feathered friend circling over us. "What kinds of things? So far, she's only told me her name and given us some warning of danger."

"She also brought healing to Liam. Leighis berries are scarce and don't grow anywhere near here." A soft scolding tone replaces Jadar's shyness.

"That's true." It's not that I don't appreciate the beautiful white raven and her attachment to me. It just feels as if there should be more.

"The scrolls say that a witch with a familiar can tap into the senses of the animals. I read a story of an elf who saw the world through the eyes of her cat. When the cat sneaked into the enemy camp, the elf saw the number of soldiers, the layout, and how many were on watch. She was able to count the arrows and swords. That's a handy gift." Jadar shifts with the turn of the river.

Ahead of us, Liam is on Belloc's back. They're keeping

pace with Corell. Liam's shoulders are broad and his back straight as he talks to the centaur leader.

The grassland is flat and dotted with trees. Long blades sway with the wind and remind me of the Gulf of Mexico, where we'd go on vacation in the summer.

Momma is laughing with Pallon and Wellon as if they have been friends all their lives.

"Do you think it's possible I could see through Adhar's eyes?" I find her in the sky once again.

"I think you would need to ask her for that connection," he says in a sage tone, which doesn't suit him.

I try not to laugh, but a short chuckle escapes. "You say that as if I'm in communication with the bird. It's not as if she speaks words to me. It's more like impulses." I think about the moments when she did *speak* to me. "Though when she told me her name, I heard the word in my mind. However, it wasn't a voice. It's hard to explain." Even to myself.

"Ask, Wren. There is no harm." He warns me to hold on as we jump a small stream, then continue following the larger river north.

It's foolish to expect the raven to serve me. I shake off the notion. "I wasn't sure you would wish to carry me anymore."

Looking over her shoulder, he meets my gaze. A slight blush rises on his face before he looks ahead. "It is my honor to bear you. However, if you are uncomfortable, other arrangements can be made."

"No." I wonder how Momma would handle this. She'd be direct, and once everyone was mortified, they'd get over it. "I'm flattered that you're attracted to me."

"But you could never look at a centaur with those feelings." He says it matter-of-factly and without any malice.

"That's not true. I think you are very handsome."

His shoulders pull back farther, and if I were in front of him, I imagine I'd see a puffed-out chest. "Then there is hope?"

"I'm afraid there is not. I think fate decided that Liam was for me long before I met him or you. As kind as your feelings are, I was always going to love Liam." I hope not to hurt his feelings, but honesty is always best.

"I understand. Can we remain friends?" A fallen tree lies in the way, and Jadar must swerve to keep from stumbling over it. He grips my arm at his side to keep me in place.

Catching my breath, I hold him tighter and close my eyes until we're back to a steady pace. "Of course. I hope we will always be good friends."

"That gives me pleasure. Now, as your friend, I suggest you try to talk to your raven and ask to look through her eyes. There is no need to feel foolish or to be afraid. I am the only one who will know if you fail." There is no need to see his face to know he's grinning.

"Ugh. You tricked me. Fine. I'll try." I force some displeasure into my voice. "Just don't knock me to the ground while my eyes are closed."

He places his hand over mine. "I will keep you safe."

Closing my eyes, I think of Adhar. I send my thoughts to her high in the bluish-purple sky. *Adhar, can I see what you see? Will you let me?*

At first, I feel nothing but foolish for trying to send my thoughts up to an animal. The newly familiar sensation of Adhar's presence sweeps through me. It's as if another part of my mind, one that's new and different, has opened. A moment later, I open my eyes and I'm soaring through the air. I feel the lift of a current under my wings and soar higher. The clouds are so close, I can almost touch them. Below, the land is flat, and the river splits the plains as they rise toward hills. Far in the distance, I see the hazy outline of mountains. Centaurs run in a triangular formation. From here, I can see Jadar in the center with me on his back... What? How?

Adhar croaks loudly several times.

I blink and I'm disoriented and slightly dizzy. I grip Jadar for life. Then it passes, and the wonder of what I've just done rushes into me. "I did it. I saw you and the river from the air. I saw hills and trees. The wind whipped through my feathers. It was amazing."

"I wish I could fly, but I think centaurs are not meant to leave the ground."

Considering where I am, it's not strange that my mind immediately goes to Pegasus. "In my world, there are myths about flying horses. Not like centaurs, but they are winged. Now that I'm here and see how many myths from the books are real, perhaps there is a flying horse?"

"That would be something to see, but I've never heard of horses with wings. Perhaps that myth is from some other world." He slows to a trot as Corell holds up a hand, indicating we'll be resting near the river.

"How many worlds with life on them are there?" Legs tired, I slide off his back and have to hold on a moment before I can get my feet under me.

Holding an arm out for me to grab, he shrugs. "More than I can count and probably many more that we know nothing about." He cocks his head. "In your world, you don't use the portals?"

"No. No one even knows they exist. Most people think we are alone. Besides, humans don't normally have magic to open the portals." I don't bother to tell him that if they did know, they would probably be terrified and want to destroy any means of reaching Earth.

"It's arrogant to believe you are alone in the universe." His tone is flat.

"It is." What else can I say? Humans are fools to believe they are the only sentient life in the universe. Still, I won't be the one to tell them any different. They'd call me mad and lock me away.

Liam strides over without the slightest signs of having been on a centaur's back for hours. "How was your ride?"

"Fine," I lie. "I can see through Adhar's eyes. Jadar is a wealth of information about familiars."

As if hearing her name, the white raven lands atop a tree at the edge of the river. She croaks loudly and fluffs her feathers.

"That might be useful. I wonder what else your feathered friend offers." He shades his eyes to stare at her on her perch.

"I'm glad to be rescued, but my bottom feels as if a bear has mauled me," Momma says as she hobbles over.

Liam and I laugh. Jadar smiles.

I lean against Liam. "How long will we rest?"

Kissing the top of my head, he says, "Long enough to eat and drink."

A low, miserable groan rolls out of my mouth before I can stifle it. "Sorry. Momma's description isn't far off. I suppose I'll get used to it eventually." Even as I say it, I doubt it.

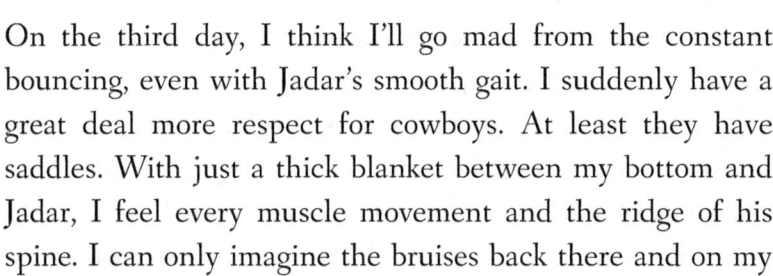

On the third day, I think I'll go mad from the constant bouncing, even with Jadar's smooth gait. I suddenly have a great deal more respect for cowboys. At least they have saddles. With just a thick blanket between my bottom and Jadar, I feel every muscle movement and the ridge of his spine. I can only imagine the bruises back there and on my inner thighs.

There's a tingle of awareness in my head, and I look up to find Adhar. She sounds a shrill alarm. I push my thoughts to hers. *Show me, Adhar.*

A moment later, I'm airborne with the sky around me and my friends far below. Adhar's cries force my attention forward. A dark cloud draws closer from the west. I wonder if the raven is telling me of bad weather coming, but my gut tightens, knowing this is something else. The cloud moves against the wind in a steady push directly toward us.

Snapping back into my own head, I scream, "Shadow demons," and point to the west.

There are no trees for cover. We're completely exposed, riding through an open plain.

Liam narrows his gaze. "It might be a cloud. Dark magic only two days from Tús Nua shouldn't be possible."

"That is no cloud. I've seen it from Adhar's eyes."

Jadar stops, and I jump down.

Corell orders, "We'll make a stand with the river beside us for Wren to use as a weapon."

My name and weapon in the same sentence still sound wrong. I should be making beautiful things for people to wear. Instead, I'm part of an army of centaurs fighting for survival. There's no time to point this out, so I nod toward Corell and take my place next to Liam.

Momma crouches behind Wellon and Pallon. They will do what they can to keep her safe.

As the cloud grows closer, the shadow demons begin to separate. There must be a hundred of them. I lose sight of Adhar and pray she's gone to ground somewhere that she won't be noticed. I grip Liam's hand. "How are we to fight so many?"

He has his mind sealed shut. "I don't know. I've never seen so many in one place. Why would she send such a force when the centaurs can't be turned?"

Horror tightens my chest. *Centaur bodies, bloody and broken, flood my mind. The ground beneath my feet is wet with blood that runs to the river. Flies swarm as there is no one left to burn them.* "They protect me, and she doesn't care about creating an army of beings she can't control. She plans to kill them. All of them."

His fingers bite into my upper arms. "What did you see?"

Tears stream down my face. "Dead. All dead." Out of the vision, the image is still burned into my memory. "I should give myself to her and save these centaurs. She'll kill them all."

"No. We will stop her." He locks his gaze with mine, and I can almost believe him.

A Crown of Wind and Water

Farther up the river, Farress lies with her head several feet from her body. The young and all the others are ripped to pieces.

I shudder. "She'll destroy their entire race just for helping me."

He shakes me and puts himself between me and the oncoming shadow demons. "That is only one possible future. We can beat her. We can win this."

"You don't even believe that. You have never believed that the elves had a chance against the witch queen." I pull back, trying to free myself. If I run forward and give myself up, these good souls will live.

Liam bands his arms around me. His voice is low and desperate in my ear. "I have changed. You have changed me. You're right, I always thought this was futile, but I never stopped fighting. Now, everything is changed. You have magic that can combat her evil. If there are three of you, who knows what is possible? Stay with me, Wren. Fight with me, please. I'm begging you. There is not one of these centaurs who would not die for the freedom of Domhan or you. They knew what they were taking on when they agreed to help us. Don't put their honor to shame by giving up."

Unable to stop my tears, I weep into his shirt. "If I give myself to her, you will live. I need you to live."

"If you die, I die. If we die fighting, then at least we do so with honor. Please. Stand with me."

My heart is breaking and coming back together so quickly, and agony erupts inside my chest. I nod. "For you. I will do what I can." I break from his embrace and look around. I expect to see blame in the eyes of the centaurs. I am the reason they will die. I am the cause of their misery and eradication. What I see are fierce warriors ready to defend their world at all costs. If they are willing, then I can do no less.

Momma stands up and looks at me. Pride and fire burn in her eyes. She lifts her chin, her faith in me shining bright.

I lower my head, then meet her gaze again. Texans don't surrender; we fight and survive. I dry my eyes and meet my fate, whatever that might be.

Turning toward the demons, I gather the magic roiling inside me and push the wind forward until they're straining to move.

Several break free and move to the east. A few more get out of my wind and break west, then swoop down.

Liam throws his light magic at them, and one by one they explode in a shower of ash and sorrow. "Ready?"

"We will add to your magic." Corell's voice is strong over the din of my wind and screaming shadow demons.

As he sends his ball of blue light into the air, my wind blows it right past the demons. Not good. Not good. "This is bad."

Liam puts his lips close to my ear. "You're going to have to let the wind go. I'll signal, and you drop your magic. Then be ready."

Oh god. "For what?"

"The gods only know." He forms another blue ball of light and lifts it into the air. "Now, Wren."

I stop the wind.

The light shoots into the middle of the cloud of demons.

They part to stay away from it.

The air sparks with centaur magic as it floods into the light, forcing it outward. It explodes, taking at least half the shadow demons with it. Ash rains down on us like the aftermath of a volcano.

The remaining shadow demons are still too many and no longer fly as one. They come down in groups of two and three.

Liam does his best to throw light on them, but there are too many, and his strength is waning.

My wind is of little use once they get close. All I can do is give Liam energy.

Corell is lifted into the air. They carry him fifty feet up and drop him.

Panicking, I draw the water from the river and catch him before he hits the ground. He tumbles and rolls as the water rushes back to its source, but he's alive.

More demons lift centaurs, and one by one they shoot into the sky. Six are taken up and dropped.

It's too many and too far apart. I lift the water again and catch Jadar. I shift the winds to force two more into the river where they sputter for air. I grab another with water, and when he lands, he hobbles to his feet.

Two more slam into the ground before I can reach them.

Belloc stares blankly at me as life leaves his body.

Fury rises inside me, and I know it's both mine and Liam's together.

He shoots a ball of light into the largest group.

Water reflects light. The words of some eighth-grade science teacher rush into my mind. I grab a stream of water, send it into the air, and wrap it around Liam's light.

The centaurs fill the elven magic with theirs until it explodes. Rainbows strike outward from the magic.

Demons screech and disintegrate as the water-infused

light streaks through them. Those few that remain flee to the east.

Pulling me into his arms, Liam sags against me. He didn't use up all of his strength this time, but enough that he's tired. "You were amazing."

A sob breaks through my control. "Check on Belloc. Maybe you can save him."

Releasing me, Liam turns. Corell and Jadar are kneeling by Belloc's still form. Corell shakes his head.

Mother kneels beside another centaur whose name is Toball. Tears roll down her cheeks. When she lifts her face and looks at me, the sorrow in her eyes breaks my heart.

Blood mars the soil and grass. I rush forward, but Jadar limps to block my path. "There is nothing for you to do here, Wren. You cannot save him."

Too many are dying. I struggle against both Jadar and the pressure in my head. I should have done more. I could have saved them if only I'd been stronger or faster. "I should try."

Liam wraps his arms around me, turns me, and pulls me into a hug. "I know this is foreign to you, but in war, there is always death, my love. These brave centaurs were not the first to die, and they will not be the last."

"Are you telling me that I'll get used to it?" My gut heaves, and I push away and run to the river. Kneeling in the grass, I vomit until my bones ache.

Liam sits next to me, rubbing my back. Tucking my hair behind my ear, he says, "I hope you never get used to death. Each loss should be felt and each person remembered."

I dip my hand in the water and rinse my mouth. Tears running freely, I sit a foot away from him. "Are you used to it?"

A Crown of Wind and Water

Stoic and calm, his eyes darken. "I have lived my entire life in a war and been a soldier since I reached my eighteenth sun. Death is my constant companion." He sighs and draws two long breaths. "No. I am not used to it. I didn't know Tobal, but he was well liked. Belloc was a fine centaur with a keen mind and a strong back. I did not know him long, but I will miss him. If ever the death of those we care about is meaningless, I fear we will have lost sight of what we're fighting for."

"If only I could have moved more water. Maybe I should have used air. I don't know how to save these beautiful people. Too many are dying." Renewed tears blind me to everything but my sorrow.

Liam reaches over and pulls me into his lap. "You were magnificent. Many more would have died if you hadn't been so brilliant. Think about your vision of them all lying dead. That was not the outcome. Your magic is a miracle. Jadar, Corell, and the others you kept from falling were lucky to have you there. You are not to blame. Venora is the villain here, not you."

Momma kneels in front of us. "I'm so proud of you, baby girl. You are so brave."

I look at her through watery eyes. "I don't feel brave, Momma. I let those centaurs die in such a horrible way."

She closes her eyes for a moment, and when she meets my gaze again, her eyes light with intensity. "You didn't let anything happen. You couldn't save them. No one could have. They died for a cause they believed in. That's what soldiers often do. You can't save everyone. What you did was amazing."

I nod.

"Good. Now, pull yourself together. The centaurs are building a pyre, and we'll need to say farewell to Belloc and Toball before we move on." Momma kisses my forehead and steps away.

Slipping out of Liam's arms, I return to the river and wash my face.

Chapter Fourteen

LIAM

The centaurs chant while the pyre burns, and they continue for hours. It's haunting and filled with sorrow. Perhaps if I knew their native language, I would also find the happy memories of Belloc and Toball.

The Martin women sit beside me by the river. We stood with the centaurs for the first hour, but backed away once the smoke became too much for Birdie. She and Wren cried for a long time, but they calmed down and started talking about the events of the day.

"How did you know to throw the water at the light?" Birdie asks.

Wren holds several pieces of grass, and she braids them into an intricate pattern. "I suddenly remembered Mr. Perkins' lesson on refraction and thought there was nothing to lose."

"Harold Perkins has a way with words." Birdie's voice gets a bit dreamy.

"Momma, did you date Mr. Perkins?"

Birdie blushes. "A few dates, but it was never going to work out, so we went our separate ways."

I have no idea who this Perkins fellow is, but my curiosity gets the better of me. "Why would it not have worked?"

With a slow, sad smile, Birdie looks me in the eyes. "Martin women only fall in love once, and as long as Wren's father lives, I'll never shake him."

This is stunning and disturbing. Even Wren looks appalled at the idea that Birdie won't let love into her heart because of a man who left her so long ago. "Do you know that he's alive?"

Taking the braided grass from Wren's hand, Birdie admires the pattern. "His name is Joe Cotton. He lives on the Atchafalaya Basin in Louisiana. He never remarried, but he lives with a woman named Jane. He still spends most of his time on a rig in the Gulf of Mexico, and he is not any more faithful to Jane than he was to me."

"How do you know all of that?" Wren takes the bracelet and ties it around her mother's wrist.

"I've shamelessly kept tabs over the years, and social media makes that pretty easy now. Maybe I should have given you his name, but I was so angry back then." She smiles at the rustic jewelry as if it were precious jewels.

Shaking her head, Wren takes her mother's hand. "No. I'm a Martin. Cotton doesn't suit. Besides, if he wanted to be part of my life, he's had twenty-six years to find me right where he left us."

"These men in your world are mad." I'll never understand any man giving up either of these women.

"Are all elves faithful?" Birdie asks with her usual openness.

"No. Not all relationships are based on trust and loyalty," I admit. "It's only my belief that you are worth staying for, my friend."

She kisses my cheek. "You are biased, son. I'll not scold you for it, though."

The chanting gets softer, and the centaurs begin walking in a circle around the pyre.

Sensing the end of the long ceremony, we three stand.

Taking Wren's hand, I feel her sorrow renewed. My ability to push death to the back of my mind is curtailed by seeing it through her eyes.

Wasting no time, we ride on in silence for the remainder of the day. It's only when the centaurs admit to growing weary that we finally stop.

I thank Pallon for transporting me. His long blond hair hangs around his face as he looks at the ground. He's thinking of Belloc, as am I. "It was my honor, Son of Riordan."

Not sure what else needs to be said, I remove the thick blanket from his back and lay it with the ones for Birdie and Wren. I wish I had words like my mother in these situations. If I've learned nothing else, I know there is nothing that will mend the pain of loss. Only time heals such wounds.

As we sit around heated rocks and eat, Wren asks, "Why is the witch queen able to use her magic so extensively without killing herself?"

"No one knows. We surmise that she needs rest and must restore her power; otherwise, she would keep attacking, but it took her three days to gain enough power after calling the demon from Coire before she could direct her shadow demons."

"I would think it would take a great deal of magic to manipulate so many for so long." Wren finishes her food and tosses her leaf into the heat of the stones. It sizzles and burns up in a moment.

Corell says, "There are those who say she pulls dark magic from Coire. After seeing that fire demon, I don't doubt that is true."

Wellon adds deer meat to the rocks, and it sizzles, its scent filling the air. "I have heard she steals magic from those she turns to shadow, and if she cannot turn them, she kills them."

"Some say it is her lovers who supply her with extra magic and life force," Jadar adds.

"Magic can be stolen?" Birdie asks. "I thought it was part of you, like blood or flesh."

Maybe it would be wiser to change the subject. Scaring Wren and her mother even more than the horrors of what they've already endured is not my intention. Still, truth always sits better with me. "Magic is an integral part of most beings who live in Domhan. It is part of our life, and to lose one's magic would be similar to going blind, maybe worse."

"Do you think she can steal my magic?" Wren holds a small stick and draws in the dirt. I think it's a design for a pendant, but it's hard to tell with the lack of light.

I wish I knew the answer. "She will try if she can, but human magic and the human world are foreign to her. She hasn't quite figured you out yet. If she knew all she needed to, she wouldn't have kept Birdie alive. She wanted to learn something."

"Maybe she did." Birdie rubs her arms as if she caught a chill on the warm night.

"What do you mean?" I pull a blanket out of my pack and wrap it around her shoulders.

Staring at Wren's drawing, Birdie won't meet my gaze. "She cast spells and did rituals while she had me. She seemed more frustrated than satisfied, but what do I know? I don't even have magic."

Wren wraps her arm about her mother. "I'm sorry I didn't insist you stay home, Momma. You'd be safe there."

"Safe, but alone and without any way to know if you were alive or dead. No. I couldn't have borne that, baby girl. I brought you into this world, and I'll defend the right of that until my dying breath. I'll not be back in Texas with no idea if I'll ever see you again. I'd suffer a thousand hours with that horrible witch rather than leave you." She lays her head on Wren's shoulder and closes her eyes.

"I don't know about the magic." Corell's voice is soft, and he smiles gently at the humans. "But the love of parent for child is the same as what we have here among the centaurs."

It's two more days to the point where the main river splits. The Giants' Bridge is within sight, and figures are crossing over the stone bridge. Its name comes from the heavy rocks that look as if they could only have been set in place by giants. In reality, no one knows who built the ancient bridge that has stood for a thousand suns.

Before I can pull my sword in case defense is necessary, the centaurs break into a gallop and start calling out the names of their loved ones from the village. A moment before, they'd been dragging and tired. Now they are imbued with a sudden burst of energy.

Farress stands on this side of the bridge, making sure each male, female, and foal crosses safely. Her blond hair blows in the wind. She turns in our direction, and even at this distance, her eyes brighten, and a broad smile shows off her beauty.

Suddenly out of place, I slip from Pallon's back and give the centaurs some privacy for their reunion.

I find Wren, and we walk to the river. She splashes water on her face, then wipes it with the shoulder of her short-sleeve shirt. "I'm happy to see the others are alright."

Taking her hand, I lead her to the bridge, and we sit on the stones where they meet land. "I'm sure it's a great relief to them all to reunite."

She cups my cheek. "You must miss your family."

Birdie does not attempt to give the centaurs space. She

hugs and greets them as if she has always been part of their community.

Farress embraces her for a long time with tears running down her face.

"I am a soldier. I am often away from home for months at a time." Still, I worry about my brothers and pray they are already back in Tús Nua, safe and with the humans they were sent to collect. They will be preparing to harass me about how long it took me to complete the mission. I kiss Wren's palm. She's so much more than a set of orders. She's everything.

"You know, Liam, you don't always have to pretend to be impervious. At least, not for my sake." She taps the side of her head, and her smile is soft and teasing.

Everything about her feeds my soul. "I miss them, and I'll be happy to get home. Now that the centaurs and your mother are safe, I will speak with Corell about our departure from the party. There's a portal not far from here. We could be home sooner."

"You want to leave them?" Horror and disappointment register like a blinking sign on her face.

Leaning over, I kiss her forehead. "It's you the witch queen wants, my love. The centaurs will be safer if we are away from them. Venora shouldn't be able to use her magic on this continent, but clearly, she's found ways around the oracle's magic. The farther away from these people we are, the better off they'll be, and they'll have a better chance of reaching the capital city."

"How do you know your city is safe?"

It's a fair question. "I can only hope the magic my mother and the oracle use to protect Tús Nua is holding better than that which is meant to protect this part of Domhan. For thirty years, the witch queen and her magic have been contained on the eastern continent. I don't know how she has breached the wards."

Wren leans into my side and rests her head on my chest. "Will you think less of me if I admit I'm afraid?"

"I'd think you foolish if you were not." I wrap my arm around her and pull her tight.

As soon as the reunion is over, I speak with Corell. He agrees that Wren's presence puts the herd at risk. To protect the children, he's more than happy to allow Jadar, Wellon, and Pallon to carry us to the portal that stands half a day's ride from here.

Corell grips my arm near the elbow in a traditional way, as friends and soldiers do when parting. "I will see you at your mother's home in a few days."

I dig in my bag, pull out my uniform jacket, and tear the patch from the shoulder. It is the deep blue of my mother's rule, with a green diamond at its center. I was given the royal color green at my birth, and this patch will let Tús Nua know I am alive, and these centaurs are my friends. There are no guarantees that either party will reach the new capital. I hand him the patch. "Should you arrive first, give this to my mother and tell her of our friendship. She will see that your people are safe and cared for."

His eyes flare with something unsaid as he turns and orders the centaurs to head north.

I get on Wellon's back, and the six of us watch the others ride away. Some weep over the loss of Belloc and Toball.

Others hug their sons who returned unharmed. Worry for my brothers does me no good, and I push it aside as best I can.

"We should put distance between us before the witch queen regains her strength."

Jadar nods as he is the senior of the three soldiers. He turns, and we ride northwest.

I send up a prayer to the old gods that the portal will bring us to safety. I'll not deny that the idea of sleeping in my bed tonight is motivating. The thought of lying in that bed with Wren in my arms makes me wish centaurs had wings.

Long grass gives way to rolling hills. Deeper greens and tall trees remind me more of home. It's harder riding, though the centaurs show no sign of tiring. They're remarkable creatures. I've come to admire their sense of honor and intelligence. In the short time I've known them, I've seen no dissidence, no betrayal, and no improper use of magic. They mostly use their magic to heal, preferring bow and arrow for battle. They transfer their magic to boost mine, but I've seen no magic used for offense.

It's shameful that elves have avoided knowing them all these many generations.

Wellon asks, "Do you think your people will be offended by our arrival?"

Wren and Birdie both turn and look at me, waiting for my answer. Wren cocks her head, her curious and stunning eyes fixed on mine.

Pallon and Jadar don't turn, but I'm sure they, too, are curious. Honestly, I'm not certain what will happen, but I have faith.

"It will be something new for them, just as it was new for

me the day we met. I want to believe the elves will embrace the changing world and accept both the centaurs' differences as well as our similarities." I know my mother will listen, and once she does, she'll be happy for the alliance. Father is always slower to change, but he'll get there in time.

"What similarities?" Pallon keeps his gaze focused on the land ahead of us.

I think about the young ones whom Birdie sacrificed and suffered to save. She still hasn't shared her experience, but it must have been terrible. "We have much in common, Pallon. We love our children. We want to protect our people. We live in the embrace of light magic and despise the use of dark. I'm sure there will be more commonalities discovered as our people mingle and learn about each other."

A smile tugs at Wren's lips. "Good people always have some common ground to unite them."

Jadar chuckles. "The elves will think we've come to attack them. It will take time to build trust." He pauses. "Still, I am curious to see the city and meet your people. I have never seen anyplace with more people than Clandunna, and that wasn't much bigger than our village."

Birdie says. "Once they see how handsome you are, you'll have all the lady elves fawning over you."

All three laugh.

Wren's smile could keep the sun from setting. "At least you're not arriving with the expectation of you saving the world. Imagine how I feel."

Before I can open my mouth, Jadar says, "If anyone can defeat the witch, it is you, Wren Martin."

I couldn't agree with him more, yet I wish I could steal her away and keep her safe.

A Crown of Wind and Water

Adhar screeches a high-pitched warning from above.

A dark mass flies toward us.

"Is that more demons? Lord above, this bitch of a witch queen has got to be shown the door." Birdie squints at whatever's coming.

My gut tightens. "Crows. Venora controls them. Get down and try to find cover. They will dive when they get close enough."

Wren and I jump to the ground as well. There's no water for Wren to use as a weapon here on higher ground. It's dry, short grass with some trees and shrubbery.

The centaurs pull out their bows and quivers.

Birdie takes cover behind a tree.

I wish Wren would stay with her mother, but she stands by my side and pulls the sword we found in Clandunna from her sheath.

The first crow dives for Jadar. He lets an arrow fly, and the bird crashes to the ground with the arrow's red feathers pointing up like a declaration of war.

More dive at the centaurs who fight with short swords for close combat. Several more crows fall, but one pecks Pallon's head.

Adhar dives like a missile and hits a crow heading for Wren. The raven kills with one strike and lands on her prey with a loud croak before flying to the tree limb above Birdie and standing guard like a sentinel.

Slicing the air, I time my strokes to take out as many birds as I can without using magic. We've used so much since arriving in Domhan, even with the help of the leighis berry, I feel drained from overusing my gifts.

Wren swings her sword at several attackers. The sudden onslaught forces her back.

The sky is black with crows, and hundreds dive and retreat, dive and retreat. Many litter the ground in pieces as their blood soaks the short grass. It feels like they will never stop coming, and we will run out of weapons and energy before this is over.

Jadar's hindquarters are gashed and bleeding, and hundreds more come in a never-ending river of cawing and clawing menace.

I'm struck, but keep swinging my sword, ignoring the blood running into my eyes.

Wren screams.

A growl sounds from the bushes. Two wolves as big as cattle and sick with dark magic stalk toward her. Their teeth bared, they focus on Wren and no other.

The crows separated her, and now the wolves are pushing her back farther.

It's a trap. "Wren, run!"

Wide-eyed, she keeps swinging her sword and looking for an escape route. Between the crows and the wolves, there's no place for her to go.

Unable to get past the crows, I double my efforts, pushing magic into my arms and sword to move faster and cut more accurately.

A wolf howls, and the second follows.

Wren calls the wind, but the wolves only lower their massive bodies to the ground, and the wind passes over them, blowing their ratty fur.

Magic, dark and nauseating, fills the air and pulses

against my flesh. The hair on the back of my neck stands up in warning.

I search for the source.

The remaining crows caw and rise into the sky.

Wren is twenty yards from the rest of us. This trap was perfectly laid. They've moved her away. I run toward her.

One wolf faces me and growls. It's bared teeth drip with saliva, brown from rot. Its hair is matted and dirty, and though twice the size of a normal wolf, its ribs strain against thin skin.

The prickling of dark magic strengthens.

A portal opens in the ground beneath Wren, her eyes go wide, and she looks at me before falling away. Her scream echoes through my mind.

"No!" I use elf speed to reach the edge of the portal without the wolves tracking me. "Get Birdie to Tús Nua," I scream, then dive into the closing portal. The wolf's claws catch my calf, but it's too late. I follow the song of Wren's soul and fall through darkness that rips at my flesh, and it feels as if my bones are coming apart.

This portal holds no light. There are no worlds flashing past or stars shooting by. There is nothing but pain and emptiness in this downward spiral.

Chapter Fifteen

WREN

This pain is like when I came through to Domhan, only worse. If a person could remember their birth, I wonder if this is what it would feel like. It's as if I'm being torn apart and remade, over and over again. My screams don't reach my ears, and only the rawness of my throat tells me I'm still making sounds.

A faint red glow in the distance grows larger. I hit something with my shoulder and my back. Pain shoots through me as my descent slows. Over and over, my body beats against walls I cannot see.

I crash into something slimy and mushy. Pushing to my hands and knees, I draw in a breath, trying to fill my aching lungs. Sulfur burns my eyes and nose.

A sickeningly sweet male voice that sounds far away and muddled as if it's underwater reaches me as my sword is taken from where it landed beside me. "You'll get used to it. Just breathe, human."

Something splashes down hard against me, pushing me back into the muck. Arms wrap around me, lifting me to standing. My vision is blurry, and my lungs feel as if they're on fire. The arms hold me against a hard surface.

"Ciaran, you treacherous pig." Liam's voice is comforting to hear, even though it sounds muddled and unclear.

Something sharp pinches my throat.

"The useless second son. I should have known you would create havoc when my plan was so perfect," presumably someone named Ciaran, says. "Throw your weapons over there or I'll cut her from chin to eye and see how her magic works from the inside out."

Liam's arms tighten, and his voice is low in my ears. "Slow your breathing. The air is nauseating but not deadly." He wipes the muck from my face. The clank of metal to my right is likely his sword and dagger hitting the floor. "Is there water in this hole?" Liam is louder, his voice harsh, and he didn't ask the question I expected him to.

A long huff that reminds me of a spoiled woman comes from Ciaran. "Bring her here. I will have water brought. I had no idea this human would be so weak. The other was much hardier."

Liam lifts me.

I try to ask about the other human, but while my brain screams the question, only garbled noises form in my mouth. A fear that whatever happened in that portal has damaged me permanently shoots through me. I stiffen, clutching at Liam.

His mind opens to me. *You are alright. Just breathe.*

A Crown of Wind and Water

Where are we?

Later. I don't want him to know we have this link. Liam sets me on hard ground. "Where is the water?"

"You never did have any patience. I would have thought all these years as a lowly soldier, you would have learned some." Ciaran's voice drips with disgust.

I can't see him, but I already hate him. That thought eases my panic, and I'm able to slow my breathing. One long inhale and another, darkness and light form distorted patterns in my vision. Liam's hand squeezes my shoulder. "The oil we fell into needs to be washed away. Water is coming."

Someone shuffles across the stone floor.

"Put it there by the prisoners." Ciaran's disdain is unmistakable. Whomever he was talking to, he despises as much as he hates Liam. "Now, get out, filth."

Cloth tears and water sloshes. Liam wipes a warm, wet rag over my forehead, then my eyes. He continues to wash my face and my ears.

"Disgusting." Ciaran makes an ugly grunt. "Fix your human, Riordan. In the meantime, know that you are now prisoners of Venora Braddish, Queen of Domhan. Do not leave this chamber. This is the only place you can survive in Coire."

The cloth stills at my chin, and Liam says, "You have fallen so far that you now tread in the underworld. Was it not bad enough to betray your people? Now you have betrayed the old gods as well?"

Heavy, booted steps draw close, followed by a loud slap of skin upon skin. Liam's touch falls away. "I would kill you if I didn't think my queen would wish to toy with you first. I have always considered you the most useless of your mother's sons, and I can see I was quite right. However, that younger brother of yours is in the running. Has he ever found a profession? At least he has magic to boast about." The boots retreat behind a door that sounds more like a vault closing with a resounding clang.

"Liam?" It comes out gurgled, but at least his name pushed out.

His rough hands touch my cheek. "I'm here. You're going to be fine. I need to wash the oil away."

My sight clears, and Liam's face comes into focus. A dark red mark on his cheek is already starting to shade blue. Reaching out, I touch the mark. He has a gash on his forehead and blood stains his hair. "Why did you provoke him?"

A wicked smile pulls at his lips. "To see if I could. He was always easily rattled, and I wanted to make sure that hadn't changed. It's a vulnerability, but he's too arrogant to realize his own weakness. I'm glad your vision has returned as well as your ability to speak." Meticulously, he continues to wash an opaque black film from my neck, chest, and arms. "I wish I had clean clothes for you, but our packs remained with the centaurs."

"Momma?" I try to stand. Fear and worry push me to my knees.

Liam holds me around the waist. "The centaurs will take care of her. They will take her to my home, and my mother will see to her safety and comfort." He looks around us. "Which is more than I'm able to do for you."

I hesitate to call the place a room. It's more of a carved-out cave with high ceilings and torches set in sconces. The black walls have ridges that follow no pattern. If this is hell, then I'd guess this is some kind of lava tube that has been modified to hold us. The stench of sulfur and burnt hair permeates everything. There is no furniture, only levels of the black stone. At the far right is an oozing puddle that I'm guessing is where I landed.

"Why were you not affected by that?" I point to the oily puddle.

"I trained for demon attacks. They've been known to use Coire oil to disorient entire armies. Of course, that was a thousand suns ago. I'll admit, I thought the training ridiculous until a few minutes ago." He shrugs.

Able to breathe normally, I only wish the air wasn't so foul. "This is hell?"

"I think this is a chamber designed to hold those from above. The rest of Coire is reported to be pure poison to you and me. Though I don't know of anyone who's returned from such a place to give an accurate report." Liam tears his pant leg, exposing a deep gash. He runs his hand over the wound, healing it. He rinses the rag he tore from the bottom of his shirt in a black cauldron filled with water. The pot appears to be made from the same substance as the walls.

"How did Ciaran leave here if the rest is unbreathable?" I stretch my arms and legs, which have nearly recovered their strength. I wince from the bruises on my back.

"Let me see." He turns me and pulls my shirt up, exposing my skin. "You may have broken ribs." He's so gentle when he runs his fingers along my side and where my ribs connect at the back, I forgive him for manhandling me. "I'd like to use magic to look."

"Um. You might need your strength for other things down here." I pull my shirt down and test my side with a stretch. The pain is sharp and forces me to breathe through it before it eases.

"It won't take much to look, and if I need to heal a bone, I'll still have plenty. Healing is not as taxing as demon slaying, at least not this kind." He pulls me close and sits behind me.

Under other circumstances, sitting between his legs in an all-black room might be romantic, but right now, I'm half furious and half terrified. I'm in hell, literally. Despite leading a mostly good life, I find myself in this place with no idea if we can get out.

Though probably hearing my thoughts, Liam gives no words of comfort. He wraps one large hand around my lats, and his warm magic tingles along my skin. "There are two breaks." *Try not to call out, my love.*

The sensation of Liam's magic grows stronger. Pain lances up my side as something snaps and cracks inside me. Blood flows through my eardrums, blocking out any other sound. I bite my bottom lip to keep from screaming.

Liam's other hand cups the side of my head. "I'm sorry."

Heat sears my flesh as if I've stepped too close to an open blaze. A moment later, the pain and heat vanish as if they'd never been there.

Removing his hand, he moves out from behind me. His voice is in my head. *The longer we can keep our feelings for each other from the witch queen and Ciaran, the better.*

I suppose he's right, but I miss his touch and his body against mine. Stretching as I did before, I'm astonished that the pain is more of a dull memory. I nod. "Thank you. That's better."

Sitting on the hard ground, we lean against the wall. No

one comes. The sounds that reach us are grating and make me cringe. I don't know what it is, but it sounds like metal upon metal. "Have I gotten used to the air here as well as the oil on my clothes?"

"Yes. It's not deadly. Only disorienting and admittedly horrible."

My stomach growls. "Do you think they intend to starve us?"

"I wish I could say no, but I have no idea what they intend. Venora needs you, or she would have had Ciaran kill you. She thought Birdie was you, and your mother suffered for it with torture. That indicates a desire for knowledge rather than destruction." He gets up and walks around the room, touching the black walls and muttering in the elven language.

"How can you be so casual about these things?" My voice bites despite an attempt to be rational. He's a soldier. He's seen much more than I have. He's trained to stay calm. I shouldn't be upset with him for being what he was trained to be.

"You mistake calm for casual, Wren. I'm not without feeling, and since you've been in my head, you already know that." The only hint that I've touched a nerve is a slight twitch in his left eye before he returns to searching our cell.

"I'm sorry. I know you care. This place has put me on edge. I wish they'd do whatever they plan. Sitting here for who knows how long is wreaking havoc on my nerves." I pick up a small black pebble and hurl it across the room. It clanks as if it were metal rather than stone.

Liam cocks his head. "Coire is not what I expected." He

walks to the wall where the pebble landed. Careful to avoid the oil, he picks up the stone and puts it in his pocket.

Before I can ask him what he's saving that for, the door opens with its vault-like clicks and pops.

Standing, I back away.

Heat permeates the chamber as three creatures enter. One carries a skinned, charred rabbit on a platter. The scent would be tempting if not for the stench of hell that's mixed in. The others haul a small cauldron and a larger tub, both filled with water that sloshes over the sides.

The creatures have arms and legs, but that is where the similarities between them and us end. They are half my size yet carry at least one hundred pounds of water, and I can't even guess the weight of the containers the water is in. Their eyes are black, with no light within and no whites, deep-set into faces shaped like foxes, but without fur or hair. Their skin is black like tar and has an oily sheen.

They do not speak or make eye contact as they place the items on the ground in front of us. Walking with heavy feet that leave tracks on the floor, they exit the way they came, with the large door slamming shut behind them. Their footsteps shine in the torchlight for a moment before being absorbed as if the stone were sand.

"This place is wrong." My stomach lurches despite my hunger.

Liam pulls a bite of meat from the bone and tastes it, then does the same with the water. "You'll get no argument from me." He hands me a piece of meat.

I push his hand away.

"Eat it. Who knows when or if they'll feed us again." He scoops water with his hand and sips it.

I force the bland rabbit down and sip some water. My hunger is at war with eating anything that comes from this place or the creatures who brought it. Still, I manage to eat enough to satisfy Liam, and I drink the slightly metallic water. "Is that for bathing?" I point to the larger tub.

"I think so."

Rather than soaking my clothes, I use the bathwater to rinse my arms, then splash some on my face. Once I've done as much as I'm willing to, I sit next to Liam. "We're going to die here. I wonder what will happen to our souls when we perish in such a place."

"I don't think our souls will be condemned by their location at our death. She can only steal our souls if she makes us shadow demons, and let's hope she wants something else from us." He shivers.

Becoming nothing but a shadow bound to an elf witch is a fate far worse than death. I hope that if that happens, one of the centaurs or one of Liam's people finds a way to kill me and set me free.

His mind at the edge of mine, he nudges my shoulder. "We're not dead yet. Don't lose hope."

It's hard not to laugh. We're in hell, and he's telling me not to lose hope. If that's not irony, I don't know what is. "Thank you for coming with me."

His eyes are warm and filled with emotions that he doesn't share, even through our mental connection. "You are welcome."

Part of me wants to pry and know precisely what he's feeling because I doubt it's hope. That was to keep my spirits up. We're probably going to die here, and who knows what we'll have to endure before that inevitability.

He pulls me close to his side. "We're safe for now. Let that be enough."

I wish I could feel as at ease as he seems. I admire how he can be prepared for disaster and remain relaxed at the same time. Maybe it's his training. However, I'm no soldier, and the notion of spending an eternity in hell has me on edge.

It's hard to say how much time has passed. We've been fed a few times and slept at least four, maybe five times. There's no change in light other than when the torches guttered out and left us in total darkness.

After a while, one of those creatures came and slipped a new torch into the sconce. Liam thanked it, but it showed no sign that it understood before stomping out of our prison cell.

My bones ache from the hard ground, and I try walking around and stretching while Liam does push-ups, sit-ups, and an assortment of other body-weight exercises. His lack of outward concern is starting to get to me. "How long do you think it's been?"

He sits up and wraps his arms around his knees. "Seven days."

"How can you know that?" My voice hides none of my fear or annoyance.

Shrugging, he continues his sit-ups. "I can tell by how often I need to sleep."

"Good for you. I need daylight and a setting sun. Why is

she keeping us here, and why doesn't she do something? What does she want?" Crossing my arms over my chest, I lean against the wall. My terror on the first day has eased into a mix of boredom and a sustainable level of fear. Maybe we're to be left here until we die. "And why feed us if she's going to let us die here?"

Backing up to the wall, he leans back and calmly watches me. "I don't have all the answers, Wren, but I'm guessing she needs you alive."

"You constantly being calm and reasonable is starting to infuriate me." I clench my fists to keep myself aware that the anger rising inside me is unfounded. Still, I want to punch someone, and Liam is the only one here.

"Would you prefer me to fly into a rage?" His jaw ticks. It's the first sign that any of this is getting to him.

I find that little signal very satisfying. "I think I would. Yes."

Suddenly, his mind is fully open to mine. His fury, rage, and fear for my life come rushing at me like an out-of-control boulder streaking down a mountainside. The enormity of his feelings batters my mind and emotions with everything he's been holding in. My knees give out, and I crumple to the floor. I press my back against the rough, hard surface to keep from total collapse. Within Liam, there is no concern for himself. He only cares that I will be hurt or worse. His greatest fear is that he might live without me. Fury and sorrow bombard me.

I shake my head, trying to push his heartbreak aside. "I'm sorry. I didn't know. I couldn't see past your calm exterior."

The images and emotions pull back.

Liam brushes away a tear that fell to his cheek. Closing

his eyes, he takes several long, slow breaths. When he opens those sapphire eyes, the soldier is back in place, and everything else is under control.

Pushing myself to my feet, tears streaming unstoppably down my face, I cross to him and kneel. "Forgive me. I'm an idiot."

He takes my hands. "No. You're afraid, which is completely normal. This entire chamber is designed to break you, and I am little help, for which I have no excuse."

"I should have realized. You followed me into this terrible place, and I've been horrible to you." Maybe this is where I belong if my character is so weak that it can be destroyed in a few days.

A hint of a smile pulls at his lips. "You are too hard on yourself. I'm trained to survive a great many things, and you now know that even I am barely holding on in this place."

Sitting beside him, I rest my head on his shoulder. "I will do better, Liam." I pray that I can live up to that vow.

Chapter Sixteen

LIAM

Try as I might, none of my magic works in this place. I can't scry in the water and reach my mother. It's not possible to blast through these walls. We eat and drink what is brought to us. We bathe to some degree, but without clean clothes, it is almost pointless. The chamber has only one exit; when closed, it is solid rock.

Coire will not offer us a way out, even though I sense the place knows we do not belong here. Much like Domhan strains against the demons when they rise, this place would expel us if it could.

The longer we are here, the quieter Wren becomes. She struggles to believe we can find our way back. I can't blame her. The evil of the underworld gnaws at anything good. Sitting beside me, she sighs. "Do you think Momma and the others made it to your home?"

I slip my fingers through hers. "Yes. Once we were taken, it's likely Venora ignored those who traveled with us."

"You mean *I* was taken. You leaped in. It was me she wanted. Though now that she has me, she seems to be leaving me here to rot." There is none of the passion I've grown accustomed to in her voice.

Wishing I had left her in her world won't make it true, but I still do. I long for the sweetness and sharp wit of the woman I fell in love with. "We're still alive, and that has to be enough for now, Wren. She's feeding us, so she wants something."

"Is this place what you expected?" Wren picks up a small pebble and turns it in her hand.

"What do you mean?"

She tosses the stone. "I guess I always expected hell to be fire and brimstone with screaming souls in torment. This is just a dank prison with that humming sound and nothing more."

"I haven't given it much thought, but this would be a perfect hell for me if you were not here."

Looking at me for the first time in a long time, she asks, "What does that mean?"

"Coire or hell is different for each person. It would be torture for me to be closeted for all eternity in a place like this. With you here, I'm not worried about my state. I'm focused on how to save you." I wish I had more eloquent words to tell her how I feel.

"Humming."

"What about it? Is it driving you as nuts as it is me?" She uses her wind magic to lift one of the small stones and swirls it around above her hand.

"Your magic works here." It's impressive that she's learning to use it without imminent death knocking on our door. *Humming*... I search my memory. "Didn't one of the young centaurs say that all they heard in their dark prison was a constant humming?"

She looks around. "Are we in the obelisk?"

"Maybe under it." My heart leaps that after all these days trapped and unable to find a way out, we've deduced something that might be useful.

"Does that help us?" A glimmer of hope shines in her eyes.

"I'm not certain, my love, but it's more than we knew a moment ago and something our captors probably don't want us to know."

"Why not?" She wipes her dirty hands on her equally filthy jeans.

"Obelisks are conduits. They are designed to draw power from the underworld and channel it for the user's purposes. I'm only guessing, but Venora might be using this one to bolster her magic." I wish I had access to all the books in the library at home. All my years of avoiding study in favor of training for battle, and now I would give anything to read about the dangers and uses of obelisks.

"But, if she's drawing power, why can't you get your magic to work here?" She scrunches her nose.

Sitting close, I place a pebble in her palm. "My magic is in the light. I would have to sully my soul to use the power of this place. Honestly, I wouldn't even know how to do such a thing. My power is replenished by the sun. If I overextended my resources down here, I would die." I shrug. "If I were certain doing so would get you to safety, I wouldn't hesitate, but so far, I haven't found a way."

She spins the stone in her palm with wind magic. Controlling the elements is strong magic that I've only seen performed by the oracle. Wren closes her fingers around the stone. "Is my magic evil?"

"No."

"But if my magic were in the light, it would be weaker down here. I don't feel weak. Other than lacking water and an abundance of air, I can do the things I did on the surface. I've even learned some control. Doesn't that mean my magic is dark?" She drops the pebble as if it might burst into flames at any moment, and it pings off the floor.

"I'm not an expert, but I don't think human magic is the same as elven magic. It feels different." When Wren uses magic, the sensation is different; it is neither light nor dark, but something else. I can't explain it.

"There is no human magic, Liam. If my people knew what I could do, they would label me a freak. Some people would think the devil was working through me. I'd be shunned or worse." She kicks the pebble away.

In the time that I've known Wren, I've grown in so many ways. She pointed out long-held prejudices I'd considered normal. It never occurred to me that she'd lived her life on the other end of similar disdain. "You are exceptional, Wren. Living in a world where magic is rare forced you to hide your gifts and kept you from learning all you are capable of. We will study your magic together. There is much to learn."

She dashes aside a tear and nods.

The metallic thunk of the door opening forces us to abandon the conversation. It's too soon for more food to be coming. My heart races as we stand. Hoping the old gods are listening, I pray that I can protect Wren from whatever comes through.

Ciaran strides in with ten demon servants, each carrying a spear two times taller than their height. I know they're strong, but how can they properly wield the weapons? "You will come with me. If you attempt anything foolish, one of you will die." He smirks at me.

I would be the one to be sacrificed. I wasn't supposed to be here at all. It's not surprising that he'll use my life and well-being as a way to keep Wren in line. "Where are you taking us?"

"Think of it as a tour of your new land." Ciaran laughs as the demons surround us and turn back toward the door. The sound is stiff, metallic, and rings with insanity.

As soon as we step toward the open door, the foul stench of sulfur fills my nose, making me gag. After the initial shock, my body adjusts, and I'm able to push aside my natural reaction to the unpleasant gases of this place.

Wren gasps for air and clutches her throat. Her eyes are wide with panic as she tries to draw air into her lungs. She coughs and retches.

I grip her shoulders. "Easy. I've got you."

Rolling his eyes, Ciaran scoffs. "The weakness of these humans is disgusting." He casts a spell and creates a sheer bubble of breathable air to encompass the three of us while the demons remain outside the protection. "They're not much different from those creatures." He points to the demons. "They don't survive above for long." The way he grins, I get the impression that he has taken pleasure in watching the demons suffocate.

Wren draws slow breaths and blinks the tears from her eyes.

My stomach lurches. They are horrible and unpleasant, but to torture anyone, let alone a lesser being, is vile. "Where are you taking us, Ciaran?"

Another baleful grin rather than answering the question.

Outside our prison cell, we walk along a precipice. Below, liquid fire boils and spits. A cacophony of wind and fire fills my head. The stench of death mixes with brimstone and sulfur. Sweat beads on my flesh, but dries before it can run. My eyes burn from the noxiousness.

This is more like Wren's vision of Coire.

She begins to breathe normally, but her skin is gray and pale. Her lips are pulled into a tight line as if holding back pain. Fisting her hands at her sides, she shuffles after Ciaran without a word.

I long to open my mind to her and comfort her, but I keep my thoughts and worries to myself, rather than risk letting anyone here know the depth of my connection to Wren. They would only use it to attack us. The less they know, the better our chances of escaping are.

In some places, the precipice narrows to barely a foot wide. Wren hesitates.

Ciaran grabs her by the hair and drags her across the twenty-foot span.

Wren screams and clutches her hair, trying to free herself.

"Stupid human with all your fears and frailties."

When he releases her, she stumbles to the hard ground and grips her head. After a moment, she looks at him. There is no fear in her gaze, only rage.

A Crown of Wind and Water

I have seen her fight and win. I've seen her anger and joy. This pure hatred is something new. It's a part of her she has never shared with me, and I can't say I mind. While I love all of Wren Martin with my entire being, to see her wrath, I'm glad it's not directed at me.

For one instant, Ciaran's jaw goes slack and his eyes widen. He might even regret his words and actions. In a flash, he fears this human woman whom he's shown only contempt. With a hesitation, he shakes his head and puts his mask of indifference in place. "Get up before I do you real harm, *chosen one*." The last words are filled with sarcasm.

I wrap my hand around Wren's upper arm and help her to her feet. It takes all my energy not to use every bit of my remaining magic and send Ciaran into the fiery pits beneath us. Reminding myself that doing so would cause more harm than good, I know this pig's time will come. If I'm lucky, it will be my sword that slits his throat.

Killing has never been something I longed for, but for him, I'll make an exception. Watching life flow out of his treacherous eyes will soothe my soul.

Wren and I walk on with the demons surrounding us and Ciaran outside of the bubble. It's clear he has spent enough time here that he's used to the gases. There's satisfaction in his preference for putrid air over being close to us.

Leaning in, I whisper, "I think you scared him."

A hint of a smile pulls at her sweet lips. "Good."

We reach black doors that stand fifteen feet high. Ciaran pushes the center, and they open. Back straight and chin high, he steps inside.

Hesitant, we don't move. A demon pokes me with the back of his spear.

Wren's arm in my grasp, we go inside.

The foul smells dissipate. The bubble around us evaporates. The room is lavish with every inch of wall space draped in red and black fabric. A similarly curtained bed sits against the wall, featuring black bedding and red pillows piled high. At the far side of the room, a chair large enough to be called a throne glows gold with black cushions. It sits on a dais but is empty.

Here, no primitive torches are burning in metal loops, as magic lights the space with the glow of pure white stones. I've only seen such creations in the mountain where the oracle lives. It's not like the magical fires that burn throughout my parents' home or the rocks heated with magic used instead of open flame. It cannot even be compared to the bulbs I first saw when I went to the human world. The white stones are old magic, and until now, I believed they could only be created with oracle magic or by the old gods themselves.

How did Venora get them? My gut tightens.

At the center of the room glows a rectangular pool with heat rising from its foreign contents, which roil like the sea.

My skin prickles with the vibration of dark magic flowing from the unnatural pool.

Bouncing like giant, deranged fleas about to leap on a new dog host, the demons stay just outside the open doors. Their eyes glow bright red, as if lit from Coire's fires.

Ciaran strides to the other end of the pool and lays his sword on a table. He removes a dagger from his hip and places it there as well. "You will see that this is the way of the new world my queen has created. You will wish to kneel before her once you learn of her true greatness." The awe in his voice is nauseating.

"Never going to happen," Wren says, giving the pool a wide berth when we round to the left side.

Seeming not to hear her, Ciaran closes his eyes and raises both his hands to shoulder level. The spell he casts is the darkest kind of magic. The words are ancient Elvish, but the dialect was banned due to its association with evil. These are the words forbidden for generations.

My ears ring from the bombardment of sounds not meant for my hearing. As my gut clenches, I hope I can hold down the meager food from earlier. This type of magic is perilous. Even without understanding the meaning of the words, my light magic recoils from the spell.

Wisdom dictates that I do nothing to provoke Ciaran until I have a way to get Wren out of this place safely. Threatening or bludgeoning him as I'd like to puts her in additional danger. If I'm killed, how will she get out? I can't risk it. If I could, I'd have broken his arm when he touched her.

Waves form in the pool, and the center darkens.

"What in the name of all that is holy is that?" Wren grips my arm but drops her hands away a moment later.

As much as I want to be her safe place, we have to keep some distance between us, or our enemies will use it against us.

A figure grows and rises to the top. The thick fluid sluices away, revealing Venora Braddish. Her skin is taut and smooth. She looks young and healthy. Whatever she's feeding from has added years back, leaving her looking like a twenty-year-old.

Without glancing at us, she steps naked from the pool. Her long black hair is slick against her pale skin and reaches nearly to her ass.

This is the first time I've ever seen the witch queen in person, though I've fought her minions all my adult life. Elves age slowly, but Venora is my mother's age. They went to school together, yet she looks younger than I. The only hint that anything has changed in her over the last fifty suns is a small scar across her left cheek.

Ciaran backs up to an armoire, gathers a black robe, and wraps it around her shoulders. "My queen, you are as beautiful as I have ever seen you."

"I do feel refreshed." Voice sultry like a woman waking from a good night's sleep, she casts a spell that dries her of the slime from the pool.

Neither Wren nor I move as we watch the destroyer of the world reclaim her youth as if she's ready to begin her rule all over again.

My heart sinks. With this kind of magic, she could live forever. Elves are already long-lived, but this could make the witch queen immortal. This is a worse nightmare than leaping into a portal to Coire.

Long black eyelashes surround her dark eyes. She is both beautiful and horrible, as the ugly she keeps inside forces its way through.

I can't take my gaze from her, and pure evil returns my stare. "One of Elspeth's spawn. How is your mother? She and I were good friends."

As much as I despise this creature speaking about my mother, I hold my biting words back. "She has told me about your friendship and your betrayal. Elspeth Riordan is the true queen of Domhan and will long survive your demise."

The silk robe clings to her as she rounds the pool toward us. "You are not half as smart as your older brother, are you? I can see why soldiering was your only option. Though, just as now, I captured his quarry." She smirks. "Did you drag this puny human here by her hair, kicking and screaming?"

Fury wells in my gut, but I force my mouth to remain shut.

"Do not speak about me as if I'm not in the room, witch." Wren lifts her chin as if that will give her petite form more presence. She doesn't know that it is her soul that fills a room more than her diminutive stature.

Ciaran steps between Wren and Venora. "Watch that tongue of yours before I cut it from your mouth and feed it to the demons."

Wren narrows her eyes at him.

Laughing, Venora turns and walks to her throne. She leans back as if there are no wars or dangers for her. She thinks herself above harm. "I can see this one is more talkative than the last. That might be a good sign. Don't cut out her tongue yet, mate. I require it for the moment."

"What did you do to the other human woman?" The fury inside Wren creates a glow around her. She intends to defend the other human despite not knowing her.

Pride wells inside me. I focus on keeping none of my emotions visible on my face. At least I have learned something already. Aaran returned from the human world with the first of the women in the prophecy. Either Venora lost her captor, or she killed her. Nothing was said about them by

Venora beyond that, which matters. She'll lie to try to get what she wants from us.

"The same thing I will do to you if you deny me, creature. You're nothing compared to an elf. An entire race of mongrels born in jungles who've learned nothing. You have magic you don't know how to use, and the few who do squander their gifts on fortune-telling." She pulls a disgusted face. "Small beings who will be easily conquered as soon as I learn the source of your magic. If you tell me now, I'll let you live out your life in the comforts of Coire. Deny me, and I'll torture you until there's nothing left but a wisp of a girl begging to tell me everything."

Wren looks at her directly. "Humans have no magic."

A lie that Wren no doubt believes.

The pleasant smile Venora has in place turns into a teeth-baring wolfish grin. "Maybe it isn't your fate that scares you, human. Who was the woman you risked so much to rescue?"

Wisely, Wren remains silent.

Venora cocks her head. "Same eyes and small stature. Same mouth, but older." Her eyes lit with realization. "I will have my creatures do whatever it takes to recapture her and rip off bits and pieces of her until you tell me the truth. I think starting with her fingers would be the most sensible approach. What do you think, Ciaran?"

"An excellent plan, my queen. Shall I send for the wolves to accompany a squadron of soldiers?" He looks from Wren to me, searching for some reaction.

"My mother is beyond your reach." Crossing her arms, Wren never takes her gaze from the witch queen.

Venora's eyes widen, and her voice rises. "No one is beyond my reach, wretch. I can get to anyone in all the worlds where I am queen, including this one. Do not test my reach. Give me what I want, or you will pay the price."

Without blinking or shrinking back, Wren again says, "Humans have no magic."

Fury burns in Venora's stare as she rises. "You think you can thwart me. Perhaps the Riordan's son is a perfect sacrifice to loosen your tongue." Her focus shifts to me. Pointing at me, she shoots dark magic from her fingertips.

My heart lurches. Pain rips through my body. No air will flow into my lungs. While I clutch my throat, my knees slam against the stone floor. I'm drawn toward the witch queen as if she were the center of the universe. My body lies on the floor, and I float above.

Wren screams my name as she kneels beside my dead form and looks up at my essence floating above.

Staring at my hands, I am a shadow.

Light magic surrounds me as Wren's prayers fill the place where my heart should be.

Come back to me. We are one, inseparable, unyielding. You cannot leave me, not like this.

The dark magic rips away, and I slam back into my body. Pain tears through me where evil claws at my soul. I can't hold on, but Wren is there with her beautiful magic, keeping me within the painful embrace of my elven form.

Both light and darkness war for my essence. The way I was bound to Venora when in shadow is terrifying. I would have served her, killed for her, died to protect her, and given all of my demon-self to her service.

Andrea Rose

Now, I am the rope tugged at both ends by two powerful women, each with their own reasons for wanting me, but only one who gives me a will of my own.

Drawing on my magic, I thrust back at Venora with all my might.

Chapter Seventeen

WREN

I will not let go. The witch will not take Liam from me. I will die before I betray him, Domhan, or the human race.

She is stronger in magic, but my skills are foreign to her, and I have the feeling that she's never been challenged before. No one has ever stopped her from taking an elf's soul and condemning it to shadow.

When Liam slams back into his body, it nearly jerks me back, but Venora stumbles and Ciaran has to catch her before she falls.

Swimming with satisfaction, I'm sure there's a smirk on my face as Liam returns from the shadow demon form. I've never been so scared or so elated in so short a span in my life. He came back to me exactly as I prayed he would.

On a furious bellow, Venora sends a ripple of her foul magic and tries to pull him away again.

Asking for the power to keep Liam intact, I hold him away from the power of the witch queen. Wrapping my arms around his chest, I pull him into my lap on the stone floor. I'll never let him go, not for her to use as a slave. Killing him would have been preferable to enslaving his soul. I'll not have it. I'd save them all, if I could, but it's our connection that keeps Liam with me. The bond between us is the only reason I can save him. I feel his mind on the fringes of mine as soon as he comes to his senses.

His pain is my pain, but I can't break Venora's magic. It's too strong, and she's too powerful.

As she keeps screaming and trying to make him a shadow demon, her skin pales, and her eyes begin to look tired. The scar on her cheek darkens and enlarges. It's a burn, and there are the same types of burns on her hands.

"Stop, my queen," Ciaran begs. "You are using too much magic at once. Please stop." He holds her around the waist to keep her upright. Worry fills his eyes.

The tingle of Liam's magic shoots along my arms as he mumbles something and throws light magic across the room. It hits them like a sonic wave, and they both fall backward to the floor with Ciaran breaking her fall.

Liam gasps for air, and his deep blue eyes lock with mine. "You wouldn't let me go."

"Never."

Across the room, Venora's skin is tinged blue. Her chest is still.

Ciaran kneels over her. He presses his hands to her abdomen. "Venora. Awake. My queen, you must awake."

The faintest hope that the witch queen is dead and this entire nightmare is over is thwarted by a low feminine moan and movement in her hands and legs. She pushes her lover's hands away. "I need the source's deepening magic."

"You will have it, my queen." Ciaran lifts her in his arms and carries her to the pool. At the edge, he lays her on the stone and removes her robe before lifting her again and walking into the thick sludge as if there are stairs within.

When his head disappears, I cup Liam's cheek. "I've never been as terrified in my life. I thought I'd lost you."

He places his hand over mine, but his smile is weak. "You nearly did. I was in shadow, and she had more than my soul. For the briefest of moments, she had my allegiance." As if rejecting the idea, his entire body shivers, and he clutches me.

"I couldn't let her take you. How did you come back?" Tears of fear, relief, and joy stream down my cheeks.

He looks almost as spent as Venora as he struggles to sit, and he wraps me in his arms. "I saw you hovering over my body. I heard your prayers to bring me back. I chose my love for you over the biting draw of her magic. I won't lie, though; it would have been easy to be lured in by her. It was as if my entire life had been stripped away, and all that was left was a desire to serve the witch queen. If not for our bond, I wouldn't have been able to come back, Wren. You saved me."

We hold each other while I weep into his chest.

Breaking the hug, he grips my face with both hands. Intensity flashes in his eyes. "Promise me you'll never leave me like that. Send light through the shadow and destroy the demon. Don't let her have my soul, love. My family couldn't bear that."

"No one is taking your soul, Liam. I'll never abandon you."

Ciaran and Venora never emerged from the pool.

After what feels like hours, the strange little demons come and force us back to our cell. Without the air bubble, my body retches, and Liam practically has to carry me through hell.

Certain I'll never make it; I press my nose to Liam's chest and breathe in his scent. It's faint under the oppressive, festering odor of hell, but I find it. I open my mind to his and listen to the song of his soul. My heart breaks at the knowledge that I nearly lost something so perfect and beautiful.

The distraction is enough to get me to the cell where the air is breathable for humans. "Why can you survive out there?" I ask him once the demons have left and sealed the door behind them.

"It's uncomfortable. I wouldn't survive long." He holds his chest and takes deep breaths.

I sit and watch him, remembering the terror of nearly losing him. "How are we ever going to get out of here?" I hate the despair flavoring my voice, but I can't help it. This is anyone's worst nightmare: a toxic environment, demons, hell, and under the thumb of a vicious enemy. I'm never going to see my mother again, and I don't know how my magic works or even how I managed to save Liam. Worse, I don't know if I can do it again if I need to.

He sits beside me, slipping his arm around my shoulder. "I've had a thought about that."

Leaning into his side, I feel his strength and relax by degrees. "What thought?"

He's pale, and without sunshine, his magic won't rejuvenate. He whispers, "I think you could make a portal, Wren."

"How in the name of Pete would I do that?" The idea of it adds to my helplessness. "Did you lose your senses when she almost took your soul? I have no control over my magic beyond lifting a pebble, Liam. It just comes whenever it wants to."

"That's not true," he says, with love in every word. "It comes when you need it most. It comes when you pray for what you want or need most. I know you can do it."

Not believing Wren Martin of Texas can create one of the holes in the world that nearly ripped me to pieces, I shrug. "Tell me how and I'll try."

For a long time, he says nothing, and I begin to wonder if he's changed his mind about the feasibility of his mad plan. "Don't scoff. You have to pray for it."

I scoff. "Sorry. But you must know how insane that sounds."

"Try, Wren."

I love him, so I hold in my second scoff. "Alright, but let's say I could do this thing, where would my portal lead?"

With a sigh, he nods. "That's a good question."

"Can you make a portal? I mean, I saw you open a portal, but that's not the same as what we're talking about, is it?" I cross my legs and face him.

"No. I don't have the skill or knowledge of portal magic. The portal in Scotland that I opened already existed. I used a specific spell to open it."

"Can other elves create portals out of thin air?"

"The oracle can." He doesn't sound as if that makes my job any easier.

"So, a group of powerful elves who have dedicated their lives to the study of magic are the only elves capable of doing this thing you want me to try. Am I missing anything?" Even though he's been through a lot today, I can't keep the sarcasm out of my voice.

Instead of being annoyed, he grins adorably at me. "Your magic is different. You could create the portal and pray for it to bring us to the training field outside of Tús Nua. It's a vast field with a stunning view of the city's white walls rising before the Great Mountains. The gates shine golden in the morning sun, and thousands of elven soldiers spar throughout the day, readying themselves for battle and defending our people." He sends the image into my mind.

I keep the picture there and think about the pain of a portal and the way it swirls with wind. Closing my eyes, I say, "I see the city and the soldiers. The mountains rise in the distance, their peaks white. It's beautiful."

"Pray for the portal that can take us there, love." His voice is barely a whisper.

As I ask god to help me make a portal to save us. I feel the wind whip around me. I open my eyes, and dust swirls a foot in front of us. A pinpoint of black appears—my heart races.

"You're doing it." Excitement bubbles in his voice.

The wind dies down, and the dot of black hope fades and dies. A heavy weight presses against my chest. "It's impossible."

Liam lets out a long breath. "It would have been amazing if you'd have succeeded on your first try, Wren. You did great. I doubt the oracle members get everything right immediately."

We sit with our backs against the wall. "I'm sorry."

He kisses the crown of my head. "You are amazing. It's been a long day. We'll try again when you've rested."

For days or weeks, we try every time we wake up. Each time I fail. Some days, I can't even get the wind to whirl. There is no way to tell how much time has passed. We're fed, though not as well as before we sent Venora back into her pool of sludgy red goop. Still, it's enough to survive.

The door opens, and a blast of magic throws Liam across the hard floor. He smacks against the wall with a grunt, then struggles to stand while the magic keeps him pinned.

I try to go to him, but Ciaran grabs me while two demons wrap a slimy black rope around my wrists. "My queen has need of you, human scum." Holding a dagger aloft and ready to throw it at Liam, where he still tries to rise, he says, "If you come quietly, I won't kill the second son."

Rage fills Liam's eyes.

Ciaran pushes his white-blond hair over his shoulder and draws back the dagger.

"I won't fight."

Victory flashes in Ciaran's evil eyes. He returns his blade to the sheath at his hip, grabs my arm, and pulls me out of the cell, leaving Liam behind.

As the door closes, I hear Liam screaming my name.

My heart clenches, and I open my mind to his. *Stay calm. She needs me, or she thinks she does.*

Love that is so pure it makes my heart ache filters through our connection. *Stay alive. Everything else we can fix.*

The demons follow behind, making noises that might be chuckling, but sound more like nails on a blackboard.

Ciaran drags me along by my bound hands at a pace that even if I were willing, I'd struggle to keep up. I fall and scrape my knee, but he barely breaks stride as he hauls me up and continues toward Venora's chamber.

Unable to breathe, I slip and stumble across the narrow stones and wonder if he intends to toss me into the molten fires of this place. However, soon we're standing before the tall black double doors.

He grips the rope and lifts until my feet dangle and the material bites into the skin at my wrists. "You should feel honored that the queen is benevolent. She should have let me kill you for making her spend another cycle inside the source. You should be flayed alive, but perhaps that's what's next for your insignificant lover once you've told us everything you know."

"Put me down before I curse you to spending all your life down here." Momma would say my mouth just wrote a check my body can't cash, but I meant every word.

His eyes widen, and the hint of fear in them is very satisfying before he returns to a hateful glare. As if he cannot find the words to put me in my place, he grunts and pushes the doors open.

Venora is seated on her throne. She's wearing a silver dress that covers her from neck to toes. It's fitted to her body and has a wide fanned piece across her shoulders as if to frame her head like something out of Earth's fourteenth century. "We started badly. Let's try again. Come and tell me your name, daughter of Birdie."

She points to a space on the dais where she wants me to either stand or kneel.

It guts me that she knows Momma's name. When I hesitate, Ciaran pushes me, and I stumble.

With my hands bound, it's all I can do to keep from landing on my face. My knees are cut and bruised, and the heels of my hands are scraped bloody. Rising, I give him a baleful glare. It's only Liam's warning to stay alive that keeps me from lashing out.

Holding my chin high, I walk to the space indicated and stand facing the witch queen. "Wren is my name."

She smiles, and pure evil pours from the expression.

My stomach lurches, and the hairs on the back of my neck stand up in warning.

"See, this is better. Isn't it? I ask you a question, and you answer. No one needs to be harmed." She takes a deep breath that brings the ridiculous fan higher. "I need information about human magic and how you restore yourselves when you expend it."

Hmm. A new tactic. "Why?"

"Why?" she bites back.

"Yes. Why do you need to know that?" I have a bad feeling about the way she's asking this.

"I need to understand human magic. The way a species rejuvenates is key to how the magic is sustained."

"So that you can invade and conquer my people? No.

That's not going to happen. Besides, humans have no magic." I stick to my guns.

Venora rises, and she towers over me. Her eyes flash red, then black. "You will tell me, either now or after I rip the magic from your rotting bones." Black shards of lightning shoot from her hands.

It lances into me like a hundred knives stabbing at the same time. I scream, but no sound comes out, or my ears have stopped working. I can't tell which. The solid rock floor rises up to meet me as I crash and writhe on my back.

The pain stops. I pull my hands away from my abdomen, expecting to find them bloody, but there is nothing but the dull ache of the torture of a moment before. My pulse races. Adrenaline flushes my skin. This world of Liam's makes me want to kill, which is something that never occurred to me in my world. The evil here is somehow greater or less shrouded. Also, no one ever tortured me or tried to turn someone I love into a demon back in Texas.

"Tell me how you restore yourself."

"Sleep." I close my eyes, hoping she'll accept that as an answer since I have no knowledge or inclination to tell her anything.

"That is not an answer, Wren Martin. Sleep restores the body but not magic." There's a pause, and then the pain begins again and lasts longer.

It's as if I'm being flayed alive. My screams echo off the walls.

Ciaran laughs from somewhere behind me.

Everything goes black.

"The human has lost consciousness, Ciaran. She is weak. Give her a taste of the power of the source."

A Crown of Wind and Water

I'm barely lucid, but the dragging of my body across the stone floor pulls me back. Cracking my lids open is the best I can do, even as the ropes around my wrists bite at my flesh.

I cry out as the two steps up to the pool bruise my ribs and hips.

His face presses to mine. "Now you will know the truth. You cannot win, stupid, weak, human."

My stomach roils as he licks my cheek. His grip is so tight, jerking back does me no good.

"I'm going to enjoy watching you die." My body is so sore and battered, it's hard to draw breath, and my words are mumbled.

At the pool's edge, the heat of whatever roils within makes it hard to breathe. As soon as my hands hit the viscous liquid, a surge a power floods me, pushing through my body, my soul, and my mind. Everything I know exists in a fog, and only the pain of too much power is real. Voices press on my consciousness. Evil. Only evil and dark. There is no light. All good has been wiped from the universe.

Barely able to form a thought, I try to push back at the fires of this energy she called the source. I realize it's where she's getting her healing. She's gaining strength by using this horrible, dark magic.

In my mind, I know that Venora has made a deal with the devil.

The voices clearly want me to hear them, but I don't want whatever they're offering. Forcing my mind away, I see Liam with his deep blue eyes filled with love, looking at me as if I'm the only woman in all the worlds. I hold the image in my mind until the voices fade and pain sears up my arms to every nerve.

I shake, and the stairs batter my side. I scream until my throat closes. Gasping for breath, I want to do as Liam asked and stay alive. Never seeing him again fills me with a worse pain than all the evil Venora and Ciaran can throw at me.

The thick liquid sluices from my hands, and the horrors of dark magic fade away as I'm dumped in a heap on the hard floor in front of the pool.

Venora lifts my chin, and her hideously beautiful face is only inches from mine. "Tell me what I want to know. How does human magic regenerate?"

The blacks of her eyes blur. My head feels as if it might explode from the pressure building within.

Pushing my face away, she growls. Standing over me, her expression softens, and she smiles. "Take her back to her cell. We have nothing but time. Perhaps tomorrow this exercise will loosen her lips. I can do this every day, and if it takes ten of your human years for you to break, I'll still have more time, Wren Martin. Day by day, night by night, I will torture you until you are encouraged to give me what I want to know."

Ciaran lifts me and throws me over his shoulder.

My head hangs, and the blood rushes there with my arms trapped between his back and my stomach. The burning in my shoulders is nothing compared to what I suffered at Venora's hands and the power of that pool—a shiver runs through me. Every day, she said. I'll pray for death. Perhaps my magic will grant me that.

I must have blacked out because a second later, I'm tossed into the cell where Liam pulls me into his arms and shouts something incomprehensible at Ciaran.

"I've got you. It's just us now, my love. Don't cry. I'm

going to kill them for what they've done to you. I promise you that." His voice is soft but filled with passion.

Forcing my eyes open, I find him holding me in his lap like a baby.

He unties the bindings at my wrists and tosses the slime-covered rope across the room. "Do you want to tell me about it?"

Shaking my head hurts, and I close my eyes. "They'll be back for me tomorrow. I can't relive it now and then go through it all again."

With the gentlest touch, he brushes my hair from my face.

The silence feels equally oppressive. I search for the song of his soul, but my mind is too full of the memory of those voices in the pool. "Tell me about something in your world that is good. I can't bear the silence, but thinking about war is too hard right now."

His deep voice is a balm to my soul. It vibrates like a bass against my head as he holds me close. "There's a fairy glen about a day's ride from my home. They are not always visible, and nothing evil can enter the glen. They reveal themselves when needed. At least, that's what the old texts say. I've only ever seen one, and it was pure light magic. I'd been riding a long way and was tired both body and mind. The glen healed me as I slept."

Closing my eyes, I listen. "Are they magic? What did it look like?"

"In a way. The fairies make them and cannot be seen by those who do not live in the light. Venora would walk right past and never see the glen. As for what it looks like, it's the most beautiful place I've ever seen."

"Tell me." I lean in tighter. My limbs shake from the aftermath of the pain I endured.

Liam brushes his fingers over my hair and down my arm. His magic tingles along my skin, taking away the sharper bits of agony, but not all. He must conserve his magic in the absence of the sun to rejuvenate.

He kisses my forehead. "At first, it just looked like a small stand of trees, but when I drew closer, I felt the warm comfort of pure light magic. I stepped through the trees, and it was exactly as the books had said. Deep green grass with flowers and mushrooms of every color spread out before me, much larger than it looked from outside the trees. At the center, a spring bubbled with cool, clean water. Sunlight shone through the canopy of leaves like a dappled painting."

"What did you do there?" The agony in my gut eases to an everlasting ache.

"I tied my horse to a tree, though I don't think he would have left the glen. The animal sensed the safety and goodness within as much as I did. Once I'd divested him of his saddle, I stripped out of my clothes and stepped into the spring. It healed my aches and pains and knitted together the scrapes on my skin. Once I was clean, I lay back in the warm, soft grass and let the fairy magic lull me to sleep. It was the best night's sleep I've ever had."

I wish I could feel the warmth of the grass and know the purity of the water in the fairy glen. I want to sleep without worrying that I'll be tortured when I wake. Reaching up, I touch his temple. "Can you show me?"

The image flows into my mind. I reach for it—magic prickles along my arms, legs, and at the back of my neck.

With what little energy I have left, I focus on the image he's sending. "I want to go to the fairy glen."

Liam's arms tighten protectively around me. "Wren, what are you doing?"

"I want to go to the fairy glen." It's all I can say or think about. If I let go of the image, all that will be left for me is pain and heartache.

"By the old gods," Liam breathes. Standing, he lifts me like a precious treasure. "You're doing it."

I try to open my eyes. "What am I doing?"

"Hold on."

As he steps forward, I manage to crack my lids and see the spinning vortex of a portal.

Liam jumps in, and I clutch around his neck, bracing myself for the agony of another portal and wondering if my poor body can survive another battering.

Chapter Eighteen

LIAM

When I carry Wren through the portal she creates, there is no sensation of being ripped to pieces. The only other painless portal I've been through was the one made by the oracle, and that one was still disorienting. However, Wren's magic wrought a gateway of swirling light, and it was like walking through a doorway. Unsure what to expect, I'm stunned we end up in the fairy glen.

Cool air caresses my skin as two moons, one full, one crescent, glow high above. Only the portal behind me is out of place compared to what I remember. "Close the portal, love."

Eyes barely open, she nods, and the swirling wind dies to a pinpoint before disappearing. "I would like to be a fly on the wall when Ciaran comes for me and finds the cell empty."

I carry her to the edge of the spring and ease her to the soft grass. "I'm not yet done with him. He'll pay for this."

Her stare grows wide, and the rage and hatred I see there make me even more determined to destroy those who put it there. "When we win this war, they'll both pay the price for their sins."

"If you need to talk about what happened, I will always listen, but for now, I'd like to take you into the water. It will heal you, and we can wash away the stink of Coire." I run my fingers through her hair, but it's knotted, and I don't get far.

She winces. "It will take a small miracle to comb through this mess." Her attempt at a smile makes me love her even more, and I wouldn't have thought that possible.

Holding her back with one hand, I lift her shirt over her head.

Weak, she tries to help the process by raising her arms. "I feel foolish to need so much help with a simple task."

After removing her shoes, I pull her jeans off and put them in a pile. Once I've stripped out of my clothes, I kneel beside her. "It's my honor to take care of you, Wren. You're the bravest person I have ever known—elf, human, or other."

"Being tortured is brave?" She wraps her arms around my neck as I lift her.

"Surviving torture and using those feelings to create magic never before seen in Domhan to facilitate our escape is more courage than most and more strength than I would have." I step into the water. "If you can float, I'll make soap."

She lets her head fall back into the water. Her blond curls spread out like a silken halo around her. As she floats, she watches me. "Magic has its benefits."

With a simple spell, I draw water up and alter its composition to shift it into a bar of soap. Starting at her feet, I wash her inch by inch, cleaning off the grime of the underworld. The fairy glen and water are sufficient restorative even in the night to feed my magic. Drawing a deep breath, I concentrate on washing her hair.

She lets out a long, satisfied moan. "That feels nice. This place is magic?"

"Fairy glens are created by magic, and the echo of it remains." I help her rinse the soap from her hair. "Shall I help you to the bank to wait while I wash?"

"I'll float here a while." She runs her fingers through her hair, tugging through the smaller knots. "Venora can't find us here?"

"No. The magic here is too full of light, even if Venora walked by the glen, she wouldn't be able to see it. If something evil did make its way in here, the glen would destroy it." I soap and rinse quickly, then put my arms under Wren to support her.

"Should we start walking to your home?" Her eyes are tired but determined.

"Not yet. The glen will restore us before we leave." I carry her from the water and turn the grass into a soft blanket before I lay her gently down. Even though I'm exhausted and worried, my body still responds to hers.

She points to the moons. "Can you tell from those how long we were down there?"

"Almost two months."

Sitting up, she winces and grunts.

I run my fingers along the deep purple bruises on her ribs. "Easy."

"Months? It seemed long, but I wouldn't have guessed that long." Lying beside me, she snuggles in at my shoulder.

"Time is hard to judge without a day and a night. Rest now, Wren. You'll feel better in the morning." I kiss her wet hair.

She sighs. "I already feel better. Safe." The last word is barely audible as she falls asleep.

Wrapping her carefully in my arms, I hold her as sleep alludes me. I watch her chest rise and fall, and I thank the old gods that she survived. My own life is a bonus. All I want is her safety. Once again, I'm struck by the realization that I should have left her in her own world, oracle be dammed. We should have tried bombarding the Watchers' Gate with magic and spared the human women our fate.

The Dagda, king of the old gods, stands before me. His face is cast in a series of connected wrinkles, and his hair and beard are long and gray. On his head, an antlered crown has grown green with leaves. His eyes stoic and filled with compassion, he levels them on me. Sitting on a throne grown from a living tree, at his feet is his cauldron, and in his right hand a tall staff. Cradled in the crook of his right arm is the harp of legend, Uaitne. He does not play nor speak, yet in his eyes the warning that I must go forward is clear.

A Crown of Wind and Water

With no memory of falling asleep, I'm startled awake when Wren stretches catlike beside me. Gloriously naked, she's perfectly lovely, and the bruises have faded from most of her skin, though the ugly one at her ribs is myriad blues, greens, and yellows.

The sun warms the glen, and I spread my fingers, testing my magic. It tingles along my nerves as if it's been waiting for this moment. Pressing my palm along her ribs, I let my fingers drape across each ripple.

She sighs and wiggles closer, pressing her ass to my thick shaft. "What are you doing?"

"Healing your ribs. I think they may be broken again." It takes a great deal of willpower to concentrate on her injury and not the wicked way she's trying to entice me into sex.

"I feel a lot better. This glen is wonderful. Can we stay here and not worry about what's happening outside?"

Wishing what she asks for were possible won't make it so. Here with Wren in my arms, I could live and die happy.

While the heat of healing rolls across her skin, the bruise lightens, and the sharp pain of her bone snapping back into place stings us both.

She gasps then relaxes. "Oh, that was almost as bad as when it happened, but the pain is easing. Thank you."

I cringe at her comparison of my healing to torture. "I'm sorry. Healing is often painful. If it makes you feel any better, I felt the pain as well."

"Of course that doesn't make me feel better." She rolls to face me. Her curls fall over her eyes.

Brushing her hair away from her face, I wish I could tell her there will be no more pain. I want to keep her safe from danger. I let the walls down so she can feel my desire.

She smiles. "I know, Liam. But there will be more trouble before this is over."

Her curls are like silk under my fingertips. "May I brush your hair?"

"You have a brush? Have you been holding out on me?"

Sitting up, I go to the edge of the spring and pull a round stone from the water's edge. Rinsing off the palm-size brown rock, I know it will serve the purpose. I carry it back to Wren. Letting the rising sun fill me with renewed magic, I focus on the stone and reform every molecule into a brush similar to the one I've watched her use on our journey.

Grinning, she takes it from me. "Amazing. I need to wet this mess."

Unashamed of her nudity, she jumps up and rushes into the water.

My cock jerks painfully, as watching her naked and healthy is always going to affect me. She's thinner than when we met. These last months have been hard on her. I love every inch of her, but I look forward to sitting at my parents' table and seeing her well-fed and happy.

Returning to me with her curls dripping, she sits and hands me the brush. "It won't be easy. We may have to cut it off. I've never gone a day without combing it, and you said it's been months. I may have to get used to a pixie cut."

Taking one knotted wad of her hair, I let my magic flow over the damp strands, separating them. "I don't know what a pixie cut is, love, but you'll not have to cut your hair unless you wish to."

Silently, she sits with her bare back to me while I work through each knot and nest of her hair. Soon, the brush combs through easily, and her curls bounce around her shoulders.

When she turns, her smile lights my heart. "Thank you."

I had no idea I was unhappy with my life until this woman filled me with more joy than I have ever known. "I'm never leaving you, Wren."

Playfully, she pushes me to my back and straddles my hips. "You've told me."

Thick and ready, my cock presses along her slit and it's hard to form words. I run my hands along her waist to her hips and settle at the crease of her thighs. "If you cannot stay here in Domhan after this war is over, I will return to your world. If you go to the top of the highest mountain, I will climb behind you. If you reject me, I will respect your decision and watch over you from afar. You will be safe and happy, as seeing you so will be my purpose in life."

Her smile fades, but emotion swims in her clear eyes. "I have not seen much in this world to recommend it, but I'm not ruling out staying here."

"Why?"

She's been attacked and tortured, demeaned and abused, not to mention being forced to kill.

She leans down and rests her forearms on my chest. Her hair creates shadows around her face as she meets my gaze. "Since coming here, Venora has influenced most of what I've seen. Her evil has clouded what must have once been an amazing world. Yet, there were still the centaurs and Adhar. I have a feeling, one day, the miracle of this place will match the magic rushing through my body. If I'm wrong, I'll return to my world, but if I'm right, what a life I might have." She blushes and rocks her hips. "And then there's you."

Rocking with her, it isn't easy to think. "I told you I would go back to your world with you."

"I don't think you'd be happy there all the time. The lure of lounging pants will not be enough for you. Here, you're a soldier with elves who follow you and obey your orders to give and take. In my world, you'd be hiding who you really are." Lowering her mouth to mine, she presses a soft kiss there.

I grip the back of her head and deepen the kiss. Her tongue meets mine with all the passion burning within me. How can anyone be so perfect? Pressing more kisses along her jaw, I rock my hips. My shaft rubs through her wetness. "I've never met anyone as good and honorable as you. Wherever we end up, I promise to make you happy, Wren Martin. If I fail, I'll have made nothing of my life."

She moans and lifts her hips.

I take her nipple into my mouth and suck as she impales herself on my cock. "Gods, Wren. I could have waited until you had time to rest."

A low moan pushes from her mouth as her body stretches around me. "Maybe you could have, but I need you. I will always need you, Liam." She sets a slow pace that drives us both to the brink. Lifting to her knees, she rides me fast and hard. Her head thrown back, she grips both breasts and tugs her nipples.

I press my thumb to her clitoris and circle the sensitive bud until she's screaming my name over and over.

Her body pulses around me, drawing my pleasure over the edge. Unable to stop, I empty into her perfection. Pulling her across my chest, I bury my face in her curls and kiss her ear. "You are magnificent."

Intimately connected, she shifts to pull me deeper and my cock hardens again. "I do like this about elves. Are you all like this?'

"For our purposes, it's just me, and only for you." There will never be another. I roll her to her back, careful to cradle her and keep my weight from pressing too hard. I may have healed her, but she's still fragile. Pulling back, I fill her again and again, slow and deliberate.

Each thrust forces the most erotic moan from her lips.

"I want to hear that sound for the rest of my life."

She lifts her knees to take me deeper and wraps her feet around my back. "Liam. I'm going to come again. I'm... You're... Oh god," she screams and pulses around me.

It's not easy, but I hold my own pleasure this time. I have time for that. Leaning on my elbows, I comb a few strands of hair from her cheek and tuck them behind her ear. "I love you."

With the sexiest smile, she makes the same gesture with my hair. "I love you, too."

Moaning as I pull from her exquisite body, I lift her and carry her to the water. If she's sore from the lovemaking, the water will heal her, and if she's not, it will renew her desires. At the very least, it will feel good to soak in the cool spring.

Without dipping her head, she paddles and watches me. "If I decide to stay here, where would we live?"

I love the way this conversation has started. "Traditionally, as I'm a son of the rightful queen, we would live in the palace."

Her adorable face scrunches like a mouse. "I can't scream while you ravage me if your parents are down the hall."

"That won't do. I'll build you a house far enough from my family that you and I will wake the birds every morning with our passionate lovemaking." I mean every word. I'd build her ten houses if that's what she wants. "If I came to Texas, where would we live?"

"I can't imagine you in Texas." She giggles. "I suppose we could move into my grandmother's house. It would need renovations, but it's a sweet place and there are a few acres between it and Momma's place."

"And you'll make your jewelry, while I figure out what uses I have in Texas?" I try to picture that outcome, but it's vague without having ever seen the land.

"Maybe." She swims forward and wraps her arms around my neck. "Do you think I could work here?"

Gripping her ass, I pull her thighs around my waist. "I know that elves would adore your unique art, and you would be a great success if you wished to continue working."

With a shift, she lifts herself higher in my arms. "Do you want to have children?"

"I'm not opposed. I like children." I consider the idea.

She cocks her head. "Have you never thought about having a family, Liam?"

I place her so she's sitting on the grassy ground with her feet dangling in the water, and I stand between her knees. Tipping her chin up, I kiss her slowly, making love to her bottom lip and then the top before swirling my tongue inside her warmth.

She threads her fingers through my hair and turns her head to allow me deeper access. One moment we're discussing the future, and I plan a chaste kiss, and the next, I can't decide if I want to taste her sweet center of bury my throbbing cock inside her again.

We're both breathless. Her chest rises and falls, and her lips are rosy from the kiss.

Pressing my forehead to hers, I say, "I never dared dream I would meet a person with whom I'd want a family."

I stop the dozen questions simmering behind her eyes by dropping to my knees and pressing my shoulders between her thighs.

She gasps, forced back on her elbows. "Liam."

Pushing her legs over my shoulders, I breathe in her heady sweetness, then run my tongue along her soft folds.

"Liam. That's teasing," she scolds with the most magical gasps.

I swirl my tongue around her clitoris then suck the bud gently at first, then harder.

Rocking against my face, she cries my name and grips my hair. Her fingers dig into my scalp and her heels into my back.

Every tiny pain adds to my pleasure. I slip a finger inside her and lick and suck until she lies back in the grass and throws her head from side to side. I add a second finger and suck hard and steadily.

With a scream that must hurt her throat, she comes in a torrent of pulsation and sweet juices that I lap up like it's the nectar of the gods. "You are magnificent." I kiss her just below her navel, then lick the rest of her juice from my fingers before I climb up the bank and fill her.

Immediately, her sheath throbs around me and she says my name like a prayer.

Without moving, I kiss her chin, her cheek, then along her jaw. "Easy, my love. Don't move until it feels good."

She wraps her legs around my hips and her arms around my neck. "Everything with you feels wonderful." Tightening her legs, she brings me all the way inside.

Nothing could ever feel as perfect as the two of us together. No victory is worth losing this woman. I slide out to the head. "Maybe we should go back to Texas now. You'd be safer. You can make a portal, and we can leave."

"That's fear talking." She pulls me in to the base and keeps her legs tight as a vise. "We'll have our time after your world is safe." She tips her pelvis and brings me even deeper.

I moan and pull back. "Do you promise?" I thrust inside her.

"Oh god. That's so good." She digs her fingers into my shoulders.

"Promise me." I fill her again and again while our gazes are locked. "Please." I meant to be gentle, but my need is too great, and her pleasure is very close.

"I promise."

My skin tingles with magic.

Wren glows, and winds whip around us as the water rises from the spring, splashing our feet.

Pleasure erupts within me, and I fill her as her body tightens with her orgasm. She pulls my mouth to hers, kissing me as if I am the air she breathes. Returning her passion, I pump the last of my seed until I can't hold my weight and collapse over her.

Worried I'll crush her, I slide from her perfect sheath and roll to lie beside her. "You are my everything, Wren. Will you marry me?" It just popped out of my mouth of its own accord. I meant it. I want that life, but I hadn't meant to ask it now in a fairy glen after the most amazing sex of my life.

Rolling to her side to face me, she toys with the hair on my chest. "Ask me again when we're calm, safe, and haven't just had magically mind-blowing sex."

Joy rushes through me. She didn't say no. "I will."

"I'm going to wash our clothes." She rises and goes to the pile of filthy clothes still in the heap where I left them after we arrived. "I don't want to meet your mother smelling like hell, literally." She sniffs the clothes. "Though I'm not sure that sulfur stink will ever come out."

Sorry to lose the view of her naked in this magical place, I get up and take the clothes from her arms. "We can wash them together."

Those lovely crystal eyes widen as she stares at me. "That's nice."

"The imbecile who left you didn't help with laundry?" I step into the spring and reach up to help her in.

"He considered housework beneath him. It's an unfortunate side effect of having a mother who doted and did everything for him." She looks at something along the edge of the water and reaches out.

I begin washing with the bar of soap. One item at a time, I scrub them and watch Wren pry something from the mud. "What did you find?"

Smiling, she holds up a perfectly round stone of brown and gold. "It's a tiger's eye and has already tumbled by the water. Do you think the fairies would mind if I kept it and made a bracelet?"

"I've never met a fairy, but once they saw how beautifully you used it, I imagine they'd be pleased." I dip her little underwear into the water, running my fingers over the lace.

Wren places the stone on the grass before snatching her intimate item away from me. "I'll wash that." Her blush is absurd and adorable.

My laughter cannot be stopped. "I wouldn't mind another day here to recover. Without horses, it will take a few days to walk home."

"Another day would be lovely." She places each item on the grass, where the sun has begun to warm the glen. "Do you think that portal I made was a one-time thing?"

I had considered the idea. "No. I suspect with practice, you could make a portal anywhere, but we don't know much about your magic, how it affects you, or how to control it. So far, you've needed dangerous situations to create wind and water magic with any power. The portal was after a terrible event, with the fear of more of the same. If you want to try, I won't object, but I would feel more comfortable if you waited until after we learn more."

With a nod, she places her torn but clean pink shirt on the grass. "I suppose there's no help for looking a shambles when I meet your family." She sighs.

"They will be happy to meet you and understand the situation." I wash the final sock and lay it beside the others.

"All the royal families I know about are pretty strict. Won't they disapprove of our relationship? Don't you have to marry someone with a good bloodline and the right connections?" She rinses the soap from her hands. Her breasts bob at the surface of the clear water, and worry creases her brow.

I wrap my arms around her. My cock seems unhindered by the fact that we've already enjoyed epic lovemaking not long ago. "My family is reasonable, though in the days before females were scarce, they would have wanted a match as you describe. I think they will be happy for us. This is meant to be, Wren. I feel it in my soul. Don't you?"

Pressing her cheek to my chest, she says, "I do, but that doesn't mean your parents will."

"No matter what they think, it will not alter my feelings or actions. I will not lose you, no matter what we face, friend or foe." I kiss the top of her head.

"That was a pretty speech." The high-pitched voice comes from the grass just beyond our drying clothes.

Chapter Nineteen

WREN

As soon as we hear the voice, Liam pushes me behind his back and stands as if he's ready for an attack.

I peek around his side.

The voice seems to be coming from a firefly. A glowing blue dot of light hovers above our clothes. "I'm not dangerous. Well, I guess I could be. But nothing evil can happen within a fairy glen. The one who gave her life for this place wouldn't allow it."

"I thought elves and fairies don't mix." I squint to try to focus on the little light as it zips around the clothes, hovers for a moment over the tiger's eye stone, and then flies around our heads.

She giggles. "That used to be true. Rían and I changed that."

"Rían Redmond? How do you know the captain of the

guard of Tús Nua?" Liam steps from the water, beautifully naked.

The fairy giggles again. In a flash of light, a woman appears with pointed ears, smaller than an elf's, and a cherubic face with large gray eyes, and short blond hair. At her back, the most beautiful butterfly wings glow with iridescent rainbow colors. She's petite, perhaps two or three inches shorter than I am. She blushes bright pink and looks anywhere but at Liam's cock, which is still at half-mast from our embrace. "Rían will not like this." She can't seem to stop giggling. "He is my mate. Who are you?"

"Mate? What in the name of all the old gods is going on here? Is this some fairy trickery?" Liam steps forward.

Getting out of the spring, I hide my nudity behind Liam. "I imagine there is a lot to tell, Miss...?"

"Not miss. I am Niamh Fiain, Daughter of Muiredach and mate to Rían Redmond. I shall ask again, who are you?" She props her hands on her slim hips, and her wings flutter.

Liam gasps. "You're the fairy princess. He lowers his head in a bow. I am Liam Riordan, son of Elspeth."

A wide smile spreads across her sweet face. "I knew it. I felt the magic and made my way here as fast as my wings could take me. I can make a portal to take you home." She swings her arm in an arch.

Liam holds up his hands. "Wait."

She stops and cocks her head.

"We're not quite dressed for court."

Another giggle. "No, I suppose not." She flies over our clothes and dries them in a moment. "You should dress first."

I reach around Liam and grab my underwear, jeans, bra, and shirt. "Um, thank you. I wonder if I might ask a favor?"

A Crown of Wind and Water

She flies around Liam and sinks so that she's eye level with me when I pull my jeans on. "Are you the second human from the prophecy?"

"Maybe. I guess we'll find out." I cinch my bra, then pull on my tattered shirt. "Can we sit a little while before you make the portal. I'm not quite ready to face...whatever I'll have to face."

She looks from me to Liam, who has his pants on and is pulling the black t-shirt over his head. "If I don't return by nightfall, Rían will come with a company of soldiers to find me. If I leave you here—" She shakes her head. "I cannot abandon you here."

I pick up the smooth stone from the grass. "What if we sit and talk a little while, and you take us through your portal before dinner is served at the castle? These fairy glens are safe, right?"

Grinning, she sits in the grass. Her wings never stop moving. "We will be safe here."

Taking my hand, Liam leads me to sit with Niamh. He crosses his legs. "Did the centaurs and Wren's mother arrive safely?"

Wings beating faster, she bubbles with energy. "Almost two months ago. We believed you were both lost. Your mothers have been mourning you all this time. They'll be so happy to learn you're alive."

"Venora brought us to Coire." Liam plucks a blade of grass and tears it into shreds.

"I thought I scented that foul place. How did you escape, and how did you get here?"

While Liam explains our journey, I can't bear to see the pity on the fairy's face. Getting up, I find some longer grasses at the back edge of the spring. Plucking them, I sit on a rock and weave a braid around the little stone, imagining it done in gold with smaller stones on each side.

"Wren?" Liam's voice is full of concern. *Are you alright? I've told her as much as I'm going to. Will you come back? I think we should go through the portal. Your mother has suffered enough.*

Swallowing down my selfish tears, I stand and join them. I hand the little bracelet to Niamh. "This is for you. A gift for finding us and saving us the long walk."

Eyes wide, she smiles softly. "This is beautiful."

My cheeks heat at her compliment. I've never been good at accepting those graciously. "If I can find some gold, I'll do it the right way when I can. That grass will dry out and crack eventually."

"I love it, and I thank you, Wren, daughter of Birdie."

My surprise must register since neither of us mentioned my name.

"Your mother has told me all about you. She is a lovely person with so many wonderful stories. My father has taken a particular liking to her." Niamh rises with her wings lifting her off the ground.

Liam stands and takes my hand. "The fairy king is in Tús Nua?"

"Not all the time, but he visits and meets with the Riordan often. It's why I sensed you. He comes through this glen, and I felt a different kind of magic. I guess that was your human portal. When he didn't portal right away to the city, I worried he was in danger and flew here as fast as I could." She ties the bracelet with magic and admires the stone.

A Crown of Wind and Water

"Why didn't you portal here?" It fills me with joy to watch her look lovingly at my work, even if it's just grass and a rock. She likes it, and that makes me happy.

"I can only portal from a glen. Even my father needs a glen's magic to create a portal. The magic of our island is similar, but no sacrifice was made, and he can only come to a glen. That is why I keep my senses open to this place to know when he's arriving."

With a gentle squeeze of my hand, Liam says, "We're ready to go home now, Princess."

"Just Niamh. We are practically family as Rían has told me he considers you like a brother." She flies to the space in front of the trees and swings her arm in a wide arc.

A portal opens.

Before we walk through, she stops Liam with a hand on his arm. "I think I should warn you that your woman will not be happy about the obvious connection between you two."

My gut lurches into my throat. "Woman?"

"She is not my woman. Dierdre is someone whom I dallied with some time ago, but she's deluded herself into making more of it. I have told her many times that we are no longer together. I told her so again just before I left to find you, Wren. I promise you, there is nothing between Dierdre and me. She is a nuisance and nothing more." There is so much anger in his voice, it startles me.

"Okay—if you say so."

From the strained expression on Niamh's face, I don't think this Dierdre will agree.

The way Liam's back is stiff and the tick in his jaw is confirmation.

I hold my breath. There's no going back. "I'm sure it's

going to be fine." My voice isn't even convincing to me. *You might have mentioned this woman.*

She's not important. You are the only woman, besides my mother, who has ever been important to me. However, I begin to wonder if Dierdre is unstable.

That's comforting. Even inside our heads, my thoughts drip with sarcasm.

We walk through the portal.

We arrive at a gate with a white city behind it. It looks like Italian marble gleaming in the midday sun. The walls holding the gate are gray stone extending out of sight in both directions. Flags fly on the ramparts, but the elf at the gate has my full attention. His gaze locks with Niamh, and he relaxes as if he were only moments away from sending out a search party and had no intention of waiting until nightfall.

When he manages to pull his attention from her, he sees Liam and his lips tick up in what might have been a smile, but I'm guessing that is a rare thing for this soldier in his blue uniform with gold trim. It's similar to the one Liam wore the first time I saw him. "I'm glad the reports of your death were exaggerated."

"Do you have Mark Twain here?" It pops out of my mouth before I can stop it.

The two men salute by coming to attention, then a brief nod. Then they hug, and I can see that the fairy was correct in calling them brothers.

Liam pounds the other man's back and breaks the embrace. "Good to see you, Rían. I have met your lovely mate. I never would have believed you would succumb to love."

"I think there is no real choice when it finds you," Captain Redmond says and pulls Niamh into his arms, careful not to damage her wings, as if he's practiced at how to hold her.

"I look forward to that story, my friend." Liam takes my hand. "This is Wren Martin. She has agreed to help us fight the witch queen and has suffered much on our behalf." His eyes fill with love as he gazes down at me. "She is mine as I am hers."

The captain's eyes widen momentarily before he bows low to me. "You have my gratitude, Wren, daughter of Birdie, and my allegiance, as the mate of one I consider my brother."

With no idea what the protocol is, I nod. "It's nice to meet you, Captain."

"We must go to the residence. Your parents will be overjoyed, and Aaran has been worried." Rían turns with Niamh's hand in his.

"Aaran is here? He's alive?" Excitement and relief fuel Liam's tone.

Stopping, Rían cocks his head. "He is well and also succeeded in his quest."

The joy of hearing that Venora had lied rushes through Liam and our connection. I'll never get used to how much he holds inside.

Niamh's feet don't touch the ground as she flies alongside Rían on the walk up the road, talking quickly about how she found us, but not mentioning that Liam was naked.

Rían is brown skinned and devastatingly handsome,

whereas she is cute and fair as a daisy petal. Their love shines like a beacon for anyone to see.

I wonder if that's what others see when they look at Liam and me.

Liam stares at the two of them, looking bewildered. "Fairies in an elven city. A fairy who will speak to elves and love one, and the fairy king, conferring with my mother. I don't know if I can take many more surprises in one day."

"I feel like a squirrel cornered by a herd of cats. If I can take it, you can."

He laughs and squeezes my hand before lifting it to his lips and kissing my knuckles. "I'll be with you the entire time. Even when I'm not, you know you can find me." He touches the side of his head.

Of course, he's right, I will be fine. I've met important people before. Corell and Farress are the leaders of their herd. I met the mayor of our small town once when he came to a craft fair. I'll be fine. I don't know who I think I'm kidding.

The main road is built of stone, and it curves upward. When we round the bend, the castle gleams at the top of a wide, terraced hill carved from marble. The castle features three white towers, with the largest one rising from the center of an enormous building.

We begin climbing stairs that seem never to end. Every twenty or so, there's a stretch of flat marble followed by more steps.

Elves begin to come out of their homes and crowd the side of the stairs. They whisper his name, and the noise grows louder until their voices rise in a cheer as they collectively realize Liam has come home.

A Crown of Wind and Water

The last set of steps is steeper and twice as high. The front of the castle is pure white, and the three towers jutting from its roof resemble a crown. Carved below the towers and above the doors are scenes of battle and triumph. Beneath are six pillars, and at the center, an enormous arched door with three diamonds carved over the top.

The door opens, and six soldiers dressed in blue and gold livery rush out to flank the door.

Momma runs out with a man and a woman dressed in white and blue.

There is no time to examine them. My heart is racing, and I run into Momma's arms. "Thank god you're okay." I hug her as tightly as I can, making sure she's real.

She pulls me back to get a look at me. "You look a bit worse for wear, baby girl." Wrapping her arms around me, she hugs me tighter than before. "I saw you go down that hole and prayed to our god and the elves' gods that I would see you again. And Liam jumped in headfirst after you. Where on earth did you get to? Elspeth used all her magic to find you, and there was nothing."

"I'm not surprised." Liam hugs us both when it becomes clear Momma is not letting me go.

Finally, Momma realizes we're not alone and lets me go. She wraps her arms around Liam. "You saved my girl. I'll never be able to thank you enough."

"I didn't save her, Birdie. She saved us both." He pulls back and takes my hand. "It's a long story and maybe not one for the middle of the concourse. Mother, Father, this is Wren Martin. She is the human from the prophecy and the love of my life. I intend to marry her as soon as she agrees. Wren, my parents, Elspeth and Brion Riordan."

"My word." Momma's voice is breathy with the romance of it.

I'd be smitten myself if this weren't so public and his parents didn't look as if they'd been hit by a truck.

Elspeth Riordan has bright blond hair, and jewels on her pointed ears sparkle in the sunlight. She recovers, and her smile is warm and welcoming. Brion doesn't smile. His hair is deep red, and his eyes are bright blue. I see a bit of him in Liam's jaw and stern expressions.

A moment later, Elspeth takes my hand. "Welcome, Wren. It is a great relief that you are alive. You must be exhausted. We shall have a room made up for you to rest."

Liam looks about to burst with whatever part of his mother's greeting he disagrees with, but she holds up a hand and silences him.

Worried that an all-out royal feud will begin on the public terrace, I force a smile. "I am exhausted, and we have been through a lot. There is much to tell you."

She threads my hand through her elbow as we turn and walk toward the castle doors.

The crowd breaks into a loud cheer.

Leaning down, Elspeth says, "They are overjoyed you have come. Now, if my youngest son would find his way home, we could start to control Domhan once again and perhaps break the curse."

What can I say? I'm one of three tools brought here for the sole purpose of saving this world. She didn't actually say that, but why should she accept a human woman into her family? I have no connections to offer.

Momma is behind me with Liam. "I cried my eyes out for both of you, though I never gave up hope."

A Crown of Wind and Water

"It's true." Elspeth smiles. "Even when Brion and I had accepted and mourned for Liam, Birdie told us to delay holding our services. She knew you were still alive."

"How did you know, Momma?" We step through the grand entrance and into an opulent foyer with sweeping staircases and a shining chandelier.

"My heart told me that my baby girl was still alive. Until it told me something else, I wouldn't let you go." She pats Liam's arm. "I want to hear everything, but you both look like you could use a hot tub and some hours to sleep."

Elspeth nods and hugs me. "Birdie is right. You'll be cared for here, Wren. I'm sure the staff already made a room ready when word of your arrival came. Will you honor us at a family dinner tonight? You can tell us all about your journey after you were separated from your mother and the centaurs."

"It's not fit conversation for dinner, your majesty, ma'am, umm, Mrs. Riordan." I have no idea how to address her. It would have been a good thing to ask thirty minutes ago.

"Elspeth and Brion will do nicely, Wren." Brion's face is still tightly held in a stern expression, but he pulls me into a quick hug. "You're most welcome here. If the story is too gruesome or painful, we can wait until you're able to tell it."

"Thank you, sir." I can't call his father Brion. "It will be difficult, but there are things you'll need to know. Maybe even things within my experience that I don't yet realize are important."

He lifts his eyebrows. "We'll see you at dinner. Get the rest you need."

"Liam!" The joyful voice comes from the top of the stairs. An elf with light blond hair and a wide smile sits on the curved railing and rides it down like he's a boy. It's not hard to guess that this is Aaran. As soon as he lands, he pulls his brother into his arms. "I never gave up hope."

Hugging his older brother tightly, Liam says, "For a time, hope was difficult to come by, Aaran. Perhaps it was yours and Birdie's that pushed Wren and me to safety."

Pulling back, Aaran's smile falters. He studies his younger brother's face. "Where did she take you?"

There is no doubt that *she* is Venora. Liam looks around at the group of mostly his family. He whispers, "Coire."

Elspeth gasps.

Momma says, "What's that, a city?"

"It's hell, Momma." My throat is so tight, I almost don't manage the short sentence.

Her hand over her mouth, Momma's eyes fill with tears. "Don't you have to be dead to go to hell?"

"Evidently, not in this world. Though there were plenty down there who were not alive as we define it." Tears spill down my cheeks, and I can't seem to stop them, even though I don't want to cry in front of Liam's family. They'll think I'm a weakling. They'll think I'm not strong enough to be Liam's wife, or mate, or whatever they call it here.

At some point, a human woman with brown hair and kind green eyes joins us. She gently takes my hand. "I'm Harper Craig. I came here from New Jersey. You need some time."

She leads me up the stairs away from the group. When we enter a long hallway, the voices from below begin talking all at once. "They'll work it out, Wren."

"Maybe I should have stayed and fought whatever fight Liam's in." I drag my feet.

Harper stops and squeezes my hand. "You can go back, but don't you think you've been through enough for now? Let Liam work on his parents. You can have a soak in the most luxurious tub you've probably ever seen, then a long nap." She opens a door on the right.

Harper is wearing black leggings and a white tunic. She's only a few inches taller than me, and from what I've seen, that makes us both pretty short by elf standards.

"I had a duffel bag before we were taken. It had a pair of jeans and a few shirts in it." I hesitate. "But what you're wearing looks more comfortable."

Nodding, she says, "They have nice things here." She points to the gowns hanging on the front of a wardrobe. Beautiful things with lace in luscious colors of green, yellow, and orange, all colors that suit Harper's complexion.

"Is this your room?" I back up to the door.

The way she laughs and takes my hand makes me like her immediately. "I moved into Aaran's room almost from the first night, but the staff insists on keeping my clothes here. They're still arranging your room, but you looked ready to fall to pieces down there, and this one is not really in use."

"Then you and Aaran are lovers?" I should have used more tact, but I'm too tired for it.

Harper blushes. "We're committed to each other in all ways. From the way Liam stared at you, I'm guessing it's much the same with the two of you."

I nod, and emotions well in my throat. "I need a good cry before I take that bath, Harper. Do you think you could keep whoever is going to fuss over me away for about an hour?"

Pulling me into a hug. "You got it, sister. When we have time, I'll tell you about the horrors of my trip here. Maybe it will make you feel better. Though, I didn't get sucked into hell."

"I'm glad you didn't."

She points to the bed. "It's a great place to cry. Believe me, I shed my fair share of tears here. Through that door is a bathroom where you'll think you've gone to heaven. I'll see that when they do come to fuss over you, they have some very comfortable elven clothes for you to change into."

"Thank you."

She waves a hand. "We humans have to stick together. Besides, I already love your mother to pieces. I'm sure we're going to be good friends."

Unable to push words out past the lump in my throat, I force a weak smile and nod.

Once Harper leaves, I lie on the large bed with its pale-peach duvet and lace trimmings, press my face into a downy pillow, and cry so hard my back hurts. It pours out of me, and I can't make it stop.

Liam's mind touches mine, but I push him away.

For some reason, now that I'm safe, I can't hold it together.

The door opens and closes. Momma's soft fingers run through my hair. "It's alright, baby girl. You just get it all out."

"I didn't want you to see me like this." My voice lacks the strength and toughness I expect from a Texas woman.

She rubs my back. "Liam said he could feel that you're upset. He wanted to come to you, but I told him that sometimes a girl needs her momma."

I nod, and fresh tears come. It's a miracle that there's any more water in me to make tears.

"Stay here. I'm gonna run you a bath then let that nice Lila in to heat the water with her magic." Momma does as she says, and I don't even look up to acknowledge Lila, whoever she is.

Once she's gone, I let Momma help me into the tub. She sits on a chair behind me and washes my hair like she did when I was a little girl.

Once I'm calm and my muscles soothed, she tucks me into bed. "Sleep now, baby girl. You're safe."

The last word sounds muddled as I fall deeply into nothing.

At one point, I think I'm awake, and a female elf with long brown hair and bright hazel eyes stares down at me. Her arms are crossed over an ample chest. She's beautiful but frowning. Maybe it's another premonition. Exhaustion pulls me back into a restless sleep.

There are loud noises in the distance. When I open my eyes again, the woman isn't there. I must have dreamed of her.

A knock at the door pulls me fully awake. "Come in."

Liam stands in the doorway. "Feeling better?"

With a few deep breaths, I assess my body's aches and pains and find them minor. "I am. How are you? Did you rest?"

Wearing clean cream-colored leggings and a belted brown tunic that ties with laces at a V-neck, he looks clean and painfully handsome as he closes the door. As he crosses to me, his steps are long and graceful. He climbs on the bed as if it's something he does every day, and pulls me close, wrapping both arms around me. "I would have slept here if your mother hadn't convinced me that you needed space. Which, she had to explain, meant time away from everyone."

"I was just emotional because of...everything. I don't need space from you, Liam. Momma doesn't understand yet." I lay my head back on his chest.

"Then you don't mind that I've had them put your things in my room?"

My pulse speeds. "I don't mind, but what will your mother and father think?"

"They think it's impulsive and lacks propriety." He laughs. "I cannot bear the idea of you sleeping elsewhere."

"Close is good." It's strange to be in a relationship where I have no doubts about the man's feelings. I feel what he feels. My only worries are from people outside of the two of us, and that we are literally from different worlds.

He kisses the top of my head and points to a pile of clothes folded neatly on a chair near the window and a blue dress hanging on the wardrobe that glimmers in the late-day sun. "Someone brought you something to wear to dinner and an option if you'd prefer to be comfortable."

"Will you be changing for dinner?"

His chin rubs along the side of my head. "I will wear my uniform. It's customary to dress for dinner. Lila will probably be here soon to help you."

"There was a woman in here. I wonder if that was Lila?" I push my memory to bring back the hazy image.

"What woman?" His voice sharpens.

"An elf with long brown hair and hazel eyes. I thought she stared down at me while I slept, but I might have dreamed her."

A Crown of Wind and Water

He stiffens, then pulls away and rises from the bed. "You didn't dream her." Without an explanation, he leans down and kisses my cheek. "I'll come to escort you to dinner."

I jump out of bed. His demeanor makes the hair on the back of my neck stand up. "Liam, who was it?"

Softening his expression, he returns and pulls me into his arms. "I suspect it was Dierdre, but I will deal with her. You have nothing to worry about."

"I wasn't worried until you said that." In truth, I thought I had dreamed the elf woman and that she was a product of the stress of being in a new place and all that had come before.

Taking my face in his hands, he presses a kiss to my lips.

There's a light knock on the door, and an elf with light brown hair and brown eyes steps in. She sees Liam and gives him a schoolmarmish look that should have quelled him.

He laughs and turns back to me. "I will speak to Dierdre. Everyone here is happy you have come, and you already know how I feel." The warmth of his love washes over me.

My cheeks heat as he kisses me again and rushes from the room, giving Lila a peck on the cheek on his way out.

She slaps his shoulder. "You need to dress for dinner," she calls after him, but he's long gone. "I am Lila. Would you like me to do your hair, Miss Martin?"

"Please call me Wren. Is it inappropriate here to leave it down for dinner?" I touch my wild curls. I wish I had one of my combs. I suppose the witch queen will throw my treasures into the fires of hell. I can't even remember when she took my bracelet.

"Not at all." Lila takes the blue gown from the wardrobe. "They told me you were fair, and I thought this color would suit, but I can see I'll need to shorten the length."

"The dress is lovely. I'm sorry to cause you more work. I can find my duffel and wear my own clothes." I have no idea where Liam's room is, but I'm sure that's where my duffel bag was put after whatever occurred below with his parents.

"It's nothing. You forget we have magic for such tasks when they must be done in a hurry." She winks.

"I suppose I didn't think of that." I laugh and try on the beautiful gown of periwinkle, watching in awe as Lila uses the gentlest magic to adjust the material to fit me, as if it were made just for me. If only this world fit as easily. "Do you think I can have access to the bag that the centaurs brought for me? It has some jewelry in it that I'd like to wear."

"Of course. I'll have someone bring it right away." After going to the door and speaking to someone in the hall, she asks me to sit in front of a small mirrored vanity table, and fusses with my hair and smiles. "Curls are rare in elves. Your hair is beautiful."

An elf in blue livery knocks and then trips into the room. "Your bag, my lady." He thrusts my duffel toward me.

Lila frowns. "By the old gods, Paddy. You are too clumsy by half."

"I apologize." Paddy bows, places my bag on the floor, and backs out of the room.

I giggle. "I'm glad not all elves are self-assured and graceful. I thought I would feel quite frumpy here." Lifting my bag, I dig in the side pocket until I feel the small jewelry bag, and pull it out. I roll it out on the little vanity table, revealing the few pieces I brought for the trip to England.

"Oh, how beautiful." Lila stares over my shoulder.

"Thank you." I pick up a silver necklace with a swallow in flight and a pair of silver earrings that I noticed Liam admired when we were in a pub one night. "I thought these might look nice with the dress."

Lila picks up the necklace and examines it with a softness of expression and a slight smile. "And you made this? Your mother told me that you were a remarkable artist, but I never expected... This is exquisite." She pushes my hair aside and clips the chain around my neck.

"You are too kind." I slip the earrings through my piercings and pinch my cheeks. "Do you think they'll like me, Lila?"

Her expression is kind as she meets my gaze in the mirror. "I think they will adore you. I think this world is grateful to you. I knew Liam is in love with you from the moment I saw the two of you together. If that were all that were true, would it be enough to ease your worry, Wren?"

I dab the corner of my eye before I burst into tears again. I've got to get these emotions under control. "It would be more than enough."

She pats my shoulder. "Have a lovely evening. I'm going to go and see if Harper needs anything. Liam will return to escort you in a few minutes."

"Thank you, Lila." I stare at my reflection for a long time, wondering how in the world I went from hell to wearing a beautiful gown such a short time.

Chapter Twenty

LIAM

As I escort Wren into the private dining room in the blue dress, my heart leaps in my chest. She is stunning and wears a charming smile. Not even my father is immune to her warm, kind nature as she thanks him for the hospitality.

Mother has had the dinner delayed slightly in favor of some light snacks and wine in the sitting area at the far side of the room. "I thought we might sit and hear about your journey before beginning dinner, as Wren is concerned for our appetites once we hear the tale."

Besides my family, Wren, and Birdie, the group includes Harper, Rían, and Niamh. Father told me that Corell and Farress were invited but declined as the centaurs are celebrating at their encampment this evening, which has been planned for a few weeks. They will visit tomorrow.

Several footmen offer wine, but as soon as their duties are complete, Father asks them to step out.

Mother says, "Corell and Birdie told us everything up until you were pulled through a ground portal."

"Are we late?" A blond elf accompanied by a stocky man with dark curly hair and wrinkles rush in.

It strikes me a second later that the man is human. Moreover, the woman is familiar.

"No. We're just going to hear about Liam's journey." Aaran takes Harper's hand, and they sit together.

The familiar elf stares at me and grins. "You've grown, Liam."

"Nainsi?" My memories are scattered because I was young, and she went to live with an aunt and uncle. Then she went with my parents to the human world and never came back. But this is my adopted sister. I pull her into my arms. "Nainsi. How is this possible?"

"We came back with Aaran and Harper." She touches my cheek. "This is my husband, Bert. Bert Donaldson, my brother, Liam."

Bert's handshake is firm, and he looks me in the eyes. "It's good to meet you. We've been praying you'd make it back."

"Nice to meet you." I'm still bewildered.

Father clears his throat. "I know there's a lot of catching up to do, but perhaps we'd better start with your journey, son."

"You're right, Father. Nainsi and I will have time to get reacquainted. The tale Wren and I need to share isn't pretty, but we did learn some things. Most of them don't bode well for elvenkind."

"You brought us the centaurs, Liam. That is a fascinating and favorable alliance." My mother's eyes shine with pride, and I'm honest enough with myself to accept that I covet that from her.

Wren takes my hand as I sit next to her. "Before we tell the story, has anyone seen Adhar?"

"Who is that?" Father looks to Birdie for clarification.

"The raven." Sitting on Wren's other side, Birdie pats her knee. "She left us as soon as you were taken. She flew north, and I haven't seen hide nor hair of her since."

I'll have to ask about that phrase later.

Wren sips her wine, then puts it on the low table. "I suppose she'll return if she's needed."

I wish there was something I could do to comfort her. "Wren was separated from the rest of us by the crows and the wolves. The portal opened, and she fell through. I dove in after her," I begin the story, letting Wren take over when she wishes.

When we reach the part where I was turned into a shadow demon, my mother and father both inhale sharply.

Nainsi clutches my shoulder.

They all relax a degree at the realization that Wren saved me from a fate much worse than death.

Wren keeps her voice level as she describes the scene in Venora's chamber and the torture she endured.

I have to force my breathing to remain steady and hold my rage deep inside. I never should have allowed her to be harmed in any way, let alone tortured for information.

Birdie weeps quietly.

"When they returned her to the cell, Wren was hurting, and I told her about the fairy glen a day's ride from here. I used my mind to show her the place. She opened the portal. I lifted her and walked through. There was no pain or sensation of spinning. One moment we were in the cell in Coire, and the next we stood in the glen with the moons and stars shining down on us. Wren closed the portal. We healed and would have stayed another day before daring the walk home, had Niamh not come for us."

"Liam healed my broken ribs." Wren chimes in as I skipped that part as well as our lovemaking.

No one speaks or sips their wine. They barely breathe as they stare at us in stunned silence.

Harper dashes away a tear, and Aaran wraps an arm around her. She takes a deep breath. "I know the pain you endured from the black lightning. I'm so sorry, Wren. If the dark magic in the pool was worse, I can't imagine what you have suffered."

Mother stands and turns away for a long moment. "My sons and their mates have endured much at Venora's hands, and I am to blame. I should have known what she was capable of many years ago and stopped her. I let the memory of our friendship blind me, and you have all paid the price. Even Birdie suffered because of my failings." She faces us. "You have my deepest apologies. I promise that I will do better, and you will always have my support and allegiance."

The fact that Mother accepted Wren as my mate means more to me than the fealty. It shouldn't, but it does.

"Thank you," Wren says. "I will do what I can to help save this world. I'd like to see it as it should be, rather than how the witch queen has altered it."

Mother's eyes shine with emotion. "We don't deserve you humans."

Nodding, Father squeezes her shoulder.

"Something has just occurred to me." Niamh's wings flutter faster. "The pool where the witch queen healed herself, you say it harmed you. That is probably because human magic is neither light nor dark, the way elven and fairy magic is. She must have known or at least suspected this, and your torture was to confirm that there is more than what we know. Human magic, from what we know, is neutral, and it can be used for good or evil."

"Perhaps she was trying to turn Wren to darkness so that she could recruit her." Father crosses his arms, a stance he always takes when contemplating or protecting.

Niamh rocks her head from side to side, and her eyes remain unfocused while she thinks about the idea. "It's possible. It's equally possible that the substance in the pool is a living source of magic, and if that's the case, it may have learned something about humans."

Mother's eyes are wide and her voice is soft with tension. "And that knowledge could be transferred to Venora. By the old gods, I hope you're wrong."

"I think Wren could use her magic to send herself and her mother back to Texas, where they would be safe. If Venora knows how to use magic against her and Harper, this battle is lost." Part of me thinks we all should make our way to the human world and cut our losses with Domhan. That decision is up to my mother, not me, so I keep it to myself.

Wren's mind nudges at mine, forcing me to meet her gaze. "I know you want to protect me, Liam. I appreciate that more than you know. But if she knows how to push through to the human world, if that knowledge was in me, I'm not leaving here until we stop her. I don't speak for Harper, but

I'm not going to stand by while Verona destroys our world. It's not perfect, and there's plenty of evil there, but there's a whole lot of good too. If I have to die, let it be for a good cause and not because I ran home with my tail between my legs and let a villain into my home."

"Amen," Harper says.

By the old gods, this woman could ask anything of me, and I would jump to give it to her. She's magnificent. "Venora may have already learned enough. She may already be laying siege in your world."

Niamh shakes her head. "I don't think so. If she had gotten all she needed, she would have had no reason to keep Wren alive. You, Liam, she might have tried again to turn or used as bait for your family, but Wren would have been useless to her." She gives Wren a sweet smile. "I'm sorry to be so blunt."

"Not at all. You're right. She stopped her torture once it was clear I wasn't going to survive much longer. She planned to bring me back to that pool day after day until she had what she wanted. At the time, I thought it was getting me to tell her how human magic works. Of course, I have no idea the answer to that question, so it was easy enough to keep telling her that humans have no magic. She might have meant for the pool to tell her by draining me of the knowledge, then absorbing it when she soaks in that horrible slime." Wren shivers as if a cold breeze just blew through.

"Would the knowledge be compatible with the source?" Rían asks.

We all turn and stare at him.

I have to admit that even I'm surprised by the depth of thought that the question holds. Rían Redmond is the captain of the Tús Nua guard. He is an innovative leader and an outstanding soldier. His ability to identify a set of conditions and apply them to a successfully mounted offense or defense is why he has climbed in rank. Clearly, I've underestimated his magical aptitude. I've known him all my life, and this is the first time I've seen him think beyond what is presented to him, or at least, the first time he's voiced those thoughts. This fairy he loves is good for him.

"Good question," Niamh leans into his side. "We don't know that. It's possible Venora's plan could backfire."

"Meaning, she might absorb something harmful?" Father asks.

"Or it might damage her healing source." I would pay a mountain of gold to see her face when she realized that Wren's magic would be her destruction. "Of course, we have no way of knowing the answers."

"Dinner is served," the butler, Perri, announces in a firm voice from the dining area.

Mother rises, and so do the rest. She takes a deep breath and leads us to the table. As father holds her chair for her, she says, "Liam is right, we can't know. We can only hope it is a miscalculation on Venora's part. Her shortsightedness has saved us on more than one occasion. Let's hope she continues to resist change. In the meantime, we shall continue as planned. We train and wait for Raith and the third human to arrive. We'll nurture the new friendships we've made, and together, somehow, we will save this world."

As soon as Mother is seated, we all take our places around the table. The meal is so good, I stuff myself. Of course, it's been an age since I had a fully cooked meal with all the fixings. "Mother, how do you like the centaurs?"

She smiles. "Intelligent and thoughtful people. I wonder why we ever believed them to be savages?"

Niamh shakes her head. "I wonder if the old gods didn't put these false notions of each other into our cultures."

"But why would they keep you apart and fill you with bigotry?" Harper puts her fork down and presses her napkin to her lips. She's a lovely woman with a forthright gaze.

"Good question." Aaran lets out a long breath.

"I suppose they had their reasons." I can't imagine what they were, but I'm a soldier, not a philosopher.

Aaran has never liked anything that takes away his free will. He shakes his head. "Perhaps when we open the Watchers' Gate, we can ask them."

"I certainly hope if you meet the old gods, you won't be impertinent," Mother scolds.

"I would be," Birdie announces with gusto.

We all laugh and make it through the dessert without any new revelations or arguments.

An hour later, Aaran lies across the bench in the garden sitting area, where we always gathered as brothers. Resting his head on Harper's lap, he smiles. "I'm truly relieved you've come home, Liam. I refused to believe you were dead, but that doesn't mean I didn't miss you."

"Thank you. It's good to be home. I hope Raith will survive." Our younger brother can be impulsive and irresponsible, but he has the kindest heart, and when he focuses, he also has a good head on his shoulders.

Wren has changed into comfortable brown leggings and a white tunic that she looks adorable in. She sits beside me with her hands pressed to the bench on either side of her thighs. "Do you think he'll encounter more trouble than we did?"

"It's hard to imagine," I admit. I wish I could do something to ease the strain visible in her eyes. We're to go to the oracle tomorrow. Perhaps they can help.

Laughing, Aaran says, "If there is more trouble to be found, Raith will find it and then find a creative way to make the situation worse."

"Oh dear." Wren shifts slightly toward me so that her arm touches mine.

I hug her and shift her so she's nearly sitting in my lap. "I think we should give Raith credit. His magic is strong even if he struggles with control."

"Some people need an urgent situation to present itself before they find their path. Raith might surprise you both." There are hard edges to Harper's accent, so different from Wren's.

"When I realized how long we'd been in Coire, I thought both of my brothers would have made it back here by now."

"He'll make it." Aaran's voice is sober and strong.

"Do you think he's fallen in love with the woman he's meant to bring home?" Wren's cheeks turn pink.

I run my thumb along the warm, soft blush. "It seems inevitable."

We sit in silence, each to their own thoughts, until a soft

huff and leaves moving in the bushes to our south force us all to turn.

"Dierdre is spying again, Liam." Aaran sounds annoyed enough that if I asked him to handle my old lover, I think he would.

Wren stiffens and crosses her arms. "I'll go inside."

I tighten my hug before releasing her and getting up. "Stay here. I'll deal with her."

The look I get from Wren is tight, as if to say, *Who do you think you're ordering around?*

"Please."

Her expression softens.

Harper chuckles.

I step out of the private sitting area and walk past where I know Dierdre is spying. When she follows, I continue a few yards more. "Did you break into the castle today and stand over Wren while she slept?" There is no disguising my anger simmering just under the surface.

Her footsteps stop before she reaches me. "I-I-I just wanted to see the tiny human who has stolen you from me."

At least she didn't lie. Still, it's unforgivable. "Wren deserves your reverence, not to be hovered over in anger. She nearly died to get here to save our world. You have no idea what she endured, and yet you call her tiny human as if you are above her. She far surpasses you in every way. You are even worse than I thought. I don't know what mental break you've had that, after our last several conversations, you still believe we are lovers, but if you need help from the doctors, you should seek it. Go home and never step foot on these grounds again, Dierdre. I will write to your father this night and tell him to keep you under control before you shame his family irrevocably."

As if none of what I've said made it past her hearing, she rushes forward with her arms out.

I step back and avoid her unwanted embrace. Her eyes, which always looked bright and sexy, are filled with a measure of insanity that I'd not seen before.

Tears fall down her cheeks. "Kyle and I are no longer together. Don't you see, Liam, I am free to be your wife, your mate. I am the one you need by your side. I'm an elven woman who could rule all of Domhan the way it's meant to be ruled."

Her words and the passion in them send a chill down my spine. Lifting my hand, I send a golden shard of light into the night sky. There's no sense in provoking her. "You need to rest, Dierdre. Go home now."

Two guards arrive and stand at attention.

She rushes toward me again, but I hold her firmly away from my chest. Backing her to the guards, I say, "Take her to her father's house and let him know she's unwell and will need attention."

Before she's fully out of sight, Wren stands beside me.

Aaran and Harper, too. Aaran's eyes are wide. "We heard everything. You didn't move far enough away, brother."

"I'll have to go to Mother and tell her about this." I sigh.

"Dierdre is ill; it's not your fault." Aaran pats my shoulder.

Wren wraps her arm around my waist. "She said she would rule with you. Does that mean she's expecting something bad to happen to Aaran?"

"It does." I look at my brother. "You know that I do not, nor have I ever, shared those thoughts or feelings. You will be an excellent leader should the curse be broken, and I would be honored to serve in your army."

Giving my shoulder a tight squeeze, he smiles. "I know. I also know you would make an excellent king should my journey take a different path." His eyes shift to Harper.

"I assume we have time for those decisions after the Watchers' Gate?" I look at Wren in the same manner.

We both laugh.

Taking Wren's hand, I lead the way to the castle. "Wren, I'm going to take you to my room. All of your things are there, and a maid has been assigned to help you."

"I don't need help." She looks down at her simple clothes.

She's so perfect, capable, different from anyone else. My heart expands with every moment I spend in her company. "Then send her away. Whatever you want. I have to speak to my parents before I join you."

Wren's trepidation about Dierdre bubbles along our connection. "You think she wants to hurt me?"

We enter through the back patio and use the central hall to reach the stairs. "I don't know. She seemed unstable. I've known her a long time, and something isn't right within her."

"Has she suffered from mental illness before?" Wren's soft, kind voice shows empathy rather than disdain.

"Not that I ever noticed. Though, before I left to find you, she came to the garden on my last night, and some of the things she said were similar to tonight. I thought it was rude and lacked awareness of the situation, but tonight was far worse." We reach the door, and I open it. "Bolt the door, please. I'll be back as soon as I can."

I wait until I hear the bolt sliding into place before I head up the hallway to the queen's apartment. If not for our connection, I'm sure my very independent woman would argue with me. However, she can feel my worry. Something isn't right with Dierdre. She's unstable.

I nod to the guards flanking the large double doors before knocking.

"Come in," Father says.

I enter the elaborate main chamber. The living area is decorated in the Riordan blue with gold and white accents. Mother and Father sit on the couch, each with a wineglass in hand. I step closer and bow formally. "I'm sorry to disturb you, but something has happened that concerns me. I wanted your opinion and to inform you of the possible danger."

Putting down her glass, Mother frowns. "Sit, Liam. What's happened?"

I'm anxious and sitting isn't easy, but I do as she asks and stay seated in the overstuffed chair across from them. "Dierdre Byrne has displayed some concerning behavior."

"I thought you ended that relationship long ago." Father narrows his gaze on me, ready to reprimand, but patient for the moment.

"That's true. I ended our arrangement several months before I went to the human world. She had begun another relationship with Kyle Mahony, and I was well rid of her. However, she sought me out the last evening before I portaled and made a comment about the two of us ruling Domhan." I raise a hand to keep Father from flying into a rage. I completely understand and concur with this. "My feelings mirror yours, Father. I told her as much and had her removed from the garden."

"Something else happened tonight?" Mother's perception is keen, and in part it's due to her magic, but mostly because she's my mother and knows I wouldn't be bothering them to gossip about something that happened months ago after they've retired for the night.

"Two things," I begin. "This afternoon, Wren was sleeping when she woke and thought she saw a woman staring at her. She wasn't sure it had been real since she was exhausted and still half asleep, but the woman she described may have been Dierdre."

"That hardly sounds like the behavior of Donovan Byrne's child." Mother and Lord Byrne grew up together.

I can understand why she would wish to protect his child. "I went to ask Dierdre before dinner but couldn't find her. Then she sneaked into the garden a short while ago and confirmed the incident. She wasn't stable, Mother. She made threats and again mentioned Aaran's demise and, in a way, yours as well. She spoke of ruling herself, until the curse was lifted."

"By the old gods. I knew she was spoiled as she's one of the last female elves born, but I had no idea..." Mother's eyes are sad and tired. "I'll go to Donavan's home tomorrow and see her for myself."

Liam. Dierdre is here. Hurry! Wren's voice screams in my head.

Turning, I run out of the royal rooms and use elf speed to traverse the hall. *Move away from the door.* I crash into my bedroom door so hard that the wood splinters around the bolt, and one of the hinges breaks in two.

With my parents at my side, I freeze. Wind rushes through the window like a summer storm. Wren stands at the bottom end of my bed, her arms outstretched, her curly hair wild around her fierce face.

Every other piece of furniture in the room is turned to rubble and crashed against the opposite wall. Dierdre is five feet off the floor and pressed to the painting of the great mountains that hang there. The wind holds her in place with her mouth open and her hair plastered to the wall.

"By all the old gods," Father mutters.

There's genuine fear in Dierdre's eyes. The wind must carry away her screams. She shifts her terror-filled gaze to me.

It would behoove me to feel concern for her situation, but my pride for Wren overrides any sympathy I might have felt for Dierdre. She could only have had one reason for invading this room.

"It's dragon wind. You should stop her, Liam. Wren will wear herself out." Mother nudges me out of my shocked state.

Skirting around the outside of the room, I manage to avoid the dragon wind. I step between Wren and the footboard. "You can stop now, my love. She won't harm you or anyone else."

The wind strengthens.

"Wren, we will keep Dierdre from getting away. I swear to you, she will answer for whatever she has done." Mother's voice is barely loud enough to breach the roar of the wind.

I try to put my arms around Wren, but magic pulses

from her like an aura, and I cannot touch her. "Please, Wren. Let her go."

As if her arms are on threads, she lowers them slowly, and the dragon wind diminishes.

Father catches Dierdre before she hits the broken furniture strewn beneath her.

"She was hiding in the wardrobe. I opened it to see if my bag was in there, and she leaped out at me with some jeweled knife." Wren doesn't take her eyes off Dierdre. "The only reason she didn't cut me is I clutched some of your clothes and pulled them down on her."

"She's a monster." Dierdre's mad eyes barely focus as she tries to pull out of my father's arms. "You saw the wind. She's a witch like Venora. You've made a mistake, Liam. Don't worry. It's not too late. You can still send her back to where she came from and make amends. She's evil."

Rather than defend herself, Wren crosses her arms and leans back against the bed. Her crystal eyes stay alert and leveled on her attacker, but she does not need to make her case.

Wren risked her life and her soul to be here, and she didn't have to do it. "No one is sending her back, Dierdre."

Holding up a hand for silence, Mother steps forward. "Dierdre Byrne, what were you doing in the wardrobe?"

"I was going to surprise Liam." By the gods, she even manages a blush.

Raising an eyebrow, Mother crosses to the corner where a jeweled athame is stuck into the wall. "What was the ceremonial dagger for?"

Panic widens Dierdre's eyes, then, an instant later, it's gone. "It was hers." She points a bony finger at Wren.

A Crown of Wind and Water

"Where would a human obtain an elven athame?" Mother's voice remains calm and without accusation.

"How would I know? Perhaps she is more than she seems. She is here to ruin Domhan with her stealing of the next to wear the crown." The wildness is back in her expression.

Mother grips Dierdre's chin and stares into her eyes. "I'm going to be sorry to explain this to your father, child." She turns to the royal guards standing at the threshold. "Fetch Captain Redmond to take her to the oracle. They'll evaluate whether or not she can be rehabilitated. They will care for her properly."

A guard leaves, his heavy boots pounding the floor.

"Patrick, hold her, please." Father hands her over to the other guard. "How did she get in here? You said you sent her home with the guards."

It hasn't escaped me that one or both of those men must have either helped her or, at the very least, disobeyed my order to see her home. Without a breach of orders, she couldn't have been taken all the way to her father's house and returned here before Wren and I arrived. "I will begin an investigation immediately, Father."

With a sigh, my father looks from me to Wren, who remains with her arms crossed and watching Dierdre as if another attack is imminent. "Wren, I am very sorry for the events of this night. We shall do better."

Finally shifting her gaze, she nods at Father.

He looks at me. "Have the two guards held for questioning but wait until morning to deal with them. Stay with your mate. She'll need to feel safe."

Wren cocks her head and regards my father as if she's seeing him again for the first time.

"You will all be sorry when she slits your throats in the night," Dierdre shrieks.

Rían rushes into the room. He evaluates the state of the room and his officer, restraining the hysterical woman. "Your orders, Majesty?"

Mother repeats the order to take Dierdre to the mountain. "Give me an hour to summon her father. She can survive an hour in a cell, but make sure she doesn't injure herself, Captain."

"Yes, ma'am." Rían shifts his chin toward the door, and the two royal guards take Dierdre out while she struggles and screams about Wren being our doom.

With a long look around the room, Mother says, "A guest room was arranged for Wren down the hall. It might be best if you both stayed in there until this can be restored."

Six guards arrive.

"Find Dole and Crain and detain them until morning," I order.

Wren flinches.

Four guards rush to do my bidding. The other two stand waiting for my parents to leave.

Mother approaches Wren with her hands out for taking.

After a long pause, Wren uncrosses her arms and takes them.

Smiling, my mother says, "What happened tonight is not an example of who we are as a people. I'm very sorry for what you have suffered. You are right not to defend yourself or offer an explanation. No one in this room believes you would attack another woman unprovoked. I'm glad you were able to defend yourself. You must show me this dragon wind when there isn't danger."

"I don't think I can. My magic comes when I'm scared, angry, or desperate." Wren's voice rings with apology.

Mother squeezes her hands. "So far. You have had no training. Don't be hard on yourself. Get some rest. Tomorrow we'll go to the oracle."

"Thank you, your majesty. I'll try."

Once my parents are gone, I look around the room and laugh. I pull Wren into my arms. "Well, once the rumors get out, no one else will try to harm you. Though most elves are happy you've come."

"Most?" She rests her cheek on my chest.

I wish I could tell her the sentiment was as universal as it ought to be. "There will always be those who believe the old gods separated elves and humans for good reason."

"Maybe they're right."

Taking her hand, I grab the strap of her duffel bag from the rubble and sling it over my shoulder. We step into the hall and walk to the guest suite. "They are not right. You and I were meant to meet and fall in love."

Chapter Twenty-One

WREN

Liam kisses me goodbye, and as he's leaving, Momma pushes through the half-open door. "I heard there was some trouble last night?"

Once he's hugged her, Liam says, "You can find out everything from Wren. Food to break your fast should arrive shortly."

Momma sits at the small table near a window that overlooks the garden we were in last night. "It's beautiful here."

"Dangerous and beautiful." I finish dressing and sit opposite her.

Before I can tell her what happened, there's a knock, and when I call come in, Harper peeks her head in. "I wanted to check to see if you're alright."

"Have a seat." I get up and pull a chair over from the corner.

Joining us, Harper says, "I heard you broke every piece of furniture in Liam's room."

"Did you?" Momma asks.

I shrug. "Most of it, but that woman came at me with a knife and said some terrible things about humans."

The door opens again, and three maids come in carrying trays of food. A whiff of fresh yeasty bread, eggs, and tea instantly makes my stomach growl. Lila smiles. "I had enough brought up for all of you ladies."

"Lila, we could have gone down for the meal." Harper's warm smile shows familiarity and respect.

"It's nothing," Lila says. "Miss Wren had a difficult evening, and I heard you ladies joined her this morning."

Two footmen carry in a larger table, which is placed beside the first.

Before I can think to protest, all the fuss, dishes, and food are placed before us.

Niamh flies in. "Oh, isn't this lovely?"

"Won't you join us?" I get up to find another chair, but Lila is faster and brings one from the wall near the fireplace.

"Only if I'm not intruding. I'm not human, and if you have human things to discuss…"

Momma chuckles. "No special human discussions. Fairies, elves, and centaurs would all be welcome at our table."

"And dwarves," Harper adds.

As she sits and her wings tuck in behind her, Niamh asks, "Are all humans so accepting of those different from you?"

"No." I take a warm roll from the basket. "Unfortunately, humans have plenty of bigotry and hatred."

A Crown of Wind and Water

The pretty fairy frowns and eats a berry that looks similar to a strawberry, but it's purple like a grape. "Do you really have dragon wind, Wren?"

"It would seem so." I spread butter and purple jam on my roll, then close my eyes as the flavors wake up my palate.

"And the woman was an old flame of Liam's?" Momma scoops an egg that looks poached onto a slice of bread and pours gravy over the top.

Rather than vilify Dierdre, I say, "They did have a relationship of some kind, but it ended months before Liam came to find me." The hours since the incident have left me feeling sorry for her. She's clearly suffering from mental health issues.

Harper drinks tea and makes a face. "All I know is, I thought Jersey Girls were badasses, but now I know not to mess with a Texas woman."

"True enough," Momma says around a mouth full of bread and eggs.

With a laugh and another sour face, Harper adds, "I'd give all of the gold in this castle for a cup of coffee."

"I'm getting used to the tea." Momma sips happily.

I can't help laughing at the horrified expression on Harper's pretty face. "This is nice."

"It is." Niamh's wings flutter.

There's another knock.

"Come in," I call, as all heads turn to see who it is.

Bert swings the door open. "I heard there was a gathering of humans and wondered if you'd mind one more." He smiles at Niamh. "But if it's ladies only, I'll understand."

"Nonsense," I say. "Come and join us. We were lamenting the lack of coffee in Domhan."

He grumbles. "I lived on the stuff back home. I make them use double the tea, and it's still just dirty water." After grabbing a chair from near the fireplace, he sits across from Niamh.

"Other than the lack of coffee and the mad witch trying to kill me, it's a wonderful place." Harper takes a bite of a berry.

"I have two mad women trying to kill me. Count yourself lucky." It's meant as a joke, but it falls flat.

Niamh looks from me to Harper. "Will you stay here after the witch queen is defeated?"

"I don't know." Harper shrugs. "I can't imagine never returning to my mother in New Jersey, but leaving Aaran seems impossible. He's said he would return to our world with me, but I don't think he'd be happy in a world where he has to hide his nature. For now, I'm here, and we have a job ahead of us that might kill us. If that happens, then I'd have worried over nothing. So, for now, I'm not thinking about it."

The truth of that should be sobering, but I can't help laughing at the easy way she says it. "I think surviving this long has been a kind of miracle."

"When Nainsi came to Montague, that's on the Labrador Coast, she used to tell me stories of this place and all its wonders. I believe most of what she told me remains true. The elves are wonderful, even after thirty years of being beaten down and losing loved ones in this war. Many have family who were turned into shadow demons, yet they honor them as beloved dead. The land is still beautiful, but when you see how things look near the tower in the east, you can get a glimpse of what Venora will do to all of Domhan. I'm not part of the prophecy, but I do think this place is worth saving. Besides, we have to protect our own world. After what Wren and Liam said about human magic and that obelisk, we don't have much time."

Momma nods. "Humans don't fare well in this world, but we do seem to pull through. I hope the youngest brother and his lady find their way back soon."

Leave it to my mother to remind us that there's still another one of us in the wind. I wonder where they are. "Considering how long ago the three of them left to find us, things are probably not going well. I wish we could help them the way Niamh helped Liam and me."

"If I sense them, I'll go to them, but so far, I only felt the portal at the one glen you came to." She brushes her short hair behind her pointed ear.

I suppose I should be worrying about my own problems, but after the journey here, my heart goes out to any human beyond the safety of the city walls. However, the walls didn't protect me last night. No, I did that myself.

The sun is high when Momma and I walk to the woods where the centaurs have made their encampment.

A company of dwarves came down from the mountains earlier, and we met a very interesting one named Fancor. Harper treated him like a favorite uncle. I liked him immediately.

"Momma, maybe the reason the elves needed us was to bring all the creatures of this world together." The irony of that is not lost on me, considering that humans can't find peace in our world, and it's just us.

She wraps an arm around my waist. "It could be. Strange as that sounds. It seems that embracing a few humans has opened them up to the people right here in Domhan. Maybe it's not the reason, but the nice side effect."

"Maybe." I step in front of her as we enter the wooded area. Before my second foot crunches the underbrush, a hand grabs my shoulder. Gasping, I turn to the left. "Jadar!"

He hugs me. "We heard you survived. Come. Corell and Farress will scold me if I don't bring you to them immediately."

The woods are not as dense as those in the south, nor are the trees as tall. This must be a younger forest. Still, the path is not an easy one to follow, and I'm glad to have a guide other than Momma. "It's pretty here."

"It will suffice for the time being. I hope one day we will return to the south, and pray that our true home will be rebuilt after the witch queen's reign is over." He huffs out a long sigh.

Patting his back, I say, "I will keep your hopes in my prayers, my friend."

A wide grin washes away all worry. "If you pray for it, I know it will come to pass."

It takes all my restraint not to tell him that I don't have that kind of power. Why dash his hopes? They are just as valid as my prayers.

We break through the shadows of the trees into a wide-open space with a small creek running through. Centaur homes have been built to shelter them, and a large cook fire smolders at the center of the camp.

A Crown of Wind and Water

Corell gallops over. "Wren." He lifts me in a hug. "We were very worried."

Through my squashed lungs, I manage, "It's good to see you. Thank you for getting my mother here safely."

"Put her down before you harm her," Farress scolds but chuckles at the same time.

I pat Corell's back as he puts me on the ground and greets my mother in a similar manner. "Come. Sit. We heard you had come, but the celebration to dedicate our temporary home was already underway. We planned to join you in the city this evening. The Riordan invited us to dine."

I sit on a stump arranged near the fire. It's a good sign that the centaurs have added seating for species with two legs as well as four. "I hope you'll still come. I wanted to see everyone and assumed the entire village wouldn't be invited to dinner in the castle."

"Wouldn't that be a sight?" Farress simmers a pot in the still-smoldering coals of an earlier fire.

Corell and Jadar tell us about the rest of the journey to Tús Nua as well as the unexpectedly warm welcome they received. "Elspeth offered to build us homes, but the elven homes would not suit centaurs. Then she said we could look around the land in the area and perhaps find someplace that would work until we're able to return to our home, if that's our intention."

"That was kind of her." I'm not surprised. Liam's mother is a wise woman. She'll need these centaurs before this war is over. "I'm glad you've had a good experience with the elves."

"Not all." Jadar's voice is grave.

We're interrupted by Wellon and Pallon joining the circle.

I'm happy to see them all looking well and happy despite their losses.

Once everyone is settled, Farress hands me a cup of tea. "We don't have our leaves from home, but this is a nice substitute."

It's good tea and I thank her. "What did you mean, Jadar? Was there trouble?"

Corell gives Jadar a hard look. "It was nothing. A small group of elves protested our coming, but once Elspeth made a public announcement that she was happy to have us here and thanked us for joining the fight against the witch queen, we've had no problems."

"Was anyone harmed?" I don't like this one bit.

When her mate doesn't respond, Farress says, "A few bruises. The elves were from the outskirts of the city. They wouldn't say who led them."

"I have a good guess." Momma's voice is low and muttered into her teacup.

If that's the case, the trouble should die down now that Dierdre is getting help. "I also had some unwanted excitement last night. There was a woman who opposed my being here. She's unstable and needs medical help. I think she'll get it now. I think Birdie believes she may have organized the others. Perhaps that will be the end of it."

Jadar stands and paces. "You came here to help them. You almost died more than once, and so did Birdie. How dare anyone try to harm you within the city?"

I go to him and pat his back. "You lost friends in the same journey. How dare anyone oppose you being here?" I smile and wait for him to calm down. "There will always be those who want things to remain the same, even when that isn't possible and the current situation is untenable."

"Historically, that's true." Momma sighs and puts down her empty cup. "In our world, there are always groups who push for change and those who hold fast to the old ways. Sometimes they're right and sometimes they're wrong. This is the nature of evolution."

An hour later, Liam steps into the clearing and the reunion continues until he says, "I'm sorry to break this up, but Wren and I have to go to the oracle with Aaran and Harper."

I was having such a good time, I'd nearly forgotten about the stress of being brought before some group of high-up muckety-mucks.

We say our goodbyes for now and take the winding path out of the forest.

Liam takes my hand and offers Momma his arm. He leans in toward me. "I heard something from your mind when I said we had to go. What is a high-up muckety-muck?"

The outburst of laughter from Momma is a little over the top, but I can't help laughing right along with her.

"You shouldn't listen when you're not invited."

Grinning, he swings our arms as we walk. "I apologize, but will you tell me what it means?"

"People too big for their britches." Momma is not helping.

Liam's blank expression is priceless. "That made my understanding even worse, Birdie. Though I suspect that was the point."

Once I get my laughter under control, I say, "It's someone in authority who is pompous or self-important."

While I was hoping he would say that my description is unfair to the oracle, Liam smiles and nods. "They have cause to be self-important. They are the oracle. They live longer than even a normal elf. They possess magic and knowledge that is unique to their vows. They've left behind all worldly things and live within a mountain, which they never leave. What I've seen of it is very comfortable, but a beautiful prison is still a prison. Though they made the choice, I suppose."

"Great. Now you've made me feel bad for something I thought. It's not as if I said it out loud." I try to pull my hand away.

Holding it tighter, he lifts my fingers to his lips. "We all think they're high-up muckety-mucks, my love. I suspect they know they are, too."

"Well then, bring them on."

Momma says, "They never come out of the mountain and see the state of the elves they serve?"

Shaking his head, he lets out a long breath. "I've never seen a member of the oracle outside of their mountain, and the only way in is through a portal they control. They are removed from the lives of ordinary elves."

"How can they advise then?" Momma's line of questioning is not making me feel any better about the coming meeting.

Liam looks into the sky. His handsome face is made even

more irresistible by a slow smile. He points. "I think your friend is back."

Squinting, I follow the direction of his finger, and the tiny movement of Adhar among the fluffy clouds catches my eye. "Oh! She's come back." I send her a warm greeting through my mind.

Her *craa* sounds far away, but hearing it fills me with joy.

As we continue the walk toward the castle, Liam says, "To answer your question, Birdie, the queen and our family spend a great deal of time with the elves we lead. We know of their pains and pleasures. We make it our priority to not only take advice from the oracle, but to advise them in turn."

"I'm relieved to hear that, Liam," Momma says it in a way that reminds me of how she spoke to a student who'd given a particularly thoughtful response to a question.

Despite all that's happened and the stress of going to see the haughty oracle, I'm happy. It's absurd, but being with Liam fills me with the kind of joy I've only dreamed about. The type that many girls dream about, but few ever find.

Rather than meeting Aaran and Harper in the castle, we say goodbye to Momma and continue around the north side to a stable, though it's the fanciest one I've ever been in. The floors are wooden, but the rest of the structure is stone, and the stall doors are steel.

Aaran stands an inch or two taller than Liam, and he is dwarfed by the horses, which are taller than the centaurs. He helps Harper onto a white horse, then mounts a black before spotting us and grinning. "I thought you decided not to go."

A pair of gorgeous grays stand waiting with a groom holding the reins.

Liam stands next to one and looks at me with raised eyebrows.

I jump up with one foot on his thigh and hoist myself into the saddle. "I'm from Texas. We don't scare easily." I thank the groom for the reins and wait for Liam to mount.

"I hadn't been on a horse in years when I got here. I had to learn all over again." Harper stares at me with her mouth agape. "You look like you were born on a horse."

"I spent a lot of time on the back of a centaur when I got here, Harper. This lovely beast has a saddle. It's already easier."

Impossibly, her eyes and mouth get wider. "Holy crap."

The road to the oracle is more of a well-kept path. It would be tough for a cart or carriage to make this trip, but perhaps they're not meant to. We don't rush, and Aaran tells us about their journey and when they realized Venora could gain access to this continent via water.

"That's likely why she built her obelisk in the lost lands, but it was dry where we were taken. She's gaining strength, as is Ciaran." Liam spits out his name.

"He nearly killed Niamh. Well, I suppose he did kill her, but Rían was able to pull her back to her body. You can imagine, he wants Ciaran dead." Aaran doesn't sound as if he minds the idea.

A low growl rises from Liam. His eyes narrow. "I love Rían like one of my brothers, but he'll have to fight me for that honor."

"I wouldn't mind a crack at him." Harper breaks the uncomfortable moment.

The men look at her, then grin.

"What? The guy is the worst kind of traitor. And he

poked around in my head where he wasn't welcome. He held me while Venora tortured me. I deserve a shot at him." She sits up taller in her saddle and stares them down.

"By those standards, I should put my hat in the ring." I give my horse a nudge to keep up.

Eyes filled with regret, Liam nods at me. "One thing is certain: Ciaran Seveline will not find justice in a courtroom."

My heart pounds and my stomach tightens. I grip the reins too tightly, and the horse shifts until I'm nearly in the bushes. I force myself to relax and pat her neck. "Would a court here let him free after all he's done?"

When Liam doesn't respond, Aaran says, "It's unlikely, but he could claim Venora had bewitched him. If that argument held, he'd likely be sent to the oracle for rehabilitation."

There's that growl again. Liam's temper is far too close to the edge. "He's not going to be rehabilitated."

No one disagrees with him.

I open my mind and send my love through our connection.

Liam's shoulders relax as we arrive at an archway that leads to nothing but rock.

Inside, Aaran rings a bell or something that's tucked inside an alcove to gain us entry through a portal. I'm too focused on Liam and the diminished bloodlust he's trying to get under his complete control to see the process for entry.

Once through the portal, we enter another chamber through heavy wooden doors. Liam and Aaran cover their left fist with their right hand and lower their chins in a kind of reverent greeting for the ten elves seated behind a high desk that wraps the circular room.

Everything is white with no adornments of any kind. All

ten men and women are dressed in white robes. They stare at me, yet there's a peacefulness about them that is reassuring. Sconces burning all around the chamber light the space.

"My brother has returned successfully." Aaran's words are good news, but his tone is grave.

One of the oracle elves appears in front of us.

I stagger back, not expecting her to be there. One second, she was behind the desk thing, and the next, she landed like a bright light a few feet from us. Her dark skin gleams in the fire's glow, her eyes are dark, and her stare is direct. She places her hand on Liam's forehead. "The journey was more than you expected, Liam Riordan?"

"In all ways, oracle." He steps back from her touch and offers me his hand.

Taking it, I step next to him.

She studies me.

"This is Wren Martin. She has suffered much on our behalf." Liam gives the information like a warning.

The oracle almost smiles, but doesn't. "She'll come to no harm here."

She lifts her hand to touch my forehead the same way she touched Liam's.

I back up.

Cocking her head, she closes her eyes, as do the other nine around the desk. Opening them, she asks, "May we touch you? It will not harm you."

I look at Liam, and he nods. I lift my chin and say, "You may, and thank you for asking."

The sarcasm doesn't register with the oracle, but Harper tries to stifle her chuckle.

A Crown of Wind and Water

The oracle's hand is warm and soft. There's a murmuring of voices along my consciousness, and then it's gone. Lowering her hand, she stares for a long time. So long, I think she may never say anything. All ten close their eyes, and I have the impression that some communication is happening between them.

It's a little rude, but Liam seems not to mind, so I ignore it.

Finally, they open their eyes, and sorrow flickers there in the one close to me. "We are sorry for what you have endured. Coire is not meant for the living. Coire is not meant for the pure of heart. This breach by Venora Braddish is beyond what we thought even she was capable of."

"I don't think anything that witch does should surprise you. There are no lengths she won't go to for the things she wants. Power is her drug of choice, and she's long addicted, with no hope of recovery." I have no idea what these people want from me, but the one thing they'll get is the truth, whether they like it or not.

"You are frank, like Harper. This seems to be a human trait. We are glad." She moves her hand to indicate we should walk with her.

"Not all humans," I say. "But likely the ones who are willing to jump through a magic portal into a war to help a group of people they didn't know existed before, those are bound to be direct."

Liam and Harper laugh.

We walk through an archway into a long hall that leads to a bright room with windows facing the city. It's beautiful and full of life.

The oracle steps into the center of the room. "This is the

room where you will train with Harper. We will show you how to use your magic if you are willing."

I get the feeling the last part was added on for my benefit, and I appreciate it. "I would like to be able to use it without my life or the lives of others being at risk. Especially the portal thing. It would be nice to use that to find Liam's younger brother. It would also be nice to feel closer to home."

"Portal thing?" The oracle narrows her eyes in the first sign of confusion.

"Wren created the portal that allowed us to escape from Coire. She tried and failed before being tortured, but after being dunked in the source, and with the threat of more of the same, she succeeded in making the gentlest portal I've ever stepped through. It took us from the underworld to the fairy glen I showed her in my mind." Liam puffs out his chest and beams at me.

After a long pause where the oracle stares at me as if I'm shiny and new, she says, "We will certainly try. Come again tomorrow with Harper when the sun is in the west. We will start your training then. Harper has learned much in the weeks she's been visiting us."

I swear I detect a hint of pride, but I have no idea if it's for Harper's progress or the fact that the oracle managed to teach something to a human. It might be best if I never knew the answer to that question. "I will come and do my best to learn from you."

With a deep breath, she turns to the arch where we entered.

"How is Dierdre?" I ask before she can dismiss us.

Slowly, she turns back. Her eyes are shadowed. "I'm

surprised you care about the well-being of one who wishes you dead."

I shrug. "I can't change who I am."

Another long look at me makes my skin tingle with magic. "She is sick in mind. We are letting her rest. It has not yet been decided how to help her or if she can be helped. Like Venora, she may have taken her darkness too far."

"You didn't find any good in her?" My chest is tight. I look at Liam. "Was there good in her when you were lovers?"

He lets out a long breath, and his shoulders slump. "Yes. There was good in her when our affair began. She slowly became obsessed with court and getting more from me than I was willing to give. That was when I ended it."

A trill of jealousy rushes through me, but I push it aside. Liam loves me. He doesn't love any other woman. "If she had good in her, it must still be there. You should try to help her."

There's a flash of light, and we're all standing in the center of the circular desk again. The oracle all close their eyes, and the sense of magic flowing between them returns. When they open their eyes, the one who's been speaking to me says, "It's important to you, second of the prophecy, Wren Martin?"

"It is. If you don't try, then she's just the first to be lost." I have no idea how I know this. "There are others who I think she led to attack the centaurs. Perhaps they will need help finding their way back into the light as well."

Another long pause as she studies me. "We have heard what you say, and we will take it into account as we make our decision." She looks at Aaran. "Tell your mother that if she wishes to send the ones who followed Dierdre Byrne, we would accept them. It is sometimes possible to pull darkness from an elf if it is born of something foreign and not ingrained."

"Yes, Oracle." Aaran bows and makes the sign with his hands.

"Thank you," I say.

Liam smiles at me and bows to the oracle.

An instant later, we are all four outside the mountain, standing next to our horses.

"Damn, Wren, you have balls." Harper's laughter is contagious.

Smiling, I shrug. "I'm from Texas, Jersey Girl. Besides, if you don't ask, then the answer is always no. We don't know what happened to Dierdre. Maybe Venora got to her with magic. Maybe not. It's important we know the truth."

We mount and head back the way we came.

Liam won't stop grinning at me, and it's making me blush. "What happened with the guards?"

His smile slips too easily into a frown. "Crain admitted he's been seduced over the past months by her. He told the other guard he would take her home, then he let her go. He didn't know she had plans to attack you. At least that's what he said, and based on his level of shock, I believed him. I still took him off active duty, and he'll be cleaning floors and stalls for a long while."

"Maybe he needs a trip to the oracle. Maybe Dierdre is passing along a dark spell." Aaran shivers in his saddle.

I don't blame him. The idea is like a computer virus poisoning everything, one program at a time, but these are living elves she may have poisoned.

Chapter Twenty-Two

LIAM

In the week since our arrival, dwarves in great numbers have come down from the mountains. They've made camp in the foothills, and their leader, Sandon, her mate, Fan, and their son Fancor are staying in the castle as my parents' guests. Fancor assisted Aaran and Harper during their journey home and is not at all princely, which I appreciate.

The fairy king, Muiredach, has joined the household with the promise of five thousand soldiers ready to come through the portal in the fairy glen.

Mother has arranged a formal dinner followed by a ball and dancing. Never before have so many different people gathered. As the first event of its kind, it will host elves, centaurs, dwarves, fairies, and humans. The household is in an uproar.

Before the festivities, I have been asked by the oracle to

visit Dierdre. I protested. It's a bad idea, but they insisted, so I'm making my way down the sterile halls within the mountain. This part is a kind of sanitarium, though very few rooms are occupied. I fear that is about to change.

Two members of the oracle stand in the hallway waiting for me, the one with long black hair who spoke to us when Wren first came here, and the other is a man with gray hair. There are very few elves old enough for their hair to go gray. I would guess he's two hundred suns, probably more. Still, he's tall and fit.

I bow to them when I approach. "I still feel this is a mistake. The last two times I saw her, she was unreasonable."

The man speaks. "And yet, since she's been with us, she's been calm and logical."

"It's a test?" I still don't like it.

"We're trying to evaluate her, and she's blocked all attempts to see within." The woman says. "From the outside, she appears like a good citizen of the community."

"Very well. Open the door." If she's not mentally ill, she can stand trial for her crimes against Wren.

"She has no weapons or means to make them," the man says.

"Have you bound her magic?"

The woman shakes her head. "She's not gifted enough for that to be a concern to us."

"Then she's fooled you more than I thought possible. She's armed." I step into the small chamber. The walls are soft gray. There is a window, but I can feel the magic rolling off it. It's not real, merely an illusion meant to give comfort. The single bed is the only furniture.

Lying in the bed, in a white robe that reaches her bare

feet, Dierdre could almost pass for an oracle. Her expression is soft and calm. Her gaze shifts to me. She jumps from the bed and launches herself at me with arms wide and a bright smile. "Liam, you came. I knew you would come."

Easing her away, I hold her at arm's length. "Nothing has changed, Dierdre. I came because the oracle asked me to. Though I do care that you might be ill."

Turning away, she drops her smile. "My only illness is this place."

"You tried to kill one of the humans from the prophecy. Don't you think some concern about you is valid?" I keep my voice even and without emotion.

"I did no such thing. That's just what she said. I only wished to have a look at her." Her voice has taken on a petulance that belongs in a child, not a grown woman.

"You hid in the wardrobe and jumped out at her with an athame, Dierdre. What were you going to do with the blade?"

She looks out the fake window. "It's a nice day. Shall we go for a walk?"

"No. We cannot leave here. Will you tell me why you wanted to hurt Wren?"

Spinning, she looks at me as if the name stirred rage in her. "You can fuck who you want, Liam. Just remember you belong to me. When you tire of the human, I will take you back."

"You're mistaken, Dierdre. I will not tire of Wren. She's my destiny. She and I have a bond that only occurs when two souls are meant to be joined. I will never return to your bed, and what we did there was all there ever was between us." This entire thing begins to feel cruel. I look toward the door, but the oracle doesn't open it.

"Liar!" She digs her nails into the side of my face, missing my eye by a half inch.

My inattention cost me. Blood streams down my face.

Dierdre's hand goes back, and a red ball of energy forms in her palm. Hatred burns in her eyes. Here is the evidence the oracle was looking for.

I grab my cheek with one hand, and not wishing to harm her, I build a blockade with my magic. When she throws her orb, it shatters against my shield. Dark magic prickles along my skin as it might when a viper hides in the tall grass.

She screams and hurls more magic at me.

The door flies open and the oracles rush in. They use magic to pin Dierdre to the wall where the window was, but now there's only more of the soft gray wall. The male keeps her still while the woman presses her palm to Dierdre's forehead.

Dierdre screams and curses at me and the oracle. She struggles against the magic bonds that keep her still. "You let them do this to me. You tricked me."

I ask the male oracle. "Is she hurting her?"

He shakes his head. "She's reading her. It causes no pain, but the walls that were built up fell when she attacked you. If she is poisoned by dark magic, we will know."

Part of me wants to help her. This is better than the penalty for treason, but my gut still tightens. "I'm going now."

When only Dierdre protests, I step into the hallway and find my way out of the mountain.

When I reach my room, Wren is sitting in the middle of the bed, dressed for the evening, her deep-green gown fluffed out around her like a flower, and she is the precious center. With calm concentration, she weaves some bits of fabric in an intricate pattern. The dress shimmers in the late afternoon sun shining through the window. Her hair is pinned up in perfect curls, and a few dangle around her face.

For a long moment, she doesn't look up, and I am free to admire her at work.

When she feels me watching, she smiles and shifts her attention. As soon as she sees me, her expression falls. Leaping from the bed, she rushes to me and touches my cheek. "You're hurt. What happened?"

I pull my blood-stained shirt over my head and toss it into the laundry. "The oracle got what they wanted. She let her guard down, and now they'll know if she's turned to dark magic, has been poisoned by it, or if she's ill. I didn't stay to hear the verdict."

Stepping into the bathroom, I check my injury in the mirror. Four angry streaks of red run from below my left eye to my chin. I press my hand to my cheek and send healing magic to the deep scratches.

"They tricked her?" Wren looks almost as torn as I feel.

When I pull my hand away, the wounds are gone, save for pink lines. "I tricked her. I pushed all the right buttons to prove she wasn't the calm, steady elf she was pretending to be. When I succeeded, the oracle came in and accessed her mind."

Rather than expressing the disappointment I deserve, Wren wraps her arms around my waist and holds me. "That must have been terrible for you."

"How will I ever deserve you, my love?" I hug her tight and kiss the top of her head. "It was terrible, but if she's under Venora's influence, Dierdre is the injured party."

Tipping her chin to look at me, she says, "Maybe, but she did attack me. Not to mention the underlying plot to do away with your mother and brother so that she could become queen. I'm pretty sure she deserved what she got, but you didn't. I know it was difficult for you to bait her."

I let out the breath I've been holding. "Thank you, Wren."

"You should bathe and get dressed for dinner. I sat for an hour while three of the maids fussed over me to get me to look like this." She steps out of my arms and holds the gown's skirt out for viewing.

"As beautiful as you look, you were perfect before they fussed over you."

Her cheeks grow pink at the compliment. "Just a bit of a glow up. In all the important ways, I'll be the same."

I kiss her forehead. "Truer words were never spoken. What were you working on when I came in?"

"Nothing, just a bit of braiding. Lila brought me some pieces of cloth. I find that I miss my craft." She shrugs.

"I'm sorry. I thought we'd have made it back here months ago." I should have done more, been better, and protected her from harm. I've failed in every way.

"It's not your fault, Liam. As much as it pains you, you

don't control everything." She taps my chest, then lets her hand linger on my skin. "I suppose it would be terrible if we were late for an important dinner."

As I pull her close, my cock has already alerted to the invitation in her voice. "What did you learn today when you went to the mountain?"

She presses her center tight against me and makes a little feline sound. "I learned how to make wind without the danger of death surrounding me. I almost made a portal, but it collapsed." There's fire in her eyes and excitement that has nothing to do with the way she's rubbing against me.

"You like the magic lessons?" I grip her ass and lift her, but miles of fabric bunch between us as she wraps her legs around me. Another woman might worry about her clothes getting wrinkled, but not my Wren.

"I do like the magic growing inside me. I'm forever amazed that I have power after a lifetime of being small and soft." She kisses my neck and runs her tongue to my ear. "Do you have magic that will whisk these clothes away?"

Calling my magic, I send our clothes into a neat pile on the chair. "You have always been the strongest person I've ever known, with or without magic."

She presses her arms on my shoulders and lifts herself so my cock is precariously close to paradise. As she eases down, my head slips inside her soft wetness. "We're going to be so late for dinner."

Backing up to the bed, I sit and thrust deep inside her. "Gods, you're perfect."

Wren pushes me to my back and rides me hard and fast. "If we're quick, no one will notice." She pants and digs her fingers into my chest while lifting and lowering her core to take me, over and over.

I grip her hips and lift my knees and press my feet against the footboard so that I can push us to the center of the bed. "I don't care who knows as long as you come so hard, you're smiling all through dinner and still thinking about this while we're dancing later."

Staring at me with her mouth and eyes wide, she bursts out laughing. "I hope none of the guests are mind readers."

I lift my hips and slowly fill her. "If they are, they'll know I love you. I want you. I'm never going to get enough of you. You are the other half of me that I didn't know I'd been waiting my lifetime for."

"The things you say." She grips her tits and throws her head back. Those adorable curls come loose and bounce around her head as she lets me fuck her from below.

I press my thumb to her clit and rub until she's screaming my name and meeting my thrusts by slamming down in time.

As my orgasm takes control of me, I rub faster, bringing her with me. Her sheath tugs and pulls at my cock, drawing out the last drop and leaving me saying her name over and over as she collapses on my chest.

"If I promised to go back to the human world with you, would you agree to be mine for the rest of our lives?" For a second time, I'm compelled to beg her to marry me.

With a long, satisfied sigh and our bodies still connected, she says, "I was thinking..."

"What?" Having expected her to say no, or that I had to ask after we defeat the witch queen, I'm buoyed by hope. My heart races. "What were you thinking?"

"Just that if I can learn to make portals that don't feel like death, and I can make them reach Earth, maybe I would like to stay here in Domhan and visit home a few times a year."

The shock of what she's saying is so thorough, I must see her face. I roll us so that she's on her back, and I'm on my elbows hovering over her. "Do you mean that?"

"I don't think I could go back to never using magic or hiding my magic all day, every day, for the rest of my life. I can't bear the notion of you pretending to be something or someone you're not. Here we can be ourselves, and I think we could be happy." While I'm too stunned to speak, her expression becomes guarded. "Unless you don't want that."

What is she talking about?

She wiggles to get out from under me. "Maybe it was just the sex talking. I can be impulsive. Momma always says so."

Before she can get to the edge of the bed, I wrap my arms around her middle and pull her so that she is sitting between my legs. I press my mouth to her ear. "I want to marry you. I promise to love you until the end of time, both in this life and the next. All that I am belongs to you, heart and soul, Wren Martin. Living here would be an amazing bonus."

"But you didn't say anything." Worry laces her voice.

"Only because in my life, all I have known is fighting for everything. Victories are hard-won and short-lived. I'm not used to having what I want most handed to me so beautifully." I have to take a moment to catch my breath. Emotions fight to escape. "Nothing in my life has prepared me for this moment, Wren. If I didn't respond the way you imagined, forgive me. I want to be with you, and if that's here in Domhan, where we can live honestly, it will be perfect. But if you wish to return to your world, I will support that as long as I'm allowed to follow you there for a lifetime."

She turns in my arms and runs her thumb across my damp cheek. Tears sparkle in her eyes, illuminating them like clear blue crystals. "Marry me?"

This woman is perfect. "Yes. Is tomorrow too soon?"

I have attended many celebrations in the grand ballroom of Tús Nua. I've been required to go to these events since I turned sixteen suns. My brothers enjoy the fuss and flirting that is paramount to these things. I generally stay in the background and do my duty, but no more.

Tonight is different. With Wren on my arm, I'm able to experience the gala from her point of view. As she stares up with a look of wonder on her beautiful face, I see the six crystal chandeliers, the arched ceiling, and the painted scenes of the old gods in a new light. Fresh and beautiful, even the smallest bit of gold paint isn't lost on her discerning eye.

"This is heavenly." She points to the scene where Dagda plays the harp Uaithne and defeats the Fomorians by causing the harp to evoke laughter, sorrow, and finally, slumber. "We read about that."

I take her hand and lead her to the dance floor. It takes only a moment to remember my instructions. With Wren in my arms, the simple steps in three beats feel sensual and right. "I've always hated these events." I twirl her, then reclaim her waist.

"You dance very well for someone who hates it." Every time she smiles, my heart and pulse speed up, and I want to make her smile for the rest of my life.

Lifting her to avoid a dwarf couple who have lost the motion of the dance, but appear to be having a fine time, I spin us out of their path, and Wren giggles. "It seems that having you with me has altered my view on balls."

"How so?" She giggles as more dwarves balter around the floor.

I steer us clear of danger, but it's becoming increasingly more difficult. "Thank goodness Farress and Corell are not much for indoor dancing." I point to the pair as they clomp out of the large, arched double doors.

Wren's eyes sparkle with joy, and we continue to keep time as we watch our friends clear the garden and take off at a gallop toward the forest.

A fairy the size of a butterfly zips between our faces and up to the chandelier, where he sits with a dozen others who watch the ball. Several have changed to full size and are watching and learning the dance from Niamh and Rían, who must have been practicing because they look as if they were made for the dance.

"I never thought I would see Rían Redmond, Captain of the Queen's Guard, dancing, or smiling for that matter." Still keeping her hand in mine, I point to the couple.

"They look perfect together."

"I suppose they do." The world changed while I was away, and in ways I could never have dreamed. "Rían is the least likely man I know to fall in love. The fact that he did so with a fairy seems inconceivable, yet, there is the proof."

She leans in and presses her cheek to my chest. "You don't like change, and having so much of it foisted on you makes you feel like a cat in the bathtub." She pats my shoulder.

"A cat in the bathtub? I suppose that might have been true a few months ago when I burst into your life, my love, but now it's an everyday occurrence. You changed my life. You make me a better man. I always thought that to be a good soldier, I had to remove all feelings from every aspect of my life. You taught me that..."

"Feelings give us something worth fighting for." She says the words I'm fumbling for.

I twirl us around the floor to the edge, then take her hand. "Let's go into the garden."

There are so many couples dancing, it's lost its attraction, and the heat in the ballroom has become stifling.

Once outside, we walk to the center where a large fountain bubbles. I take several deep breaths and sit on the edge of the fountain. "Did I tell you how beautiful you look tonight?"

She saunters over and sits on my knee. "You did, but I don't mind hearing it again."

Birdie's laugh fills the garden.

We both turn to find her standing on the veranda, talking to a dwarf.

"Momma likes it here. She's been studying Domhan's history and examining how human myth and Domhan's historical facts have many similarities." Wren lays her head on my shoulder.

I wrap my arms around her and breathe in her warm, flowery scent. "Do you think she'd stay?"

Shrugging, she says, "Maybe. Why do you ask?"

"You will be happier if your mother is near." I could stay like this for all my days. However, wishing a war were not happening won't make it so. The battle is coming.

"She would be safer in Texas."

"I suppose she'll decide for herself, but I want you to know there will always be a place for her in our home."

Pressing her lips to mine, she sighs against my mouth and sucks my bottom lip between hers. The kiss is soft and slow with none of the desperation of our earlier lovemaking. "You are the best man I have ever known. I'll tell her and also ask her to go home until this war is over."

From her tone, she already knows Birdie will not leave. I have to agree. From what I know of Birdie, she's not one to run for safety. "Perhaps it would be wise to give her some training with a blade."

Wren's warm laughter fills me with joy. "It's a good idea."

We remain by the fountain until voices find their way toward us. The ballroom begins to empty into the garden as Mother commands the fireworks to start.

Bright colors fill the sky and reflect in Wren's upturned eyes. It's the most mesmerizing sight I've ever beheld. Even without the pyrotechnics, I feel the same way every time I look at my perfect human mate.

Epilogue

WREN

Memories of the ball float through my mind as I return from training with the oracle. I pat Fior's thick neck. Liam's mother gave me the beautiful gray horse as a gift. The mare's hair is the color of a storm cloud while her mane and tail are jet black. Maybe I should have refused her, but I was already in love with her.

"Are you gathering wool, or is it something serious?" Harper asks as she rides beside me on her white horse.

I like my new friend from New Jersey. I don't imagine we ever would have crossed paths if not for our elves. "I was thinking that the ball was a beautiful affair. My first since senior prom."

"Mine too. I would have thought you southern girls have debutante balls all the time."

We round the final bend, and the castle rises, shining bright white in the late-day sun. In the east, dark clouds gather. It looks as if we've returned just in time to stay out of the storm. "I'm not that kind of southern girl. Momma and I live modestly on property that's been in our family for generations."

Harper points toward the coming weather. "Looks like we'd better dash for the barn or we'll be soaked through."

Thinking the same thing, I follow her at a gallop to the yard in front of the elaborate stone barn. A groom waits. He's tall and thin with long black hair and an easy smile.

I toss him my reins and jump to the ground. "Thank you, Dane."

Harper and I make a dash for the door on the side of the castle nearest us and make it just as the sky opens up. We're giggling like girls as we continue to run down the hallway.

"I didn't think we'd make it." Harper fixes the ribbon holding her hair back. "If I ever go home, I'm bringing scrunchies back by the dozen."

Ahead, there are several voices in the foyer. As we step through the door under the stairs, the voices stop.

Liam, Elspeth, Niamh, and Fancor all stare at us as if they've been caught with their hands in the cookie jar.

"What are you all up to?" I ask.

Momma rushes in from the far door. "Are we ready?" She looks up, sees me, and presses her hand to her mouth.

I look at the guilty expression on all their faces and know something is going on.

Liam grins. "We thought we'd have a few more minutes."

"We had to run to avoid the rain." I take his offered hand. "What's going on?"

He kisses my fingers. "I have a surprise for you. Everyone here helped make it happen."

A Crown of Wind and Water

Despite the strange behavior of everyone besides Liam, I feel the rush of excitement building inside me. "What surprise? I don't need anything."

Tugging my hand, he leads me up the stairs, past our room, then up another set of stairs to a door that looks like all the others on the guest level of the castle.

The others troop behind us, and even Harper has joined the parade.

Liam takes both my hands. "I wanted to marry you right after the ball. Mother asked us to wait for a *proper* wedding. She didn't say I couldn't give you your wedding gift. In fact, she helped arrange this. Harper told me in your world, a ring is offered from the groom to the bride as a promise. Here, it is usually a bracelet." He turns the knob and pushes the door open. "I thought you might like to decide on the exact piece you would like, as your work is far more unique than anything made by elven jewelry makers."

The small room is flush with light despite the rain teaming outside. A long table holds a small lathe, light, pliers in different shapes and sizes, an adorable hammer, wire, a melting pot, and trays of stones in every color. It's a jeweler's dream to have a workshop like this.

"This is..." I have no words.

"Is it what you need to continue with your art? If something is missing, tell me and we'll try to get it for you." Worry runs through his words.

"It's perfect. It's a dream. How do these things work without plugs?" I run my hand lovingly along the top of the lathe.

Elspeth says, "They are powered by magic. They will run for as long as you live."

I hug her. "Thank you."

Liam says, "Your mother told us what you would need. Niamh and Fancor were able to get the shiny bits from their people. Harper and Aaran helped me set everything up."

I hug Fancor.

He chortles and turns red. Patting my back, he says, "I'm pleased you're happy, Wren. You should be able to continue your passions in whatever world you choose."

Squealing with joy, Niamh joins in the hug. "Many of those pretty stones came from the waters of the glen. The wire was made here in Tús Nua, but the silver and gold came from the dwarves."

"I also brought you some raw materials to melt into whatever shape you wish." Fancor pats my head.

Tears flow freely down my face as my joy cannot be contained. "Thank you all. This is more than I ever could have expected."

One by one, they hug me and leave. Elspeth cups my cheek. "I wouldn't want you to give up anything you love to stay here and make my son happy."

My emotions are so overwhelming, I can only squeak out, "Thank you."

She kisses my forehead and joins Momma at the door. They leave together, giving Liam and me a long look before they leave us.

Looking in every direction of my stunning workshop, my heart overflows with love and gratitude. I leap into Liam's arms. "You are amazing. Thank you."

He grips my bottom and kisses me hard on the lips.

Threading my fingers through his hair, I pull it loose from the ribbon and deepen the kiss. My tongue searches his for more. Breathless, I break the kiss. "I can't believe you did all of this. How did you even know?"

"Every day, I find new braided chains of grass or fabric in our room. It was a good clue. You need your craft to be truly happy. I promise you, Wren, your happiness is the most important thing in my life. I will strive to bring you joy for as long as I live." He carries me around the workbench to the chair and sits with me in his lap. "Fancor will help you trade for the minerals that come from his mountains whenever you need more."

"There is enough here to keep me busy for a year." My voice is thready with joy and gratitude. "Thank you." I bury my teary eyes in his shoulder.

Kissing my ear, he says, "I love you. Anything you need, I will provide or help you obtain."

"What is left for me to give to you?" I hadn't meant to say it out loud. I will never be able to repay such a thoughtful gift.

With one hand, he combs his fingers through my curls and cups the back of my head. "You are all the gift I will ever need. Telling me you will be my wife, my mate, my life partner, is far greater than this room."

My heart is near bursting. "The things you say." I dash away my tears.

From the moment I made the decision to stay in Domhan and make this place and this man my home, I never doubted that it was the right thing. Now I can visualize what life could be like once the battle is won.

"We will beat her. For many years, I didn't believe it, but now I know in my heart that we cannot lose." Liam's eyes are filled with passion and truth.

Andrea Rose

I lean into his body and revel in his embrace. "There's nothing we can't do as long as we're together."

I love how this book came together. I hope you enjoyed *A Crown of Wind and Water*.
It would be a big help if you would leave a review.
Keep on reading Reign of the Witch Queen and see how the youngest Riordan son does in *A Crown of Fire and Ice*.

A Crown of Wind and Water

A CROWN OF FIRE AND ICE
Book 3
Reign of the Witch Queen

***One reckless leap. One broken portal.
A love forged in chaos and fire.***

LAYLA

I've never belonged anywhere.
So when I hit rock bottom, fresh off losing a nationally televised "superhero" competition, a devastatingly handsome man with pointed ears asks me to jump into a swirling vortex and help save his world...

I jump.

Was it reckless? Absolutely.
Was it smart? Not even a little.

Within minutes of landing, we're attacked by shadow demons. Two things are clear: my beautiful elf is not as competent with portals as advertised, and dying might be the *best* outcome, because whatever these creatures are, becoming one of them would be far worse.

RAITH

Convincing a human to fight in Domhan should have been the hardest part.
Instead, Layla leaps into the portal without hesitation, and that's when everything goes wrong.

I've spent my life failing to live up to my family's legacy. I'm not the perfect son, like Aaran. Not the honored soldier, like Liam. I'm the third son, the disappointment who has too much power and not enough discipline.

My magic is strong, but my focus slips at the worst possible moment. The portal shifts and drops us onto the wrong world—a dying hell, crawling with the witch queen's minions.

I've made another catastrophic mistake, and this time an extraordinary human is paying the price. I'm going to make this right, even if it means walking through fire and ice to get her home.

***

Join my Newsletter – A wonderful way to stay in touch and always know what's new and exciting in the Andrea Rose, Andie, and A.S. Fenichel book universe is to sign up for my weekly newsletter. You'll automatically receive a free book, but beyond that, you'll love all the sales, news, and book talk: www.asfenichel.com/newsletter

Also by Andrea Rose

FANTASY ROMANCE

Reign of the Witch Queen Series

A Crown of Light and Shadow

A Crown of Wind and Water

A Crown of Fire and Ice

A Crown of Stars and Sea (Prequel Novella)

A Crown of Blood and Duty (Novella)

Writing as A.S. Fenichel

HISTORICAL PARANORMAL ROMANCE

Witches of Windsor Series

Magic Touch

Magic Word

Pure Magic

The Demon Hunters Series

Ascension

Deception

Betrayal

Defiance

Vengeance

HISTORICAL ROMANCE

The Wallflowers of West Lane Series

The Earl Not Taken

Misleading A Duke

Capturing the Earl

Not Even For A Duke

The Everton Domestic Society Series

A Lady's Honor

A Lady's Escape

A Lady's Virtue

A Lady's Doubt

A Lady's Past

A Lady's Christmas

A Lady's Curves

The Forever Brides Series

Tainted Bride

Foolish Bride

Desperate Bride

Single Title Books

Wishing Game

Christmas Bliss

An Honorable Arrangement

CONTEMPORARY PARANORMAL EROTIC ROMANCE

The Psychic Mates Series

Kane's Bounty

Joshua's Mistake

Training Rain

The End of Days Series

Mayan Afterglow

Mayan Craving

Mayan Inferno

End of Days Trilogy

CONTEMPORARY EROTIC ROMANCE

Single Title Books

Alaskan Exposure

Revving Up the Holidays

Writing as Andie Fenichel

Dragon of My Dreams (Monster Between the Sheets)

Turnabout is Fairy Play (Monster Between the Sheets)

Soul of a Vampire (Brothers of Scrim Hall)

Soul of a Reaper (Brothers of Scrim Hall)

Soul of a Dragon (Brothers of Scrim Hall)

Soul of a Wolf (Brothers of Scrim Hall)

Soul of a Demon (Brothers of Scrim Hall)

Soul of a Phoenix (Brothers of Scrim Hall)

Soul of a Monster (Brothers of Scrim Hall)

The Manticore's Mate (Catskills Mountain Monsters)

Promised to the Satyr (Catskills Mountain Monsters)

Wild for the Wyvern (Catskills Mountain Monsters)

Big Enough to Bite (Harmony Glen)

Biting Bigfoot (Harmony Glen)

Bitten by Love (Harmony Glen)

Mantus

Riding With the Panther

Dad Bod Handyman (Lane Family)

Carnival Lane (Lane Family)

Lane to Fame (Lane Family)

Changing Lanes (Lane Family)

Heavy Petting (Lane Family)

Summer Lane (Lane Family)

Hero's Lane (Lane Family)

Icing It (Lane Family)

Mountain Lane (Lane Family)

Christmas Lane (Lane Family)

Texas Lane (Lane Family)

Building Lane (Lane Family)

Humbug Lane (Lane Family)

High Voltage Lane (Lane Family)

For Letter or Worse (Lane Family)

**Visit Andrea Rose's website
for a complete and up-to-date list of all her books.
http://andrearoseauthor.com**

About the Author

Andrea Rose is a pen name for author A.S. Fenichel. She also writes as Andie Fenichel. Andrea gave up a successful career in New York City to pursue her lifelong dream of being a professional writer. She's never looked back.

Andrea adores writing stories filled with love, passion, desire, magic, and maybe a little mayhem tossed in for good measure. Books have always been her perfect escape, and she still relishes diving into one and staying up all night to finish a good story.

With over 60 published books, Andrea Rose/Andie Fenichel/A.S. Fenichel has written historical romance, fantasy romance, contemporary romance, and mixed-genre romances. She has authored several series, including Reign of the Witch Queen, Everton Domestic Society, Witches of Windsor, and more. Strong, empowered heroines from Regency London to modern-day New York are what you'll find in all her books.

A Jersey Girl at heart, she now makes her home in Southern Missouri with her real-life hero, her wonderful husband. When not reading or writing, she enjoys cooking, traveling, history, and puttering in her garden.

Visit Andrea Rose's Website:
http://andrearoseauthor.com

Send Andrea Rose an Email:
andrearoseauthor@outlook.com

Join Andrea's Newsletter:
www.asfenichel.com/newsletter/

instagram.com/asfenichel
facebook.com/a.s.fenichel
tiktok.com/@asfenichel
bookbub.com/authors/andrea-rose
pinterest.com/asfenichel
x.com/asfenichel
amazon.com/author/andrearoseauthor

www.ingramcontent.com/pod-product-compliance
Lightning Source LLC
LaVergne TN
LVHW021051100526
838202LV00082B/5461